OVERRIDE

ALSO BY HEATHER ANASTASIU

Glitch

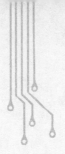

OVERRIDE

HEATHER ANASTASIU

ST. MARTIN'S GRIFFIN
NEW YORK

This is a work of fiction. All of the characters, organizations, and events portrayed in this novel are either products of the author's imagination or are used fictitiously.

OVERRIDE. Copyright © 2013 by Heather Anastasiu. All rights reserved. Printed in the United States of America. For information, address St. Martin's Press, 175 Fifth Avenue, New York, N.Y. 10010.

www.stmartins.com

Library of Congress Cataloging-in-Publication Data

Anastasiu, Heather.
     Override / Heather Anastasiu.—1st ed.
        p. cm.
     ISBN 978-1-250-00300-3 (pbk.)
     ISBN 978-1-250-02234-9 (e-book)
     [1. Individuality—Fiction.   2. Emotions—Fiction.   3. Thought and thinking—Fiction.
4. Psychic ability—Fiction.   5. Government, Resistance to—Fiction.   6. Science fiction.]   I. Title.
     PZ7.A51852Ove 2013
     [Fic]—dc23

2012042134

ISBN 978-1-250-00300-3 (trade paperback)
ISBN 978-1-250-02234-9 (e-book)

First Edition: February 2013

10   9   8   7   6   5   4   3   2   1

*For Dragos, you're the reason I know how
to write about love*

Acknowledgments

Second books can be dreadfully hard, and I owe so many thanks to the people who helped me push through to find the story and get this book to where it needed to be.

First of all, thanks to my editor, Terra Layton, who was *infinitely* patient as we went round for round through so many drafts until we got one that finally clicked. I so appreciate your ideas, suggestions, and continued enthusiasm even though this one was a beast at times! And thank you to the rest of the team at St. Martin's!

Thanks as always to my awesome agent, Charlie Olsen.

The amazing Lenore Appelhans deserves a huge shout-out. You read some truly dreadful early drafts and helped me realize that sometimes you have to just start over from scratch. You rock my socks off. Thanks also to my other fabulous beta readers, Paula Stokes and McCormick Templeman.

Huge thanks to my critique group here in Minneapolis, Anne Greenwood Brown, David Nunez, Natalie Boyd, Lauren Peck, and Carolyn Hall. You guys always call me out on my crap, help me write better characters and fuller scenes, and are all around just awesome people. I always look forward to Thursdays!

And thanks to the Apocalypsies for helping me stay sane through this whole crazy process. Apoca-hugs :)

Chapter 1

MY HEART POUNDED in my ears. The low humming sound, muffled by the wall, was just loud enough to hear over my shallow, panicked breaths. I sat up on my loft bed and paused to listen before carefully easing myself down the ladder. The pads of my bare feet landed on the cold floor. There was barely enough space to stand up and I had to squeeze between the treadmill that pulled down from the wall and the shower and toilet at the foot of my bed.

I moved silently. Only two people at the lab knew I hid right behind their walls, and today couldn't be the day the rest of them found out. My life depended on it. The Resistance had been careful enough to erase the tiny alcove from the schematics. Officially, the room, just like me, didn't exist.

I paused with my ear inches from the wall. In the three months I'd spent hidden in this confined space, I had come to know every sound. Learning them was a matter of habit almost as much as it was a matter of survival. I paused, focusing intently on the rhythmic *click-click-click*.

I leaned my forehead against the wall, letting out the breath I held. It was just an ordinary sound, a normal shift in the perfectly regulated air system. I should have known. This lab was one of the few places with the kind of heavy air-filtration system I needed to survive. It worked like clockwork, and, without it, almost any surface allergen would kill me quickly.

I closed my eyes and my heart rate slowed. It was remarkable how quickly I could move from alarm to complete relaxation and back again. Another matter of habit.

I climbed slowly back up to my bed. This alcove might be my safe haven, but sometimes it felt more like a prison. The bed was too short to stretch out and the ceiling too low to sit up completely. The confinement was strangling. Sometimes I'd look at the walls and they seemed nearer than before, like the room was closing in on me, inch by inch.

I slept during the day, for as many hours as I could, but time still stretched out endlessly. Lately I'd begun parsing the days into manageable thirty-minute pieces to make the long and painful monotony less overwhelming: drawing, jogging on the treadmill, unfolding and then refolding my clothes, pacing back and forth across the narrow floor, counting the objects in my room, studying the history texts the Resistance gave me—the real histories, not the lies we learned in the Community. And training, endless training.

In the early mornings I'd spend countless more half hours staring at the cool slab of ceiling above me, watching as the thin string hanging from the air duct blew back and forth in the allergen-free air. It was maddening to sit here knowing Adrien and the rest of the Resistance were fighting the Chancellor and the Community while I was stuck caged in this tiny room. I was tired of being the helpless prisoner. I wanted to be out there with them.

I closed my eyes and swallowed.

Most of all, I wanted to feel like I had some control again. When we escaped from the Community, I had reached into people's bodies and crumpled the miniscule hardware in their brains with my telekinetic power. I had ripped heavy lockdown doors off their tracks. But now . . .

Now, no matter how much I trained—or at least tried to—it was no use. I'd stare at my tablet for thirty minutes straight, willing it to move just an inch. It never budged. Not because the power wasn't there. Exactly the opposite—there was too much of it. I could feel it expanding inside me even now, pressing against the backs of my eyes and making my hands twitch. But I could never direct it the way I meant to. And then sometimes, when it had built up for too long, it would erupt like a boiling geyser.

I shook my twitching hand and then made a fist. I didn't want to think about it anymore. I propped myself up on my elbow and looked at the drawings papering the wall by my bed instead. Mom, Dad, my younger brother, Markan. The people I'd left behind. And the people I'd lost. Max.

I reached out and touched the picture of Max's face. I'd tried to capture how he looked when I first knew him, when everything had been simpler and we'd been friends. We'd been drones together, subjects in the Community where we were tightly controlled by emotion-suppressing hardware. It was a dangerous place for anyone who managed to break free, but somehow we'd found each other. We'd protected each other as we explored the new incredible powers that developed as a side effect of the hardware glitches. I'd trusted him, before I even fully understood what that word meant.

But that was all a long time ago now. That was before I'd

3

learned that someone you think you know can look you in the face and tell you lies.

I thought about the last time I'd seen Max, right after I found out he'd been working for the Chancellor as a Monitor the whole time. He was an informant, reporting on people who were glitchers like us, getting them captured and "repaired," or worse, deactivated. And he hadn't felt remorse for any of it.

"I was going to protect you from it all," he'd said. "We were going to live a life beyond your best dreams, you and me together forever. It would have been perfect." His voice had turned bitter. "You were supposed to be mine."

My face burned hot at the memory, and I shook my head. I remembered the disgust on his face when I told him to escape with us.

"And do what? Join your little band of Resistance fighters? Spend every day watching someone else live the life I always wanted with you? Don't think so."

It was a wound I opened and salted over and over again. It tortured me to remember, and the anger felt fresh and hot every time I repeated his words. But the truth was, I needed the anger and the pain. I dug it deep into my chest like an anchor holding me in place. It reminded me that I was alive even if this alcove sometimes felt like a tomb, that I was free, and that one day soon I'd be able to join the others to fight against the many injustices that had enslaved us.

I turned my eyes away from Max to the other face that was featured most often in my drawings. Adrien, with that smile he saved for me when no one else was looking. I sighed. His was the only face on my wall that didn't fill me with regret.

The last time I'd seen him had been ages ago, while he was passing through on his way to the Foundation. It was going to be a school for glitchers, and, best of all, it would have an air-filtration system equal to the research lab here. I'd be able to join him there without fear of the air I breathed or worrying that any sound I made might get me caught and killed.

As I reached up to trace Adrien's face, a tremor ran through my hand. The gentle quaking had been plaguing me all night, first in my thighs, now my hand. A flash of fear washed over me.

Not again. It shouldn't be happening again so soon.

I flexed my hand, then made a fist, and the shaking stopped. I swallowed hard, trying to quiet my rising alarm. I hadn't gotten my telekinesis to function properly in weeks, and the power raged like a wild beast clawing underneath my skin. Adrien always called our glitcher powers Gifts, but I was beginning to suspect that he was wrong.

I clicked the light off and settled into my pillow. Our minds may have evolved to develop superhuman abilities, but what if our bodies hadn't? Maybe we were too fragile to contain that kind of power. Maybe our Gifts were actually a curse.

I'd only been asleep for a few minutes when I woke to my knuckles banging repeatedly into my cheek.

"Shunt," I murmured, suddenly fully awake. My arm kept at it, but now the shaking had moved up to my shoulder. The normal telltale buzz of my power grew louder in my ears until it was a high-pitched screech.

"No, no, no," I whispered, clicking on my light and climbing awkwardly down from the bed. I glanced at the clock on the wall above my head. It was an hour into the workday. Somehow I had to stop myself from going into full eruption mode, or else I'd be caught for sure.

The first time my power had gotten uncontrollable like this I'd been lucky; it was nighttime, when no one was around. Milton, one of the two people at the research lab who knew I was hiding here, had been slack-jawed when he finally pushed his way into my trashed room the morning after. The metal frame of the bed had been twisted in on itself like a figure eight, and the toilet had come loose and made a dent in the concrete of the opposite wall. All my drawings and clothes had been shredded, and I'd sat huddled in the far corner with my arms over my head, bruised and bleeding.

But Milton had been kind. He said I reminded him a little of his sister, a drone he had to leave behind in the Community's control. He told me stories about her while he helped me clean up. He said maybe the outburst had happened because I was boxed in here and not able to use my power often. But he didn't understand, not really. It was more than that. My power was changing, and I was changing with it. I couldn't control it anymore. I didn't know how I ever had. Sometimes I imagined it consuming me from the inside like a slowly fattening parasite.

I reached up and managed to grab my pillow and blanket right before my legs buckled and I landed on the ground. There was barely enough space to lay flat, but the floor was safer than the bed. With what little muscle control I had left, I wedged myself between the shelf and the toilet to keep myself as secure as possible. I squeezed my eyes shut. I knew what was coming next, and it was going to hurt. I clenched my teeth in the darkness, willing my body to stay still and quiet. Above all, I had to stay quiet.

Both my arms shook uncontrollably now. I flipped myself onto my side to get the pillow under my head and put part of the twisted-up blanket between my teeth. The tremors moved to my torso and down to my legs. My elbows, shoulder blades, and heels jerked up and down, slamming painfully into the cold floor. I wanted to scream into the blanket, but I was afraid that if I opened my mouth even the tiniest bit, all my power might accidentally burst out.

The screech inside my head became a long howl. The beast wanted release. I ground my teeth further into the blanket and tried to brace myself for each time my body smacked into the ground. Again and again and again. I winced with each hit, aching from the impact on bruises that had never fully healed.

I just had to get through this and then I could rest.

The shaking became wilder, and as it reached an apex my foot banged against the wall, making a loud *tap, tap, tap* noise every time it hit. I focused all my energy on my legs, trying to hold them still, but my body was out of my control. A whimper of fear escaped my lips. If the wrong person heard me, it was over.

I thought I was going to pass out from the pain and panic. I prepared for the worst, knowing I couldn't hold on much longer. The power built up like expanding gas in an enclosed space, begging for release.

I couldn't keep it in. It was going to explode. I clamped my mouth shut tighter, but it felt like I was ripping apart from the inside. I clenched my teeth and felt sweat dripping down my face from the effort.

Right when I felt like I was about to burst wide open, the seizing began to quiet down. The shakes slowed to trembles, then to just a shiver, and then I lay still. Sweat dripped down my temple and slid into my eyes with a salty sting. I wanted to wipe it away, but I was so tired, my arm felt leaden. I rolled over onto my side and breathed slowly as I gathered my strength. Then I eased my way to my knees, pausing with each movement, and eventually rose to my feet.

I felt like I'd been running on the treadmill for a day and a half. But at least I'd be able to sleep now. I climbed tiredly up the ladder to my bed. My arms shook again, this time not from excess power but from exhaustion.

But right when my body finally rested on the thin mattress, a scratching sounded from the wall, right at the hidden entrance to my room. I froze. Milton shouldn't be bringing me food yet. Someone must have heard my foot banging into the wall and was coming to investigate. They could have easily followed the sound back to the wall panel that doubled as the secret entrance to the alcove.

Fat tears squeezed out of my eyes. I wasn't strong enough to fight. I rolled my tired body over toward the wall. Whoever came in wouldn't see me right away, but I knew it would only buy me a few moments. I was a muddle of fear and exhaustion. After so much effort, so much sacrifice and patience, I couldn't lose it all like this, facing my enemies while weak and afraid—

The door opened and immediately I heard a whisper. "Zoe, it's me."

It was Adrien's voice. All the tension flooded out of my body. I half climbed, half fell down the ladder and launched myself into his outstretched arms. He wasn't supposed to be here until next week. Was he here to take me to the Foundation early? I parted my lips to ask but couldn't find the strength to care about anything other than his warm arms around me.

My hair had come undone from its braid during the shaking episode, and Adrien curled his fingers into it. I sank against him, breathing him in. Even my exhaustion lightened in his embrace. It was always like that when I was with him. I tipped my head back and he kissed me. His lips were gentle, and for a moment I forgot all the loneliness and fear of the past few months. All I could think about was the soft texture of his lips and the way love for him bloomed inside me like a light cell blinking to life in a pitch-black room.

But all too soon he pulled away. His eyes were cloudy. "There's not much time. We've gotta move. Now."

He turned and let go of me, and my weakened legs gave out from under me.

"Zoe!" Adrien caught me around the waist, pulling me back up. "What's going on, are you okay?" He set me down on the closed toilet lid, the only place to sit other than up on my bed.

"I'm fine," I lied, blinking and trying to get a breath. "I just gotta get some rest. Can we leave in the morning?"

But when I looked back over at Adrien, he was already pulling out the biosuit box and opening it up.

"We gotta leave now Zoe, not tomorrow morning. Fit your feet into the rubber boots first, then we'll pull the rest of the suit up."

"Why now?" I asked, blinking and trying to make sense of everything that was happening. I stepped into the boots.

"I had a vision. They're gonna raid this place soon."

It took a few more moments for what he'd said to sink in. "Wait, you mean . . . they know I'm here?"

"Not yet," Adrien said, managing to sound halfway calm. "Chancellor Bright was just named Underchancellor of Defense. Right off, she ordered inspections on any place with the kind of air-filtration system she knows you need to survive. I thought we'd have more time. I mean, there's about fifty facilities like this in the Sector, and there's no way she'd know this is the only one the Resistance has access to." He shook his head. "But I saw it."

"When will it happen?"

"I don't know." He ran a hand roughly through his hair. "It felt like a short-term vision, like it might happen in the next few days." He looked back up at me.

I felt a fresh wave of panic. They were coming for me. The horrifying reality of the situation settled in, clearing away some of my remaining cloudiness and exhaustion.

"I was gonna send a com," Adrien said, "but I was afraid any communications would get intercepted and decrypted. I didn't wanna accidentally *be* the cause of the inspection."

Another cold realization swept through me. "But wait. Where are we going?" I asked. "If the Foundation isn't ready yet, this lab's the only place we have access to with air I can breathe. What happens when my biosuit runs out of oxygen in twelve hours?"

"We're going to a beta site nearby. They have a few spare oxy tanks there. It'll buy us some time to figure out the rest."

He held out an arm to help me stand and then pulled the heavy padded suit up to my waist. There were three separate layers to it, and it smelled strongly of plastic and stale air.

"It's dangerous, I know," he continued. "But we don't have a choice. If we move fast enough, maybe we can get out of here safely. Maybe we can change the vision." His jaw tensed for a moment. "Otherwise what's the point of seeing the future?" I wasn't sure if he was talking more to me or to himself.

"Have you ever done it? Changed something you've seen?"

He didn't answer me, just lifted up the top half of the suit. "Here, fit your arms in."

I shrugged my arms into the heavy sleeves of the suit and sat down again to rest while Adrien clipped one of the compressed oxygen packs onto the belt at my hip and hooked it up. He fit the thick helmet with a see-through face mask over my head, adjusting it so the edges were firmly aligned with the body of the suit. The whir of precious air circulating through the mask filled my ears. He reached for the suit's forearm panel to run a quick diagnostic that would check for tears or leaks, and that's when I saw it: the red alarm light began flashing silently in the corner.

I gasped and looked over at Adrien. We both knew what it meant.

The Inspector was already here.

Chapter 2

ADRIEN'S FINGERS MET my fumbling ones as we attached the other tank to my waist.

"How do we get out of here?" he asked.

"If they came down the main elevator, we follow the escape route I've practiced." My voice was low and muted through the mask. There was a microphone option for normal speech, but I wasn't sure how loud it would be, so I didn't switch it on. "Head to the west end of the complex and take the stairs." I'd memorized the lab schematics and drilled the best escape routes. The lab had three exits—two elevators and one set of stairs. The stairs were closest and the best option for getting out unnoticed. "As long as no one sees us, we'll be fine."

Adrien nodded. The diagnostic clicked in my ear, and I looked down at the readout panel on my forearm. All systems clear. At least that was one piece of good news. I also felt steadier on my feet. The adrenaline pumping through my body was briefly giving me strength. I took a deep breath and pushed my gloved finger against the button that released the sliding door to the adjacent room in the laboratory.

Voices sounded from another room nearby, but the lab was

empty. The room was all clean lines and antiseptic lab tables covered with equipment. The smooth, burnished metal floors glinted. I paused to listen, but, within the echoing space, it was impossible to tell how close the voices were.

I ducked low and crept behind one of the laboratory tables, careful not to knock into any of the test tubes in my bulky suit. Adrien shut the door to the hidden room behind us. It looked like every other chrome-lined panel that formed the wall. But before Adrien could slide a table in front of it to complete the illusion, the click of boot heels and voices from the hall echoed louder. Adrien dropped down beside me.

My heart thumped wildly, and I instinctively put my hand to my heart monitor. I was glad the Rez had disabled it months ago; otherwise it would have been beeping loudly to signal my rapid heartbeat.

The room only had one exit. In my emergency evacuation plans, I'd always taken for granted the flashing alarm in the alcove would go off in time to make it clear of this room. Before I could even try to think what to do next, the voices were in the room with us.

Adrien huddled with me behind the black-topped table, eyes flicking around and mouth pursed tightly. I didn't know what he was looking for. To get to the stairs, we first had to get out of this room and past the doorway, right where it sounded like the Inspector was standing. Panic bubbled up inside me.

"What is it you say you study here, again?" The Inspector's clipped tones echoed off the chrome walls of the spotless lab. There was a moment's silence before Milton's voice piped up.

"We study viral pathogens, such as Flu 216 and its various permutations. Also," Milton continued, his voice shaky and high-pitched, "we're doing some innovative research into the application of nanotechnology to viral pathogens. The Cabinet of Medical Technology is very interested in our progress."

"I see," said the Inspector, his boots thudding as he stepped further into the room and closer to the table we hid behind. "And have you noticed anything . . . anomalous?"

"N-no, sir," Milton said. I squeezed my eyes shut. Milton was a painfully bad liar. He was younger than most others at the lab, but he was a genius, the top viral tech. Like most researchers, he didn't have the emotion-numbing V-chip installed. Which was a problem right now.

Usually Veri, our other Rez insider, was the one who handled communicating with officials on behalf of the lab. She was far more skilled in the art of subversion and misdirection. But she must not be here yet, and Milton stumbled over every other word.

Footsteps came closer. Sweat beaded on my forehead and dripped down my face beneath the mask. I looked frantically at Adrien.

"What's this?" The Inspector paused near the false wall to my hidden room and tapped the paneling. Had Adrien not shut the door completely? I cringed at the hollow ping of the Inspector's knuckles on the chrome and my heartbeat sped up even more. He was close enough that I could see the tip of his shiny black boot.

I wanted to crawl around the other side of the table, but Adrien sensed my panic and shook his head. His eyes darted in every direction. We both knew the crinkling noise my suit would make. There was no way we could sneak out of the room unnoticed.

A hiss sounded. The Inspector had found the small catch that opened the hidden door. In our haste, Adrien must have forgotten to replace the cover. He leaned in and whispered frantically in my ear. "Knock him out with your telek, like you did with the Chancellor that time."

"But—"

"Anomalous contraband." The Inspector's voice came from inside the small alcove. I heard the sound of papers being ripped off the walls.

I tried to listen, to see if there was any buzzing in my ears, any whisper of power left that I could try to harness. But all I could hear were Milton's weak excuses. He backed away from the other man, moving closer to us. "I didn't know that was there," he said. "I swear I've never seen that room before!"

I squeezed my eyes shut and tried again to draw on my power. None of this was going according to plan. No one was ever supposed to find the hidden room. I had to disable the Inspector if any of us were going to make it out of here alive.

I closed my eyes and tried to call on my telek. Moments earlier, my power had nearly consumed me. Now, no matter how much I strained, it wouldn't come. The beast was gone.

I shook my head frantically at Adrien. He seemed to understand and tugged me forward while the Inspector was busy looking through the things in my alcove. But we weren't fast enough. As soon as we rounded the corner of the table, the Inspector's voice rang out. "You there! Stop!"

Adrien bolted for the door, dragging me along with him. My feet were heavy from the weighty suit, but I managed to stay upright. Milton ran after us.

The Inspector's voice rang out behind as he spoke into his arm com, "Possible fugitive sighting in sublevel lab 810. Subjects are heading west!"

I cursed. Reinforcements would be coming.

"They'll be covering the west stairs," Adrien said.

I nodded and when we came to a fork in the hallway, pulled him left instead of right toward the stairs. "Let's try for the freight elevator in the central lab."

I tried to shut out all other thoughts and focus on moving one foot in front of the other. Adrien pulled Milton in front of me as we ran down the narrow hallway. "Get your elevator access card ready!"

The floors and walls were made of a dulled gray metal and our pounding footsteps broadcast our every move. Ahead, I saw where the hallway opened into the central lab.

Almost there.

We raced toward the opening, close enough now that I could see the elevator across the expanse of the lab.

But right as we closed the distance and were almost into the room, a shadow darkened the opening, and then another and another. Three Regulators stood in front of us, the metal plating on their faces glinting from the light in the hallway. They were the Community's soulless soldiers, almost as much machine as they were man. Adrien stopped cold, but Milton wasn't as quick. He tripped over Adrien, taking both of them down. My breath stopped in my chest and the moment seemed to slow. I looked from Adrien to the Regulators right as they raised their forearms, each with a triple-barreled laser weapon attached.

We were all going to die.

A jolt rocked involuntarily through my body. I must be hit. They must have fired in the instant I'd taken to blink. But I was shocked when I realized it was the Regulators who were blown backward, not me. They landed heavily on their backs halfway across the lab, bloodied chunks of alloy flying from their chests and arms as they went. I felt my eyes widen as I looked down at my outstretched arms in shock. My power. It had worked.

Adrien was on his feet. He pulled Milton up again just as one of the Regulators stirred.

"Go back!" Adrien shouted. He pulled a gun from his hip and let out several bright red blasts.

Milton and I raced back down the hallway. I looked over my shoulder. All three of the Regs were getting up now. Two of them were bloodied and one looked like he was missing an arm. But still, I knew I hadn't done enough damage. I'd only slowed them down for a moment. Regulators never stopped, no matter what.

Adrien kept firing behind us, but I didn't pause to look again. I was too slow already. The hallway was long and straight. The Regs would have a clear shot at us as soon as they were on their feet. We'd never make it if we kept going forward. My mind raced as we passed several numbered doors down the hallway. I thought about the schematics of the lab I'd memorized. These were research rooms. If we went into one of them, we'd only get ourselves trapped. Unless . . .

Two more doors down, I paused and slammed my gloved hand on the door release pad. Milton kept going.

"In here," I shouted. Adrien ran a few steps past me and grabbed Milton, yanking him through the doorway right as a quick stream of red burned into the wall where we'd been standing only moments before.

Adrien closed the door behind us. The door was made of reinforced steel, meant to seal shut in case of any pathogen leaks or disruptions to the ventilation system. But even though it shut with a satisfyingly heavy clang, I knew it wouldn't stop the Regulators for long.

"What now?" Adrien asked, clicking the button for the lock mechanism.

"The waste chute," I said, nodding toward the wall where a small door was embedded in the wall. We were eight stories underground, and the lab had a separate waste-disposal system for the hazardous materials they dealt with.

This was the central disposal room. Bottles of thick liquids lined the walls, full of acids to break down organic matter before it was loaded into disposal barrels and sent up the chute. The whole place smelled like antiseptic and lye. "Milton, can you get it open?"

Milton's whole body shook, his face pale. He gave a quick nod and went to the control panel beside the small door. His fingers tapped quickly on the interface. Adrien slid another energy tube into the bottom of his gun handle and aimed it at the door to the hallway. He didn't have to wait long.

A sizzling noise sounded as a bright molten line appeared from the Regs' laser weapons, firing from the other side.

"Hurry," I said to Milton, who was still typing furiously.

"Got it!" He let out a triumphant whoop as the chute door slid sideways into the wall. My eyes were on the chute—it was a rounded chamber three feet in diameter, meant for sending barrels of waste up to the trash room by the loading bay.

"You two first," Adrien said, walking backward across the room toward us, his weapon still trained at the door. He pushed me toward the opening.

Then the door to the hallway blew inward and the Regs charged into the room one after another.

Adrien fired, blasting one straight in the chest. The laser round knocked the Reg backward, but he got back to his feet with only a singe on the front of his metal breastplate.

The other Reg lunged toward Milton and me. I stumbled backward, tripping over the heavy suit and landing half in the chute. I pulled my legs inside.

"Come on, Milton!" I screamed. But when I looked up again, the Regulator had clapped his hands on both sides of Milton's head. In an instant, he crushed Milton's skull like an overripe watermelon. I stared in shock as Milton slumped to the floor.

A shriek of grief and terror ripped its way out of me, and suddenly all the bottles lining the wall started vibrating. Adrien dropped to the ground and rolled behind several barrels stacked beside the counter as the bottles exploded. The acid spray from the broken containers hit the three Regulators straight in the face.

They stumbled blindly, one falling into the other until they tumbled into a heap. Adrien took the moment of confusion and launched past them. He pushed me to my feet and squeezed into the chute with me. The chute door closed right as a Regulator climbed to his knees and aimed his weapon.

Adrien wrapped his arms around me as a deafening rush of air surrounded us, and then we were sucked upward with nauseating speed. But the chute was meant for barrels, not people. Adrien and I bounced painfully back and forth between the walls. Within a few heartbeats, another chute door opened and we tumbled out into a trash container half-filled with barrels labeled HAZARDOUS WASTE. The back of Adrien's tunic was ripped up and the skin underneath looked scraped raw. He got to his feet as if he didn't feel it and hurried over to me.

"Oh god, Zoe, your suit."

I looked down dazedly and saw that part of my suit hung in shredded ribbons off my arm. Adrien grabbed my left arm to check the diagnostic readout, his face a mask of fear. After a moment he let out the breath he'd been holding. "Only two layers were breached. You're okay. Come on."

"We've got to go back," I said, finally finding my voice. "We need to get Milton to a medic—"

Adrien shook his head, his jaw tensed. "He's dead, Zo. But the Regs aren't, and they'll stop at nothing. We've gotta go."

"But—"

He took my shoulders and forced me to look him in the eye. "It's how we survive in the Rez. The living matter, not the dead."

It made me sick to my stomach, but I knew he was right. My mind seemed to finally catch up with what was happening. Milton was dead, and every second I didn't get moving, I was only putting our lives in danger.

I nodded and followed Adrien as he scrambled over the piles of trash barrels spread haphazardly between us and the exit. My boots weighed so much I could barely lift my legs high enough to step over some of them. I stumbled once, but caught myself before I fell, while Adrien punched the button to open the door. The large bay door rolled slowly into the ceiling, groaning as it went. We bent down and scooted under as soon as it was high enough.

The sunlight was blinding. I'd spent three months in a room with only a dim light cell, and the intensity of the day-light seared through my eyes to the back of my skull. There was no time to adjust, so I squeezed my eyes closed except for a tiny crack and let Adrien pull me ahead.

"We're on the east end of the building, right?" Adrien asked.

"Yeah."

"Good." He sounded relieved. "That means my duo-rider is around the corner."

I had no idea what a duo-rider was, but I just focused on running as fast as I could and watching the concrete under my feet so I didn't trip.

"There!"

I looked up and saw a small egg-shaped vehicle by the wall. The engine was already running and it hovered a few feet off the ground, though I didn't quite know how. There weren't any of the fuel-burning propulsion modules roaring along the bottom like I'd seen in other flying transports. The engine was just quietly whirring. The top half of the vehicle was made of one solid oval window. Adrien raised his hand and clicked a small hand-held device. The window lifted up and backward to reveal two seats, one behind the other, and a small stepladder dropped down the side.

I tried to step up with my thick, booted foot, but it didn't fit into the ladder rung.

"Come on," I said to myself, as I tried again and managed to get my boot tip wedged in enough to hike myself up. I heaved my body over the side and into the narrow backseat, looking up just in time to see a Reg burst out of the backside of the building.

"Adrien, get in!"

His wiry body moved faster than I'd ever seen as he leapt into the front seat and sealed the window shut in the same motion. The Regulator ran straight at us.

"Why isn't he shooting?" My voice was near hysterical. We were a clear target out in the open like this.

Adrien grabbed the steering controls. "He's the one missing his firing arm." We lifted off the ground.

I sat back and buckled myself in. After another moment, I breathed out in relief as the vehicle rose higher and higher into the air.

We were safe.

Then the vehicle rocked forward suddenly, making me lurch in my seat. I looked ahead and saw a metal hand clamped on the small hood of the duo, inches away from the window. We were almost twenty feet in the air now, but the Reg had still managed to launch himself high enough to grab hold.

He pulled himself up over the front edge with his one arm. The flesh portions of his face were blistered from the acid, parts of his nose and his bionic eye missing entirely. Even the metal on part of his face had melted and partially slid off, revealing the bone underneath. But none of it stopped him. He pulled himself higher up the hood of the duo with single-minded determination.

Adrien fought with the steering, veering wildly left then right in an attempt to shake him, but the Reg had gotten an iron grip on the lip of the front windshield.

I closed my eyes and tried to focus. I needed to use my telek. I could easily dislodge him.

Nothing happened.

With a giant crack, the Reg smashed his head against the window. It was reinforced plastic, so it only cracked and dented inward, but a couple more hits like that, and he'd make it through and get to Adrien. The image of Milton's crushed skull flashed in my mind.

There was no more time to try accessing my power. I reached over to the front seat and grabbed the weapon holstered at Adrien's hip.

"Open the top," I yelled. Adrien didn't look my way, but he reached forward and clicked a switch. The window started lifting up and backward, creating a crazy rush of air that almost knocked the weapon out of my hand. I managed to keep a grip and pushed the trigger. A burst of red light flared straight into the Reg's face with enough momentum that he was blown backward. He didn't release the metal shell as he tumbled down. The duo's hood peeled off with him, leaving the engine underneath exposed.

Still the Reg held on.

Adrien flipped the switch so the roof sealed shut again, then swung the steering stick back and forth in a zigzag. We could only see the Reg's hand, gripping the shredded metal of the hood, but the rest of his body bobbed below, his weight still throwing us off balance. He wasn't letting go, no matter how much we swerved and twisted.

"Hold on to something," Adrien said. I was already nauseated from the movement, but I gripped the armrests.

Adrien jerked the stick full backward, and we headed straight up into the sky. My head knocked against the back of my helmet at the sudden movement. Then he rammed it back down and sent us in a spiraling freefall. My stomach dropped and I clung to the armrests, trying to contain the terrified scream that rose in my throat at the sight of the rapidly approaching ground. As we spun, the centrifugal force pushed the flap of hood metal outward. The Reg flew out with it away from the body of the duo, but he still held on. His added weight threw us into an even more intense spin.

After a few more dizzy, chaotic seconds, the piece of hood the Reg gripped so tightly ripped off with a screeching tear, and he was flung off into the air.

The vehicle rocked heavily as the Reg fell free, and Adrien's knuckles were white on the steering stick as he attempted to right us. But we still spiraled downward and the ground was so close that I could begin to make out the leaves on trees.

"Adrien!" I shouted, bracing my hands against the back of his seat.

He strained with his whole body to pull the stick backward.

My heart lodged in my throat as I waited for the impact, but finally we pulled up out of the spin, and after another few moments we were flying straight again.

It was suddenly bizarrely quiet.

"We made it," I finally whispered, barely believing it.

But Adrien shook his head. "We've only just begun."

Chapter 3

ADRIEN'S BACK WAS RIGID as we flew. The only hint that he was rattled at all was a slight tremble in his hand as he punched through an interface cube that rose as a projection from the duo's console.

I looked behind us. The lab was only a square dot now with the outline of city buildings jutting up behind it in the far distance. No one was following us.

I looked back at Adrien. I could see in the small mirror that his face was taut with focus and his thick hair was matted around his forehead. I'd never really seen him like this. I'd known Adrien as the quiet voice talking to me late at night in my room about beauty and the human soul, not as Adrien the soldier. I'd known vaguely that he used to run missions like this all the time. He'd lived on the run and then joined up with the Rez when he was fourteen. But seeing him in action was something totally different.

"Are you okay?" I asked.

He pressed his lips together tighter. He looked almost angry. For a second, I thought he wasn't going to answer me, but he finally said, "I should have been there earlier. I was so stupid. I should have found a way to get an encoded message out. I could have warned Milton not to come into work to-day and gotten you out another way. Now he's gone, and I almost lost you—" He stopped and clenched his jaw like he was physically holding words back. "I should have done things differently."

"It's not your fault, Adrien." I tried to reach out to touch his shoulder, but my strap held me back.

"I can see the future," he said, his voice hard. "Whose fault is it but mine?"

"Without you that Inspector would have captured me. You saved me."

His jaw stayed just as tight. I couldn't tell if he believed me.

"We're not safe yet," he finally said. "Those Regs will be calling for an armada to find us," he said. "The duo's cloaking mechanism isn't built for long runs, but the beta site's nearby. I should be able to get us there before it wears off." His voice dropped. "At least I can do this one thing right."

I stared at him a moment longer in the mirror. My eyes traced the line of his cheekbone down to his strong jaw, clenched in frustration. I took a breath, determined to find the right words to comfort him, but nothing came.

My stomach churned from the speed and sudden drops as we flew on. I squeezed my eyes shut and put a hand on my stomach to try to settle it. I hated the sky. I'd grown up in an underground city in the Community and didn't think I'd ever get used to the empty expanse above. It was unnatural—all that *space*. And now we were suspended in it, with only the duo's whirring engine keeping us from crashing back to earth.

Adrien was quiet for the next half hour as we flew, but he

kept running scans for the attack transports who could find us if our cloak wore off. I had time to finally think and process everything that had just happened. I shivered with the realization that Chancellor Bright was enacting her plan. She was the Underchancellor of Defense now. I knew she'd never intended to remain the Chancellor of the Academy for long, but I hadn't expected her to move so fast. She'd already begun her quiet takeover, and, with her glitcher Gift of compulsion, none of the Uppers in power would see her coming.

I remembered the forced sincerity on her face when she'd offered for me to join her. She promised a utopia with glitchers in charge instead of the corrupt Uppers. I'd even been tempted, until I realized her plan only replaced one oppressive government with another, never changing anything about the Link system that enslaved millions. I'd rejected her offer. And barely escaped with my life.

"Hold on," Adrien said, breaking into my thoughts. "We're gonna make our descent now."

I gripped the black armrests hard as we dropped again, but it wasn't a quick dive this time. We kept falling and falling until I was sure the engine had failed. I opened my eyes just as the duo slowed suddenly, jerking me forward in my harness strap.

We'd dropped down into a forest. Green surrounded us on all sides, and Adrien slowly navigated the duo through the trees. Leaves slapped at the windows. It was as if the very air sprouted green. Leafy bushes and gigantic trees surrounded us, from above and on every side and the ground below.

I leaned away from the window, remembering the last time I'd been in a forest. It was when I had first met Adrien, six months ago. He'd tried to rescue me from the Community, only to discover once we left the underground city that I was deadly allergic to almost everything on the Surface. I looked down at the rip in my suit, then back out the window. I could only imagine all the billions of allergen particulates surrounding us. If something happened to the last underlayer of my suit here and I was exposed . . .

"The trees," I whispered, leaning closer to the glass in spite of my bad memories. "They're huge." The trunks were gigantic, several times wider than a person. I'd never seen anything like it.

"It's old-growth forest," Adrien said. "This area's been pretty much left alone over the last two hundred years. Look, you can barely see the sky, the canopy's so thick overhead."

I looked up through the top of the windshield, and he was right. Occasionally I'd catch a glimpse of blue, but for the most part the tops of the trees spread a dense canopy. I swallowed hard. I wasn't sure which was worse—being in the duo up in the open sky or being here surrounded on all sides by deadly greenery.

"But they're so much bigger than last time."

"Different forest," he said. "We're on the other side of the Sector."

That meant my home, and my brother, were thousands of miles away. My stomach dropped. Markan was safe for now. I had to focus on that. He was only thirteen, young enough that he'd still be a drone in the underground Community, numb to all thought and emotion. He wouldn't have felt anything about my disappearance. And if he did become a glitcher like me and wake up, it wouldn't happen for a couple of years. Most importantly, he was still five years away from getting the adult

V-chip, the device that would silence his emotions forever. I had to get him out before then, or he'd be lost.

But I wasn't sure how I'd be able to rescue him. The Chancellor was hunting me, and even if she weren't, how was I going to be able to infiltrate the tightly guarded Community? Especially since I couldn't even count on my power to help me.

Another branch smacked into the window, right near where the Reg had smashed his face. Several long spider cracks spread out from the site.

"Sorry," Adrien said, gripping the control stick harder and pulling back on it. Our speed slowed more. "There we are." He slowly came to a stop with the duo hovering over an open spot of ground. A woman appeared, seemingly out of no-where, carrying a heavy green cloth with her.

She made wide gesturing motions. Adrien popped the lid.

"Out, out, out. I need to cover it so they can't catch its heat signature."

Adrien jumped nimbly over the side of the duo to the ground, then held up a hand for me. I took it and hurled myself over. I landed much less gracefully, my thick boots thudding into the ground and sinking a few inches in.

Adrien quickly grabbed the thick cloth in the woman's hands and they spread it over the vehicle.

"Were you tracked?" she asked.

"No. I think our cloak held just long enough."

"There," the woman smiled and let out a breath. Her brown hair was pulled up in a loose bun and she had warm brown eyes. "You took a long time. You don't know how relieved I was to see the duo's beacon light. Though I'm surprised it still works, this thing looks so mangled." She gestured to the ripped-up hood.

"We barely got away." Adrien's said, his voice quiet. "And Milton didn't make it."

Jilia's eyebrows furrowed together. "I didn't know him, but I'm sorry." She pulled Adrien into a loose hug. "It's so good to see you." She was so short, the top of her head only reached the middle of his chest. She pulled back and turned to me. "And you must be Zoe. I'm Jilia, but everyone calls me Doc."

"Hi." I tried to take a step toward her, but my boot was stuck. I tugged a little harder and heard a slight suction noise as the ground released it. The bottom half of my boot was covered in a mixture of green and brown sludge. "Ugh," I muttered, just as I heard a gentle *tap, tap, tap* on the rounded top of my helmet. I looked up and several drops of water landed on my face mask.

"That's springtime for you. Mud and near constant rain. Hurry, let's get you inside and dry." She started walking.

Adrien took my hand and we made our way forward through the woods. My feet suctioned and released with every step. The trees and foliage all blended together, and I didn't understand how the woman could move so sure-footedly. She weaved around trees and over logs as if she knew exactly where she was going even though everything around us looked the same to me. The rain started to come down harder until little rivulets ran down the faceplate of my helmet. I reached up a hand to wipe the water away, but I only smeared it around and added some mud from my glove to the mix.

I stumbled on a thick root and pitched forward. Adrien

tried to catch me, but I took us both down. A long ripping noise filled the air as we fell.

The suit.

I held my breath even though I knew that wouldn't really matter. With my hyperallergies, any skin contact with the air would trigger a lethal attack. I looked down frantically, but I could barely see a thing through my smudged faceplate. "Is it ripped?"

Adrien immediately started searching my suit. An agonizing minute passed before he breathed out and held up my forearm where the outer suit material hung almost completely off now.

"It was just the two top layers that you'd already ripped. The underlayer is still safe. That was too close," Adrien said, his eyes wide. He reached up and wiped my faceplate clean with the sleeve of his tunic. His hair dripped with water.

"It's okay," I said, my heart still thrumming in my chest. "I'm fine. Let's keep going and get you out of the rain."

He let out a slow breath and nodded. He interlocked his fingers tight in mine as we started forward again.

After a few more minutes, Jilia announced that we'd arrived.

I looked ahead and frowned. I didn't see a building. Just more green. "Where?"

Jilia laughed. "Right here." She reached toward one of the trees, but when she touched it, it rippled and moved like a cloth surface. What had looked like a three-dimensional forest was actually a painted curtain.

"It doesn't work close up, but we're deep enough in the

forest that it's camouflaged from any random flyovers. The material's like the tarp I used on the duo, it covers heat signatures so thermosatellite scans don't detect us."

She gestured for us to step in, and I nudged Adrien ahead of me. I was kept dry by my suit, but he was drenched. I followed him inside to a softly lit, small interior room. Rain spattered loudly on the roof and the walls.

Adrien's wet tunic clung to him. His shoulders seemed wider than when I'd last seen him and his wiry arm muscles more sharply cut. But he looked thinner too, and when he turned I could see just how ripped-up his back was from the chute.

"Your back!" I said. His tunic hung in tatters and blood had dried from a couple of deep gashes below his shoulder blades. Deep bruises were already starting to bloom.

"Oh right, I forgot about it," he said. He turned around so Jilia could see. She immediately reached out a hand.

I winced when she touched him, placing her hand on the worst of his injuries. Then as I watched, the lacerations wove themselves shut under her touch. I looked back and forth between the now smoothed skin and Jilia's face, feeling my eyes widen. "You're a glitcher?"

"Yep," she said. "First generation, like Adrien's mom."

"Can you heal anything?" I asked.

"I can only heal minor wounds, knit tissue and sometimes bones back together, that kind of thing." She saw my face drop and smiled apologetically. "I can't deal with anything at the systemic cellular level, like allergies."

I moved closer. Within a few minutes, the skin of Adrien's back was completely smooth. Even the bruises were gone. His muscles rippled under his skin as he rotated his shoulders and breathed out a sigh of relief. "Good as new. Thanks, Doc."

"That's amazing," I whispered, still staring.

"Have you had a lot of traffic lately?" Adrien asked.

"Busier than ever," Jilia said. "A whole safe house got cracked last week, so our beds were full up. Most of them have moved on."

Adrien must have seen my questioning glance. "The Resistance uses mobile tent compounds like this one for way stations."

"We try to set them up outside all the major cities for travelers," Jilia said. "Or so Rez operatives heading into the city on raids have a base station, or if a situation gets too hot for our people living in the city and they have to run." She looked at Adrien. "But I can't remember when it's ever been this bad."

Adrien's face darkened. "It's gotta be because of Underchancellor Bright. She's got access to Rez prisoners now, and she can force them to tell her anything she wants. Safe house locations, encryption codes, anything."

Something passed between them, a quiet communication of dread, before Jilia turned to me and smiled. "Come on, let's get you inside. Tyryn was cooking up something that smelled delicious when I saw the duo beacon and came to meet you."

"Tyryn's here?" Adrien asked, his face breaking into a smile.

Jilia nodded. "And his sister Xona. You remember her?"

"She was just a kid the last time I saw her."

Jilia's face soured a bit. "She's not little anymore. Tyryn

brought her up here a few weeks ago. She's been getting into fights with the other Rez kids ever since their parents died."

"I heard about that." Adrien's voice was quiet. "Her mom and mine used to be friends."

"Anyway, let's get you cleaned up, and then you can say hi."

I looked down at my suit. Spattered mud covered my legs, and, in spite of the oxygen constantly circulating, I could smell how sweaty I was. Everything had been happening so fast, I hadn't stopped to wonder what came next. "So I guess I stay in this suit till we can get to the Foundation where I can change into another?" I asked uncertainly. I looked at the muddy, ripped outer layers.

"Oh no, no, I've got a new suit for you," Jilia assured me quickly. "We shipped some here just in case. It's much thinner and more flexible. It's made of polysurtrate, a new tribond blend that won't tear or even cut easily. And it allows a far better range of motion than the old model. You'll love it. It'll fit like a second skin."

"But how do I get from this suit," I pointed down at myself, "into another one without being exposed to the air?"

Jilia smiled. She pushed through a tent flap in front of her and gestured at us to follow. "One of the benefits of a portable research facility. This is the bathroom, normal shower and toilet on one side—" she pointed to one curtain partition covering the left half of the room, "—and this is the three-chambered, all-enclosed allergen wash-down station." She pointed to a long, rectangular container on the other side of the room that was about seven feet tall and four elevator pods wide.

"And just in case, here's an epi infuser." She handed me the thin, stylus-sized device.

"Great," I said weakly, my heart thumping at the thought of having to use it.

"I'm sure it will be fine," Jilia said quickly. "Let me go get your new suit." She turned and pushed through the flap at the far end of the room that must lead to another tent chamber.

Adrien stepped closer and put a hand on the small of my back. "You okay?"

I didn't answer, just leaned into his chest. He wrapped his strong arms around me, pulling me in tight. Even through my thick helmet, I could hear the steady beat of his heart. He dropped his chin on top of my head and rubbed my back in gentle circles. I melted against him. I was exhausted, and his arms felt so good around me, I thought I might fall asleep right there.

He pulled away, looking intently at my face. I tried to raise the sides of my mouth into something that resembled a smile, but I was sure it looked more like a grimace. He laughed. "It's gonna be okay. We're safe now," he said, giving my hand a squeeze. He nodded his head toward the container. "After you get the new suit on, you can finally rest. I'll be waiting when you come out."

Jilia came back with a shrink-wrapped plastic bag in her hands.

"After each cycle, the next door will open. Just move right through with it."

The lights turned on as I stepped inside. The tiny chamber was about the size of a square elevator pod. The door closed before I could say anything else.

Almost immediately spouts dropped from the ceiling and from the walls, and the next instant a hammering spray assaulted me from all sides. The cycle lasted for almost ten complete minutes. A drain at the button suctioned up all the water as it poured down.

I was glad to peel off the suit and my sweaty underclothes in the next chamber, but it felt strange to strip completely down, knowing that outside this container only a mere spread of tent material separated me from the dripping green forest. I clutched the epi infuser in my hand after I dropped the last bit of the suit to the floor.

I paused and closed my eyes, not daring to breathe. I waited to feel any of the telltale signs of an allergy attack. But I could only hold my breath for so long, and eventually I had to take in a gulping breath of the steamy air.

I clutched the epi infuser tighter, my thumb on the release button. One breath, and then another.

I peeked one eye open.

No swelling, no rash.

I was fine.

I breathed out again as another set of sprayers came out from the sides. Instead of water, warm white foam spurted at me, followed by another pounding spray of hot water that left me certain that every millimeter of my body had been scoured raw.

After a bracing rush of air that lasted five more minutes, even my thick curly hair was dry. I stretched my neck and took a deep breath in, taking a moment to enjoy standing free from the restrictive suit.

I opened the plastic bag that held the new suit. It was smaller than I expected, made of dark blue stretchy material that was only about a centimeter thick. There weren't any boots on the bottom, and I slipped my foot into the leg just like I would a sock. The suit pulled up snug around my waist. Really snug. I thought of Adrien holding me earlier in the bulky suit and wondered with a blush what he'd think of me in this one.

I rebraided my hair, then fit my arms in and pulled on the helmet with the built-in faceplate. The plastic glass of the face-plate was curved in closer around my face, just half an inch away from my nose at its apex, but the surface area was larger. Instead of being a tight rectangular window, the plastic was clear all the way from ear to ear so that I had much better peripheral vision. I stretched my neck. I liked the way the suit moved with me. I looked down at the front where the fabric was still slack. Even though these gloves were thinner and my fingers less clumsy, I couldn't figure out how to seal it up.

Jilia's voice came on over a small speaker. "Activate the console on the right arm of the suit, and it will self-seal."

I did what she said and the slack at the front of the suit suddenly wove itself closed. I took a little breath in as it tightened on my ribs and wondered just how formfitting it was going to be. Jilia had said it would feel like a second skin, but this left very little to the imagination. I stretched my arms and lifted my knees up to my chest a couple times, trying to get comfortable in it.

The front loosened a little and I felt like I could breathe again. I pulled on the oxygen tank that fit like a slim backpack. It clicked into place and fresh air began circulating through the mask. Finally I was able to press the release button and step back into the tent.

Adrien was waiting, all clean and in a dry tunic. I stepped out tentatively, worrying that I looked ridiculous in the tight suit. When he saw me, his eyes widened. He looked me up and down. Color bloomed in his cheeks, but he didn't look away as a sideways smile slowly spread.

His reaction made me feel bolder, and I walked around the small space and gave a little twirl, feeling more confident with every step. When I looked back at him, his bright aqua eyes twinkled.

"Nice suit," he said.

I arranged the pillow under my head and tried to get comfortable. I was so tired, I thought I'd fall asleep right away. Instead, the events of the day played like a vid screen across my closed eyelids.

I thought of Milton and wondered if even now his poor, crumpled body was being tossed into one of the incinerators. Bile rose a little in my throat at the thought. I banished the image and tried to think of something else instead. The living matter, not the dead, Adrien had said.

I looked at the thin tent wall and tried to imagine Adrien on the other side of it. Was he asleep already? I thought of his arms around me earlier and felt cold and lonely. There had been so much space separating us for so long. And now that we were finally together, we still felt too far apart.

I sat up, then after a brief moment of indecision, got to my feet and padded over to the hanging tent flap of my room and slipped into his.

He was sitting at the edge of his mattress, his forearms on his knees. His eyebrows had been bunched together as he stared at the wall with a sad, faraway look in his eyes. He blinked, surprised by my sudden appearance, and then smiled as I stepped inside.

I'd been so sure when I left my room, but suddenly I felt self-conscious. I didn't really have a reason for coming in and disturbing him. He gestured for me to sit. "Are you okay? What's going on?" he asked.

I sat down on the mattress beside his. Each room partition had several beds for when the compound was full of people traveling through. "Nothing," I said. "I just . . . didn't want to be alone." I looked down and fiddled with the tip of my glove, suddenly shy and awkward. He grabbed my hands to stop me, then moved swiftly so that he was sitting beside me. His thigh was warm next to mine.

"I'm not really in the mood to be alone either. I think too much when I'm alone." His smile was sad, but he quickly masked it with a mischievous wink. "Plus, I couldn't stop thinking of you in the other room, so close by. In that suit." I blushed.

He let go of my hand, but absentmindedly began to gently trace a line up over my wrist, to my elbow, then all the way to my shoulder. The fabric of the new suit was so thin, I could feel the pressure of his fingertip. A shiver went up and down my body, and I couldn't help arching my back.

"God, you're beautiful," he whispered.

All the day's worry and terror and chaos suddenly dropped away at his touch. I turned to him and wrapped my arms

around his neck, trying to pull him close, but I was too awkward and the movement knocked us both back onto the mattress. Adrien laughed. Our legs tangled together and he dropped
his head to nuzzle at my neck. I ran my gloved hands through
his hair, trembling at the feel of him in my arms. But the material between us was such a barrier. I was tired of barriers.

"This stupid suit," I said as my hands curved up behind his
shoulder blades.

"Hey, I am very fond of this suit. It's saving your life." His
fingers clutched at my waist, right above my hips. It sent a
burning fire racing through my stomach.

"But I know what you mean," he murmured. A low growl
escaped his throat as he pulled away.

"What's wrong?" I sat up in alarm.

"Nothing," he said with a laugh, running his hands through
his hair. "You're driving me crazy is all."

His words gave me a zing of satisfaction. "Really?" I asked,
smiling wide.

"Really. Look at you!" He gestured up and down at me.
"And I can't even kiss you!" He reached out and wove his
fingers with mine. He closed his eyes and dropped his head
slightly so that his face was shadowed in the dim light. "When
I'm touching you, it's like everything slows down for a minute. All my thoughts finally narrow down to focus only on
the feel of your hand in mine. The rest of the time everything
is pressing down so hard. The past. The future." He shook his
head and swallowed hard. "Sometimes I feel like I'm gonna
break under the strain."

"You're not going to break," I whispered, squeezing his hand
tighter. "You're the strongest person I know."

He let out a scoffing noise and shook his head again. "Hardly."

"It's true," I insisted. I paused, watching the tension tightening at the corner of Adrien's mouth.

"How are we really doing?" I asked quietly. "You've been working with the Rez. You've seen visions. Do we really have a chance? Can we really take down the Chancellor and the Community?"

He was quiet a long moment, as if he was trying to find the right words. "I don't really know how to answer you," he finally said, looking down. "Sometimes I worry we're fighting a war we can never win. We're impossibly outnumbered, we don't have enough resources, and now that the Chancellor has joined the war, we're stretched too thin. We were always fighting an impossible fight—that's life in the Rez for ya. But now . . ." his voice quieted. "I don't know. It's harder to hold on to hope. We're fighting for a dream, for a life unlike anything we've ever known. Maybe it can't be done."

"Then why—?" I stopped myself.

"Why fight?" He finished. "Why risk everything for something we might not win?" He turned his face back to me, his aqua eyes sparking to life just like they always used to when we talked. "Because if we don't fight, we've already lost. Without hope, without trying, there's no point. There's no future. And you, Zoe," his voice softened. "I would fight forever to have a future with you."

"Maybe hope alone can make a difference," I said. "Maybe having something to fight for will make us stronger than anything they can throw at us."

He nodded, but I wasn't sure if he was really agreeing with

me. Then he looked back at me and smirked. "You know, we're talking about war and revolution, but really this is supposed to be when you sneak into my room just to make out."

I laughed. "But I'm trapped in this suit."

He lifted a hand and caressed down the side of my head. "You must be exhausted."

"But I can't sleep."

"I have an idea. Here, lay down on your stomach." He moved to arrange the pillow for me.

I laid down, and he put his hands on my shoulders, squeezing and rubbing his thumbs in circles. I felt like I was about to melt into the mattress. He moved from my shoulders up to my neck, and then back down again.

I felt myself growing drowsier with each passing minute. Even though I wanted to stay awake so I didn't miss a moment with him, I quickly dropped off to sleep.

Chapter 4

I WOKE EARLY, confused about where I was until I felt Adrien's arm draped lazily across me. In spite of everything, I couldn't help smiling. I tried to slide out of Adrien's grasp without waking him, but he stirred anyway.

"Hey," he said as I sat up.

I looked down at him, his hair crumpled from sleep, his eyes blinking open slowly. I'd never seen him this way before. All dreamy, before the weight of the world had fully settled back on his shoulders. I loved the way his brow jutted out to shadow his eyes, and the smooth aquiline cut of his nose. I could have stared at him forever.

"Keep sleeping," I whispered, but he rubbed his eyes and sat up.

"Nah, I'm alright. What time is it?"

I raised my arm and looked at the readout on my suit. "Six. I'm serious, you should get more sleep."

He got to his feet. "Can't," he grinned, his eyes still sleepy. "View's too nice to close my eyes again."

I smacked him on the shoulder, but felt a slight blush come to my cheeks anyway.

He pulled me close and nuzzled a kiss in the curve of my

neck. Even through the suit I could feel the gentle pressure of his touch. But still it wasn't the same as really being able to touch him. I cursed my allergies for the millionth time.

He pulled back and gestured to the curtain that hung as a sleep partition. "After you."

Jilia was already up. She stood at the counter with her back to us.

I looked around the room, impressed again at how many conveniences they had in spite of the fact that this was a mobile building in the middle of nowhere. A small kitchen area was set up in the corner, complete with a sink and a food thermal unit. A table with six chairs took up half the room, and the other half was filled with research equipment. An extensive four-screen console was open on the desk in the corner. The screens were filled with text and diagrams of the brain.

Jilia filled a pot with steaming hot water. Her hair was in a bun again, but with the full morning light coming through the plastic window, I could see a few gray tendrils tucked in against the brown above her ears. She wore a simple faded red tunic. She paused when we came in and smiled warmly at us. "You two are up early."

"Is that coffee?" Adrien yawned loudly. "I could really use some."

"What's coffee?" I asked.

Jilia laughed. "You Community dwellers really are deprived. But since you both are up so early, there was something I was hoping to do this morning." She set the pot down.

"What is it?" Adrien asked, grabbing a mug from a hook on the wall and pouring out some of the steaming black drink.

"Well," Jilia said, "I've been studying glitcher brain phenomena for a long time, almost as soon as the Rez rescued me and I could get my hands on a console system." She turned to me. "I was hoping I could do a scan of your brain to further my research. I've been eager to study you ever since Adrien told me about the things you've been able to do with your power." Her eyebrows were raised, the excitement clear on her face. "I have some theories about glitcher mutations and I think gathering data points from a scan of your brain would really help."

I thought of all the years getting poked and prodded at the hands of the Community when they implanted new hardware. I swallowed nervously. "Will it be invasive?"

"Oh no, not at all. All external. But I'm getting ahead of myself. I should let you get some breakfast first." She leaned over to pull some protein pouches out of a box.

"No, that's fine," I said quickly, my stomach turning at the thought of the thick goo she was offering. Until they learned more about the extent of my allergies, it was all I was allowed to eat. The bottom of my helmet had a complicated mechanism whereby a straw could be inserted safely. But I knew from trying it last night that the grainy protein mix tasted horrible.

"Great." Jilia's face lit up. "Come on over here, then, I'll show you." She hurried across the room to her console station. She clicked a button and a 3-D model of the brain rotated in a projection cube beside the desk. I leaned in to look closer. It seemed like a normal brain.

"Help me grab this exam table," Jilia said, and Adrien helped her pull out a padded black table that had been folded in half against the wall.

"Zoe, if you'll just lay here."

I laid down and Jilia rolled over another machine level

with the table. She positioned three metal arms around my head.

"The suit won't interfere with the scan?" I asked.

"Nope, no problem at all. Now let me hook this up here—" She hooked a cable into the machine, then sat at the chair in front of the console. A few more clicks and I heard the machine beside my head whir to life. "Now lay as still as you can," she said.

I looked at the ceiling and tried not to twitch. The machine clicked and rotated around my head, making a complete circle. My eyes tracked the spinning metal arms.

After a few more moments, Jilia announced, "All done. Now, let's look at the data." The excitement in her voice was palpable. Adrien pulled the scanner away from the sides of my head and helped me sit up.

"If you can tell I'm a glitcher from a brain scan, why can't the Community? Or the Chancellor? She could use it to find potential glitchers and recruit them."

Jilia was typing and clicking on the console. "Luckily, their equipment isn't as fine-tuned as this. I've spent years developing software to detect these subtle differences, and only because I knew what I was looking for. The best the Chancellor could do is detect glitcher brain activity after six months of glitching. And by then, the glitcher has usually been reported and 'repaired' or been rescued by us."

She leaned in closer to the screen, looking at what was just a long string of gibberish to me. "Wow," she breathed out.

"What is it?" Adrien moved in closer.

"I'll show you," Jilia said. "It'll be easier than trying to explain it." She tapped on the screen a few more times, then turned to the projection cube. "This is a typical brain."

PEDEK 07

Remove from holdshelf on:
2017-11-20T10:12:39-0600

Title: Override #2

Request date: 2017-11-08
Slip Date: 2017-11-10 10:12
Printed at FOSSTON

An image of a brain rotated in the orange light. "This is what a non-glitcher brain looks like. The sparks of blue represent neuron activity." She pointed at various portions of the brain where minuscule blue dots lit up, making small bright clouds. "And this—" she said, then tapped the screen a few times, "is a glitcher brain."

I leaned. "They look the same to me."

"Here, I'll show them side by side. See the frontal cortex here on the glitcher brain?"

I looked closer, glancing back and forth between the two images. "There's more blue light," I said, looking up at Jilia.

She smiled. "Exactly. At first we thought glitchers simply had an increased neural capacity due to the brain adapting around the Link hardware the Community installed. But now, it's clear that the actual number of neurons has been increasing exponentially. There are genes that usually lay dormant that, in glitcher brains, are finally finding expression. The electrical impulses and connections your brain is able to make—it's not the same leap as the difference between primates and humans, but it's still impressive."

Jilia tapped in the screen a few more times. "Now, hold on. This is Zoe's brain." The blue lights on the new model covered almost the entire frontal lobe. Adrien gasped and took a step back. I blinked, certain I was seeing it wrong.

"But what does that mean?" I asked. I was suddenly queasy. My powers, the uncontrollable seizures, Adrien's visions of me as a powerful leader. All of it must be explained by the brain scan in front of me. Solid proof that I was different. My stomach dropped. I didn't want to be different. I didn't want to have all this power capped up inside me. I just wanted to be a regular glitcher.

49

"To be honest, I don't know." Jilia's eyes were still trained on the model, and as she leaned in to look closer, her face was bathed in reflected blue light. "I've never seen this before." I couldn't read the look on her face—it seemed like a mixture of surprise and excitement. It was clear Jilia only saw strength and possibility when she looked at the model of my brain, but I saw it for what it really was: dangerous.

"Do you have any unusual symptoms? Headaches? Surges in power? New abilities?"

I glanced at Adrien. "Sometimes I lose control, and I feel like it's too powerful to fit inside my skin."

Jilia nodded. "Training for you is going to be a bit difficult because we've never seen anything like you before. I'm not sure how best to tap into it and control it, but we can experiment with a few different methods."

She looked away from the screen. "You might be the most powerful glitcher in the new generation, perhaps even the most powerful we've ever seen. I can see now that there could be truth to all of Adrien's visions, Zoe. Perhaps you'll be able to save us after all." Her voice held a note of awe.

I didn't know what to say to that. I wanted to convince her that she was wrong. I wasn't special. Maybe even Adrien's visions were wrong. I didn't have a clue how to save anyone, couldn't they see that?

Adrien leaned in, his expression dark and withdrawn as his eyes flickered over the data on the scan. He didn't look at me, and I couldn't tell what he must be thinking, but his silence sent a chill through me.

Chapter 5

DURING OUR LATE BREAKFAST, Jilia explained the results of my brain scan to Tyryn. "It's like nothing we've ever seen before."

I shifted uncomfortably in my seat. Tyryn was a friendly guy, just a few years older than Adrien and me. I'd never seen anyone with such a developed physique. His arm muscles strained the sleeves of his shirt. He also had a wide scar from forehead to chin. The angry line of healed skin was shiny against the dark brown skin of his face.

"General Taylor will be pleased to hear it," Tyryn said, finishing his last bite of an omelet and then sitting back in his chair. I could feel his eyes on me, assessing me. "She's asked me to head up a new glitcher task force. We'll start training when we get to the Foundation."

"What?" I nearly choked on the gritty protein mix coming through my straw. "But—" I started, then stopped. "I'm not sure I'm ready for that."

"Don't worry," Tyryn said, his voice calm. "I've actually never trained a team of glitchers before, but I've been training Rez recruits for eight years. We won't put you in the field until you're ready."

"It's not just the, um, fighting I'm worrying about," I said, looking between him and Jilia. "It's my power. It's getting harder and harder to control."

Tyryn turned to Jilia. "You've studied glitchers. What do you think?"

"Telekinesis is a unique ability with its own set of obstacles," Jilia said. "It's not like other glitchers can tear a room apart if their power goes haywire."

I looked down. "But do you have any idea why it's gotten so out of control lately? Does that happen to other people?"

"Most glitchers experience an expansion of their powers as they grow into them. And glitcher powers are so closely connected to the emotion centers of the brain. You've been through a lot lately and you're still so new to feeling emotion of any kind, it makes sense that overwhelming emotion would make your power erupt in unpredictable ways." She leaned in, her eyes compassionate. "Most people have seventeen years to learn how to deal with emotions. You've only had eight months. But Zoe, I do think that with some discipline and practice, you'll learn to control it again."

"Jilia's helped me before," Adrien said, eyeing the older woman. "I wasn't having exactly the same kind of problems, obviously, but she worked with me to help focus my visions through meditation. She can help you, Zoe." He turned to Jilia. "You're coming with us to the Foundation, right?"

"Oh," Jilia hesitated, pushing her food around on the plate with her fork. It was the first time her excitement had flagged since she'd looked at my scans. "I'm not sure. I'm more helpful here in the field."

"From what General Taylor was saying," Tyryn cut in,

"the Foundation's almost completely finished, and it's already her new base of operations. We'll need a good doctor."

"I'm sure Professor Henry would look forward to seeing you again," Adrien added.

Jilia's face went red and she stuffed a forkful of food in her mouth. She stared at her plate and didn't respond.

Adrien's voice softened, as if he knew he'd hit a nerve. "And it would give you more chance to study Zoe and the other glitchers there."

"Either way," Tyryn said. "The sooner we head out, the better. Chancellor Bright's cracking Rez operatives faster than we can get them in place." He looked at Jilia. "Not many people know about this location, but it only takes one. We'll be heading out in a couple of days. I've already arranged transport to the Foundation, and there's plenty of space if you want to come with us. If you stay, though, you should think about going mobile again and moving this compound deeper into the forest."

Jilia pressed a napkin to her lips. "I was hoping there'd be more time."

"Time's short these days," Tyryn said, his mouth grim. "Xona and I know it better than anyone."

A girl came out from behind the flap to the other sleeping quarters, yawning and stretching her long arms. Her skin was ebony and her hair cropped short. She looked about my age, maybe a year or so younger. "Did I hear my name?" she asked through another yawn.

"Nice of you to finally grace us with your presence," Tyryn said. "Xona, this is Zoe, and you know Adrien."

Xona gave a quick nod but didn't look our way. She hopped

up on the counter with the coffee pot and poured herself a cup. It had to be cold by now, but she didn't seem to mind. She drank it down in one long gulp. Her legs dangled and I could see a small laser weapon strapped at her ankle, even though she was still in her sleep clothes.

Jilia frowned. "You know I'd prefer it if you weren't armed at the kitchen table."

Xona's eyes narrowed as she tossed the metal coffee cup into the sink. "You never know when a detachment of Regs is gonna bust in. I'd rather be prepared than have table manners."

"Xona," Tyryn said, a warning in his voice. "Jilia's place, her rules."

"Ugh, fine." Xona rolled her eyes and hopped down from the counter. She whipped the weapon out of its holster and clicked a small release switch that detached the grip from the barrel. She dropped both pieces on the table with a loud clunk. "There, not armed."

"Xona—" Tyryn started, but Jilia put a hand on his arm.

"It's fine," she said.

Xona grabbed a piece of bread from the counter and stuck half of it in her mouth, then sat down at the table and started cleaning the weapon with the edge of her tunic.

"At least get a plate," Tyryn said, his teeth gritted. "Mom didn't raise you to be an animal."

Xona glared at him. She ripped the rest of the bread into pieces and dropped it on the table beside the gun. "Don't talk about Mom."

Jilia and Adrien exchanged a silent look. Then I remembered Tyryn and Xona's parents had died recently. I cleared my throat, hoping to dispel the tension in the room by changing the subject.

"Have you met the rest of the glitcher task force?" I asked Tyryn. "What are they like?"

"I haven't met many yet," he said, finally looking away from his sister. "I just know what General Taylor's told me. Glitchers make for unique Rez fighters. Taylor ultimately wants a task force that can take on the Chancellor herself. From what I heard, everyone's really looking forward to meeting you and having you on the team. You're the only one who can even get close to the Chancellor without falling under her compulsion powers."

"Wait." I pulled my hand away from Adrien's and held on to the edge of the table to steady myself. "You expect me to take on the Chancellor?"

"You've faced her before," Tyryn said.

"Things are different now," I sputtered. "She was only the Chancellor of the Academy in one small city then. Now she's Underchancellor of Defense for all of Sector 6. She'll be surrounded by the highest security."

Xona let out a low whistle. "Shunt, that's intense."

Tyryn waved a hand and looked at me. "Adrien's had visions of you as a leader, and Jilia's scans confirm how powerful you are."

"You won't have to do anything right away," Adrien said taking my hand again. "You won't be asked until you're ready."

My chest tightened so much I could barely get a breath. Adrien knew about their plan and this task force? Of course he did. He'd probably had a vision of it. I didn't trust myself to respond, so I just shook my head.

After breakfast was cleared away and the others had gone into the other room, I grabbed Adrien. "Tell me about your visions of me. Will I really be able to do this?"

"Zo, don't worry about it. It'll all be fine." He pulled me into a hug.

I clung to him for a moment, but then pulled away. "Are you saying it will be fine because you've *seen* that it all turns out okay?"

His face clouded over. "I haven't had any visions that make it clear who wins the war, if that's what you're asking." He didn't say anything else.

"But you've seen visions of me? Me being this leader they all expect me to be?"

He was quiet a moment.

"Tell me, please."

"Zoe, maybe it's not good to know too much about your own future. I've probably told you too much already. No one would have expected you to be some great leader in the first place if I'd kept my mouth shut about what I saw."

I scoffed. "If you hadn't told people your visions, they never would have let you rescue me from the Community."

He nodded, but still didn't look certain.

"If you tell me what you see, then maybe I can start to believe it too. Maybe it will give me the strength I need."

He looked at me reluctantly for another moment, but then finally said, "Okay." He sat back down at the table and I joined him. "There's this one vision I had. Actually it was one of the first I had of you." He smiled. "The farther off in the future, the less clear it is what's going on, and this one was just flashes.

In the vision, the sun is shining overhead, but you aren't wearing a biosuit or breathing mask or anything."

"How is that possible?" I looked down at my gloves, then at the edges of the mask only inches away from my face.

"I don't know," he said. "In the first glimpse I got, all I could see was that you were running toward a house near the ocean. It looked almost like you're flying, you're running so fast. And then I got a closer image of your face, and you've got this look," he smiled again. "Like you were determined but not afraid, even though I got the feeling that you were in danger. You weren't scared."

The tightness in my chest didn't ease up at all. I thought hearing about the future would make me feel better, but it sounded like he was describing a stranger. How was I supposed to become this person?

"Were you there?" I asked.

His smile faded. "No."

"Was anyone else there?"

"No."

"Oh."

In the future I was all alone and running into danger. Great.

"But that's not what's important. It's gotta mean we'll figure out a way around your allergies someday."

I nodded, but didn't feel very reassured. "Okay," I said finally, "will you tell me another one? Maybe one that's not so far off?"

He looked down. "I really don't think it's a good idea."

"Why not?"

"Because the more I learn about how the visions work . . ."

He shook his head. "I just don't think it's a good idea." The look on his face made it sound final.

Before I could say anything, Xona stomped into the kitchen. She reached down to seal the strap closed on her shoes before hiking her foot up onto the counter beside the coffeemaker.

She noticed us sitting at the table. "Sorry, counter's got the best height for stretching."

She looked between me and Adrien like she was gauging the level of tension between us. "I'm going for a run." She kept stretching, then looked back at me. "You can come if you want. There's some extra shoes by the door."

"Really?" I asked. She'd seemed so gruff before, I was surprised by the offer.

She paused to look at me more critically. "Well, if you can keep up."

Adrien was still holding my hand. "Look Zoe, we can talk about this more—"

"No," I pushed back my chair abruptly. I didn't want to keep pressing Adrien to tell me about the future when he obviously didn't want to. "A run sounds great right now. Besides," I looked back at Adrien and tried to smile. I felt upset about our conversation, but I didn't want to take it out on him. "You said I'll be strong in the future. How else am I going to make that happen unless I train now?"

The early morning sun shone down through the layers of trees and leaves, but a lot of the ground was still in shadow. Only a few leaves were lit up bright green where the sunlight managed to break through.

"I've got a route I usually run," Xona said, jumping up and

down a few times to warm her limbs. She looked over at me. "I'm not going to slow down for you."

I nodded, fixated on all the green in the forest around us. It was still astonishing and unnerving. It wasn't just green, it was a hundred different shades, from the deeper green of the leaves hidden in shadow to the bright, almost neon green moss that covered the rocks and the bottoms of the trees.

"Ex-drones," Xona said under her breath with a smirk. "You guys always get so cracked about the Surface." Then before I could respond, she took off, racing into the forest. I followed as fast as I could, not wanting to lose sight of her in the vast green maze.

It felt good to run. The suit stretched easily with every step I took until I barely noticed I had it on. Running had always calmed me, both in my Community days and in the lab alcove. But running on the Surface was far different from running on a treadmill. On the treadmill, you could lose yourself in thought as the regular pounding of your footfalls provided a hypnotic rhythm. Out here, you had to constantly watch where you were going. The forest floor was springy and uneven, and I kept my eyes trained on the ground to make sure I didn't trip over tree roots or bushes as we went.

But the exertion did feel good. It was a relief to forget about all the insanity of the past few days and think only about where my foot would land next.

"Thanks," I said to Xona, huffing from the incline we had just run up. "I really needed a good run."

She looked at me out of the corner of her eye as she continued jogging, clearly impressed that I'd managed to catch up to her. She didn't seem winded at all. The path was wider so we jogged side by side.

"Seemed like things were intense between you two back there. Then again," she cocked her head, "Adrien was always an intense guy. That brooding stare of his used to drive all the Rez girls wild."

She looked at me like she was waiting for a reaction.

"Yeah?" I asked, not taking the bait. "Jilia said you knew each other growing up?"

"From when he was fourteen. He ran away and joined up with the Rez unit my dad led. 'Course his mom got all crazy when she found out where he'd run away to. She came into the compound where we were staying, yelling and screaming about how he was too young. My dad talked her down. Did his whole, 'the young are the future of the Rez' shtick." She sounded sarcastic as she mimicked her father. "Though from what I hear, you're supposed to be the real future of the Rez."

I felt the blood leave my face. If she was trying to get a reaction out of me, she'd finally succeeded.

"If you believe the rumors about Adrien's visions," I said, trying to shrug off the comment.

"Well, I don't. The whole idea of destiny is total piss. No offense. But I'm not going to believe one girl's gonna save the world just because someone had a vision."

"Even if Adrien's visions always seem to come true?"

Xona paused, slowing her stride. "So far, maybe. But saying something is fated sounds just like the lies my mom used to tell me about how it was all gonna turn out okay. How all the bad stuff in life was part of a bigger purpose and that everything happens for a reason. How all the lives sacrificed for the Rez will be meaningful in the end when we win."

She shook her head, looking angry. "But that's a stack of lies. Besides," she looked over at me, "if you're supposed to save the world, then that means the world was supposed to be all shunted up like this in the first place. It means this war, the V-chip, everything—" she paused, and I could tell she was thinking about her parents' deaths. "Things don't happen for a reason. If they did, what kind of sick world would this be?"

She sped up again, her face hardening. I kept pace with her, but my lungs were burning.

"Are you sure you even believe in his visions?" she asked. "Can you really handle the pressure of having to be some kind of savior?"

"I'm hoping to have some help," I said through huffing breaths. I wished I could wipe my forearm across my sweaty brow, but because of the mask all I could do was let it drip down my face. I didn't like the direction the conversation had taken. "What about the other glitchers we're going to meet at the Foundation? Do you know any of them?"

"I usually steer clear of glitchers."

"Are you always this friendly?" My voice was sharper than I meant it.

She laughed. "Look, I feel bad for you guys, okay? They put stuff in your brains, and your powers are a freak side effect. I get it, it's not your fault. But in the end," she shrugged, "you're still just another bi-product of what Comm Corp created. The Rez is fighting so that the world can go back to the way it *was*, before the Community and brain hardware and glitchers ever existed."

The path narrowed, and Xona ran ahead of me. I gave up trying to continue the conversation. We were obviously never going to be friends. Instead I thought about what she had said about the future of the Rez. I wanted to be a part of it, to help people, but there was so much responsibility being put on my shoulders. Everyone had these huge expectations of me. I thought about how Xona had said people expected *me* to be the future of the Rez. And the way Adrien had described that fearless girl in the future . . .

I just didn't understand how I went from being me to being her. Every time someone talked about me being a leader, it sounded like they were talking about someone else. Would I wake up one day and suddenly be that girl, or was I supposed to somehow be actively trying to change myself into her?

The memory of the little blue lights from Jilia's brain scan flashed in my mind. I was changing all right. I just wasn't as certain about what I'd become. I imagined the power multiplying more and more until my body split into a million pieces, little blue lights pouring out of me like water from a broken glass.

I yelped in surprise when Xona suddenly stopped in front of me and pulled me down beside her against the tree. "Don't move. Something's coming," she whispered. Her cool confidence was gone.

We hunched down into a space between two fat roots. I heard a distant humming noise that grew louder as it came closer. The noisier it got, the more my heart hammered in my chest. My telek clamored to life under my skin. I squeezed my eyes shut as my forearm began to shake. Not now. If I acciden-

tally let loose right now and was seen, we would all be caught
and delivered to the Chancellor. Or killed on the spot.

The mechanical humming got louder and louder until it was
a dull roar.

It passed directly overhead. Xona and I both tensed, curling ourselves up as small as possible against the tree trunk.
Turning my head sideways, I could just make out a flash of
metal through the tree branches. For a horrible second, I
thought it was slowing down. But then it kept going.

We stayed frozen for several more long minutes as the engine's whine became a distant hum again. It didn't loop back
around. They hadn't seen us.

Xona let out a huge sigh of relief.

"What was that?"

"Sweeper drone, scanning the area." She put her hand above
her eyes and looked upward. "The canopy should have covered us. But still," she dropped her hand and looked at me.
"They don't usually come this far out in the forest."

I swallowed hard. "They're looking for me."

Chapter 6

I WAS TIRED and about to climb into bed, wondering when Adrien would be done with his shower. We might not be able to really touch like I wanted, but having him beside me last night . . . for a while it had made all my eddying fears calm into a still pool.

I smiled at the thought of him curled around me, but then I heard the crash of something falling in the kitchen area. Followed by a scream.

I scrambled to my feet and pulled back the tent flap.

No. It wasn't possible.

Ten Regulators stood in the common area, barely able to fit in the small space. One lifted Xona off the ground by her throat. Her legs kicked in the air, heels banging spastically against the side of the kitchen counter. She tried to reach the weapon holstered at her ankle, but couldn't lift her leg high enough to get it.

Blood already soaked the far corner of the floor where Jilia lay, unmoving. A Reg lifted his huge metal hydraulic foot from her crushed chest.

Adrien sprinted into the room from the opposite entrance,

a towel around his waist. Horror registered on his face as he looked at all the blood.

"No, Adrien, don't!" I shouted. But he launched himself at the Reg nearest him anyway. I screamed as the Reg's fist connected with Adrien's lean frame, slamming him hard into the tent's struts. There was a crunch of bones breaking when he hit. He crumpled to the floor, and the Reg lifted his leg up, no doubt to crush him like he had Jilia.

"No!" I screamed. A high-pitched buzzing erupted in my ears as all the Regulators turned toward me. I felt the rage gathering in my chest, building until it pounded against my lungs. I couldn't contain it, and I didn't want to. My small frame shook until my teeth rattled, and then, with a sudden hard pulse, my power exploded outward. My ribcage cracked and split as the power burst from my mouth, my eyes, my fingertips, my chest. Blue light filled the room and I barely had a moment to look down and see my chest cleaved in two, my insides pouring out right as the last of the blue light left my body.

I felt myself crumble. I couldn't even scream.

"Zoe!"

It was Adrien's voice. I looked toward the sound, but he wasn't there. The entire scene had disappeared. Only a black abyss remained.

"Zoe, wake up, oh god, wake up!"

I blinked and found Adrien crouched over my body, shaking my shoulders. He put his hand behind my neck and helped me sit.

"Regulators!" I gasped.

"No. It was a dream," Adrien said. "But we gotta move,

babe." I put a hand to my chest, remembering the feeling of it splitting open.

I was whole and solid. But I'd felt the pain, it had seemed so real.

The tent was so dark I could just barely make out Adrien's face. I felt a storm of relief at seeing him unharmed.

But then my eyes adjusted and I saw that we weren't in the tent anymore. Or rather, the tent wasn't around us. The sides had been blown backward and several of the trees were up-rooted and had fallen sideways, the enormous trunks still taller than Adrien. The night sky was overhead. Confusion mingled with the adrenaline of the dream, and I looked around in absolute confusion. What was going on? My breath came in quick puffs, fogging up the faceplate before the suit's defroster hummed to action.

"What happened?" I asked.

"I don't know," Adrien said. "I woke up to the tent ripping apart around us."

A loud crack filled the air.

"Another tree's dropping," Jilia shouted, jumping over some fallen equipment to get to where we now stood. I looked up and saw a huge shadow, darker than the starlit night sky, fall-ing straight toward us.

"Run!" Adrien grabbed my hand and pulled me forward. I stumbled once on my blanket as I tried to direct my telek to-ward the falling tree. I managed to stay on my feet, but I couldn't feel any power or detect even the hint of a buzzing noise.

Jilia was right behind us as we ran through the barely stand-ing tent frame. The tree slammed down, the several-ton trunk flattening the remnants of the tent. The ground vibrated from the weight of the impact.

"Where are Tyryn and Xona?" I shouted, trying to clear some of the debris off my faceplate that had been blown up when the tree landed.

"Jilia!" Adrien knocked into me as he spun and turned back the way we'd come. I turned too and saw Jilia on the ground, pinned by a heavy branch.

"Are you guys okay?" Xona ran up beside us, Tyryn right behind her. "Where are the attackers?" She had two laser weapons out, and she swung them around in every direction trying to find out who had hit us.

"There's no one," Adrien said, running over to Jilia and straining to get the branch off her. "It was just an accident."

I hurried over and tried to pull with him, but the branch was still attached to the tree and didn't budge an inch.

"Is she—" Xona started, but Adrien cut her off.

"She's alive."

As if on cue, Jilia groaned, a small sound, but enough to make us redouble our efforts. Tyryn dropped to the ground beside Adrien, but even with all his muscles put to the task, the branch wasn't moving.

"Can you move the tree off with your telek?" Adrien asked.

I gritted my teeth, trying to call my strength forward with my mind. But nothing happened. I felt a slight buzz of power, but then it was gone again.

I looked at the flattened tent bits barely visible in the moonlight and then at the mangled trees all around us. Realization slowly dawned. Adrien had called it an accident, but only now did I realize what he meant. It was me. I had done this. When I'd used my power during my nightmare, I must have accidentally unleashed it in reality.

"I think I used it all up." I met Adrien's eyes. He swallowed and nodded, taking a quick look around and then turning his attention back to Jilia.

"Move out of the way," Xona said, pulling a weapon from her ankle.

"Back up, back up," Tyryn said. Adrien and I pulled back as Xona pushed the trigger. The stream of bright laser cut a shocking red in the darkness. After a couple of minutes, the laser had sliced through the thick branch and Xona set to work on the other side. Finally she'd cut through it, too.

Tyryn and Xona grabbed both ends of the log left behind and hefted it off Jilia. Jilia coughed and sputtered a few times, blood on her lips.

"What do we do?" I asked frantically.

Jilia's face was pale, but she was blinking and looked alert. Her chest rose and fell easier now that the branch was gone. "I'm healing what I can," she whispered, closing her eyes tight with her hands on her abdomen. Sweat broke out on her forehead. She worked until rivulets ran down her face.

She finally exhaled again and looked back up at us.

"Are you gonna be okay, Doc?" Xona asked.

"A few broken ribs I can't fix right now," Jilia wheezed. "But the internal bleeding is stopped."

Xona helped her up while Tyryn looked around anxiously. "What the hell happened here?"

"It was me," I whispered. The weight of guilt sank in even as I said it. "I had a bad dream."

Xona looked back and forth between the damage and me and took a step back. Tyryn just stared.

"We've got to get out of here," Adrien said, unfazed. "We're completely exposed."

Tyryn nodded. "The Sat Cams will have caught the disturbance, even all the way out here. They'll come to investigate. We gotta run."

"Shunt," Xona kicked hard at a fallen tree branch.

Tyryn bent down and gently lifted Jilia. "Xona, go get the transport started."

She nodded once and then sprinted off.

"I'm so sorry," I whispered.

"This is how life in the Rez goes." Adrien hurried forward with Tyryn and waved for me to follow. "Midnight escapes, running with only what you got on you. We're used to it."

"But it's my fault—"

"All that matters now is that we get out of here safely." Adrien took my hand as we ran.

Xona already had the transport up and hovering by the time we got there.

"Won't they be able to track us?" I asked, jumping inside and buckling the strap across my chest.

"The outer hull on the transport is built to deflect infrared screening," Tyryn said. "In the night, we should be almost invisible."

I felt my stomach rock as we lifted higher through the trees. Leaves and twigs scratched down the windows, but soon we were up past the tree line and off into the night sky.

"Where do we go now?" Xona asked.

"Henk knew we'd be headed his way in a couple of days

70

for transport to the Foundation," Tyryn said. He glanced down at the console screen. "As long as we don't bring any heat his way, he won't mind us showing up early."

I glanced out the back window at the tops of the trees. By moonlight, I could see that the circular area I'd flattened stood out like a giant target.

I turned away again and saw Adrien watching me, but I didn't meet his eyes. Guilt ate like a worm through my stomach. This was all my fault. I closed my eyes, wishing there were a way to rewind time.

Chapter 7

XONA AND TYRYN SPOKE QUIETLY in the front seats. I couldn't hear what they were saying, but Xona glanced back at me several times. Well, glared back might be a better description.

Otherwise, it was quiet, almost peaceful. Jilia and Adrien were asleep, and Adrien's head lolled against the wall behind him. I memorized his sharp cheekbones and the way his jaw tapered down to his pointy chin. His thick lips were opened slightly as he slept, and I wished that I could kiss him. Anything to wipe away the memory of what I'd just done.

I unbuckled my belt strap and moved closer to Tyryn and Xona. I didn't have a very good view out the front window, but I could see the distant bright lights ahead.

"We're heading into a city?"

Xona ignored me.

"Right outside it," Tyryn said. "There's a factory there." He pointed below, where I could just make out the outline of a cluster of structures. "The factory's chief engineer is an Upper. Officially, he works for Comm Corp, but in actuality he's a Rez spy."

"Really?" I'd never met an Upper who worked with the Rez. Uppers were usually the enemy, the privileged class who used people for drone labor without any qualms.

The engines quieted as Tyryn settled the transport down in a covered transport bay. It jolted only lightly when we made contact with the ground.

"'Allo mates!" someone called just as Tyryn opened the back door of the transport. A very tall wiry man was waiting for us. His face was covered in dark stubble as if he hadn't shaved in a week, and he smiled widely when Adrien woke up, unclipped himself, and stepped out of the transport.

"Shorty!" the man said, clapping Adrien hard on the back. Adrien was only an inch shorter than him, both of them well over six feet.

"Henk." Adrien grinned back.

"You folks are early. Glad to see ya ain't got any holes in you."

Adrien didn't say anything, but he did embrace the man.

Henk let go and turned to me, his arms open wide. "And the telek girl!" He stepped and hugged me hard right as I stepped out of the transport, lifting me up off my feet. "So good to meet ya. Shorty's talked about ya enough to make a man's ears bleed."

I turned to Adrien who smiled and looked down, his ears turning pink.

"Welcome to my factory," Henk said, gesturing behind him. "All the newest models, shiny and ready to be shipped."

As I looked around, I gasped a little to see hundreds of vehicles packed in the covered space, all in orderly rows. One

was a row of duos, another was full of large trucks, skinny in front but with wide bulbous backsides; others looked like variations on the simple quad transport design we'd come in.

Jilia stepped down from the vehicle next.

"My favorite doc! Now it's really a party." Henk spread his arms wide, but Jilia smacked them down, then winced and held her ribs.

Henk's eyebrows scrunched together. "You broke, Doc?"

"Nothing I can't fix. And don't think I've forgotten last time," she said, an eyebrow raised.

"Aw, come on," Henk said, looking almost contrite. "One little accident with blasting powder and a guy can never live it down?"

Jilia rolled her eyes. "So is the container ready? I don't want to stop here any longer than we have to."

"Did ya think I wouldn't come through for my favorite gal?" Henk grinned.

"I thought I was your favorite doctor," Jilia said.

Henk leaned in, his voice low. "Who says ya can't be both?" He wiggled his eyebrows, then pulled back. "It's over here." He gestured with his arm for us to follow.

"Top-of-the-line, next gen transports," Henk explained as we walked down between rows of vehicles. "All hover-based tech."

"No more wheeled models?" Adrien asked.

Henk laughed. "Who would drive on a road when you can fly?" He waved one hand smoothly through the air, like a vessel in flight, and let out a low whistle. "Antigravity tech's gotten good enough for these nonpropulsion engines to go mainstream. I oughta know, since I helped design 'em." He flashed a smile.

Adrien leaned over as we walked past a row of blue transports. "Henk designs transports, but he's also the Rez's best weapons expert. Unfortunately, he has a habit of testing out his favorite new toys."

Henk overheard and smiled charmingly. "They just make such a lovely *ka-boom!*" He moved his fingers outward in a wide circle to demonstrate the sight. "And it scared a stitch into the bastards craftin' V-chip parts."

"The General warned you about being too reckless. Blowing up one V-chip factory isn't going to change anything," Jilia snapped. "We're trying to win a war here!"

"Aw, it all turned out okay. And look at this," Henk lifted his arm and rotated it at the shoulder. "One factory blasted back to hell where it belongs and you got me right put together again. Not to mention I got a nifty scar out of the deal." He pulled back his tunic around the neck to show the slight line across his shoulder.

Jilia glared at him. "You're hopeless."

He sidled closer to her. "That's what all the ladies say. Wanna try and reform me anyway?"

She pushed him away, but I saw the quirk of a smile play at the edge of her mouth.

"Ah, here we are. One Grade A shipping container for my favorite fleeing misfits." Henk pointed to a row of huge boxes with the giant Comm Corp insignia on the side. Several of the hatches were open, revealing more shining transport vehicles packed up inside. But Henk led us to one that only had a few crates stacked against the walls.

"Sorry. This is the best I can do on short notice."

Xona stepped inside and looked around. "I've traveled in worse," she said. She clicked open the lid of one of the crates. "Got anything good in here?" She moved on to the next container, opening it up and rifling through some of the contents.

"Xona," Tyryn said, a warning in his voice.

Xona ignored him and kept lifting and examining items.

"Right, then," Henk said. "So I'll close you up. This here's the oxygen generator. You'll have a day's worth, though you shouldn't need it. Transports will pick up the container and drop you at the shipping yard, and then you'll be attached to a freight train heading south."

I frowned. "We'll be part of a Comm Corp freight train? Isn't that dangerous?"

Henk just grinned. "Safest way to travel long distances. Right under their noses. Then someone from the Foundation will pick up the container and voilà." He held out his hands wide. "You're delivered to your new home."

I must have still looked skeptical, because Jilia put a hand on my arm. "As much as I hate to admit it, Henk's very good at what he does."

"Wait, was that a compliment, Doc?" Henk put his hands dramatically to his chest. "I may faint."

"Now this is what I'm talking about," Xona said, pulling out a weapon as big as her forearm from the crate in the corner.

"Xona," Tyryn said, marching over and yanking the weapon out of her hand. He put it back in the crate and shut the lid.

"A girl after my own heart," Henk said. Then he nodded at the rest of us. "Safe travels."

"And Doc," Henk said. "As always, a pleasure." He stepped in and planted a kiss right on Jilia's mouth before she swatted him away, her face reddened. "You—"

Henk shut the door tight before she could finish.

Chapter 8

A JOLT WOKE ME, and I sat up. Everything around me was gray. Data sets poured down the sides of my vision, readouts of the room schematics, temperature, time of day, and in the background the monotone voice speaking the Community Creed over and over again: *The Community Link is peace. We are humanity sublime because we live in Community and favor above all else order, logic, and peace. Community first, Community always.*

"We're here, Zoe," said a voice at my side. "Un-Link yourself."

I blinked in confusion. Adrien's face was inches from mine as he whispered.

I stared at him for a moment, feeling nothing but a yawning emptiness.

"Say the trigger words to un-Link yourself. Beta Ten Gamma Link."

"Beta Ten Gamma Link," I repeated after him. Noise and color and sense washed back in a rush. After we'd left the factory, Jilia had suggested that I Link myself so that I could sleep without fear of losing control of my power. The Link controlled REM patterns, making dreaming impossible. It was horrible to have to put myself back under the Link's power. I shook my head like I could get rid of the lingering fog it created. But as I looked around me, I saw everyone was safe. It had worked.

"Where is *here* anyway?" Xona asked. She looked at Tyryn and Jilia. "You never said where the Foundation was."

"No one knows," Adrien said. "Even the driver won't know for long."

"What do you mean?"

"There's a glitcher who lives here. He makes the place invisible in people's minds, so you can't remember where you're located, even when you're here. I think." Adrien frowned. "The details are a little fuzzy. Like the more I try to think about him, the less I can remember. But I feel like maybe we're in a mountain?" He looked to Jilia.

Jilia nodded in appreciation. "It's the best defense mechanism I've ever seen. I know I've done a brain scan of the boy, but at the moment I can't even recall what his face looks like."

"Must be lonely to be him," I said.

The door to the container opened. I stood up, excited to meet more glitchers. But the person who'd opened the container was Adrien's mother, Sophia.

She hadn't exactly liked me the last time I'd met her, when Adrien and I had attempted our first escape to the Surface. If his mom had had her way then, Adrien would have left me behind and never looked back.

She glared at Adrien. "I can't believe you just left without telling me. Do you have any idea how worried I've been? What you've put me through the last forty-eight hours? Whenever it comes to that girl, it's always trouble."

Adrien stared back at her, his jaw tensing up. "I didn't have a choice."

Sophia lowered her voice. "We'll talk about this later."

We took an elevator down, and when the doors opened, a diminutive man with a cane was waiting in a brightly lit, white-paneled hallway.

"Welcome to the Foundation," he said, with an enthusiastic smile. "I'm Professor Henry."

He limped slightly as he walked, but it didn't seem to slow him down. He shook everyone's hand as introductions were made and gave Adrien a quick embrace. "Come on in, I'll show you our little operation."

He led us down the bright hallway. "Ever since we started recovering glitchers the past few years, we realized we needed a safe place for you to live and study your powers. A lot of glitchers have difficulty breathing the Surface air. It's part of living underground your whole lives. So we always intended to have a sealed-off air-controlled facility as a safe haven. Of course," he chuckled, looking back at me, "we didn't quite anticipate anyone with quite your level of difficulty, Zoe, but we've almost finished the necessary modifications."

"When do you think the air-filtration system will be ready?" Adrien asked.

"Probably a week. Maybe less if we're lucky. Ah, now we're passing some of the classrooms." He gestured to his right. The lights weren't on in the rooms, but I could see a little bit into the square spaces. Smooth metal chairs were arranged in a circle.

"So we'll have classes?" I asked. "I thought this place was mainly for Rez fighter training."

A slight cloud passed over the Professor's face. "Well, I did first envision it as primarily a school and residence for rescued glitchers, but Rosalina, I mean General Taylor, impressed upon me how important it was for us to consider the military applications of some of your gifts. Especially in these dangerous times. So we've set it up as both school and training facility."

"How many students are there?" I asked.

"About twenty glitchers," the Professor said. "All with an array of abilities."

"Is everyone here a glitcher?" Xona asked. Her mouth was a tight line.

"The students are, yes," the Professor said. "But I hope you know you are just as welcome, Xona. The Foundation has become more and more of a military base, since our invisibility gives us such a valuable tactical advantage. The military personnel are on the level below us, so you won't see them much. Since your brother will be the new head trainer for the glitcher task force, we thought you could train with them."

"So there's no other non-glitching students?" Xona asked.

"I'm afraid not, but I'm sure you'll feel right at home since all the glitchers are your age."

From the look on Xona's face, I wasn't so sure.

"Is the General here?" Tyryn asked.

"No, she's on another mission. She's embedded and on non-com."

Adrien must have seen the question on my face, because he leaned over to clarify. "Non-communication. It's standard for deep-cover missions."

"Ah, and here we are." The Professor stopped and put his finger to the touch panel beside a wide door. "The Med Center." He beamed at Jilia after the door slid up in its tracks. "Just to your specifications."

Jilia hurried past him into the room. The room was brighter than the hallway, with light cell panels installed every few inches across the ceiling. The walls and floor were the same unblemished white, and the room was filled with brand-new diagnostic machines.

Jilia looked back at the Professor, her eyes shining eyes. "It's perfect, Henry."

I saw something else I recognized—another wash-down container, and a pile of packaged blue suits.

The Professor saw where I was looking. "Until the air-filtration system is ready, you can wash and change into a new suit every day so you're comfortable."

"Thanks," I said.

"Oh look," the Professor said with a delighted smile. "Here's the rest of your team."

I turned to follow his gaze and saw a group of people crowded in the doorway. A dark-haired boy I recognized timidly stepped in front.

"Juan!" I said. We'd rescued him during our escape from the Community, but I hadn't seen him since we switched vehicles at the first safe house all those months ago.

"It's so good to finally see you again, Zoe!" Juan said, stepping closer. "I'm not on your team, but I had to come and say hello anyway." He gave me a big hug. "The only reason I'm alive is because of you." He said, his voice quieter.

"I never got the chance to thank you. I am forever in your debt."

I waved a hand, trying to hide my embarrassment. "Is Molla here, too?"

"She's here," Juan said, but then looked away. I could hear what he didn't say. Molla was here but didn't want to see me. She thought I was the reason Max stayed behind with the Chancellor. In part, she was right. The familiar pang of guilt sliced through my gut.

Adrien's face stiffened briefly, his eyes going distant. The next moment he blinked and looked at Xona standing behind him. It was brief, but I could tell he'd just had one of his short-term visions "Don't," he said, heading over to her.

At the same moment, Xona turned and saw the group crowding into the Med Center. Her eyes widened until they looked like they'd pop out of her head.

"What the shunt are *they* doing here?" she yelled. She reached under her tunic and whipped out two weapons.

I looked where Xona was pointing and gasped. Four Regulators were approaching from the back of the group.

"Lower your weapons, Xona. They aren't Regs anymore," Jilia said, her voice far calmer than mine would have been. "These are the boys Zoe rescued when she fled the Community. I've examined them myself and—"

"They're all murderers!" Xona flicked the safety off the weapons with her thumb and aimed them higher. The Regs didn't even flinch.

"Hey, calm down," said one of the glitcher boys who stood by Juan. He was dark-skinned and short but broadly built. He held out his hand, palm up. "You need to put down the weapon."

"Calm down? Calm down?" Xona's voice was almost a shriek.

"Underneath the metal, the ex-Regs are as human as you and me," Jilia said.

"They're nothing like me!"

The tips of the metal weapons Xona held began to turn a glowing orange. She didn't notice at first, but then she suddenly cried out and dropped them. She looked down at her hand in disbelief. Small welts were forming on her palm.

"Rand, you didn't have to do that," Jilia said to the boy who'd told Xona to calm down. She hurried over to Xona. "Let me see the burns."

I looked on in confusion. I had no idea what had just happened.

"Don't touch me," Xona pulled away from Jilia, her eyes flashing at Rand. "Of course you'd protect them. You glitchers are barely human either." She brushed hard past Adrien and ran from the room.

Jilia started after her, but then paused at the door and looked back at us. "I would appreciate if you would all try to be patient with her." Her words were clipped and almost angry. "She's a bit rough around the edges, but you would be, too, if you'd been through what she has."

"She's the one who pulled a weapon," a girl with long blond hair objected, putting her hands on her hips. "What were we supposed to do?"

"She protects herself the only way she knows how," Jilia said, then hurried out the door.

"And we all know you can more than protect yourself, Filicity," Adrien said to the blonde.

The girl balled up her fists and stared back. "How many times do I have to tell you, the name's *City*."

"I didn't mean to burn her hands," said Rand.

City scoffed. "You aren't the bad guy here, Rand. She pulled a laser weapon. She could have sliced someone's arm off by accident."

"What exactly just happened?" I asked.

"Rand melted her weapons." A short girl with long frizzy brown hair got to her feet from where she'd been crouching on the ground with her arms covering her head. She beamed at Rand. "He can turn metal molten."

He winked and waved at me, his palms turning a glowing orange. City smacked him hard in the shoulder. "Now if he just could learn to tone it down sometimes."

He rolled his eyes. "Because you are always so controlled with your lightning."

"It's electricity, not lightning. And it's not supposed to be subtle."

"Why don't I introduce you all officially," Adrien said. He gestured to the blonde. "Zoe, this is City. She can produce spirals of electricity from her bare hands. Then there's Eli, Wytt, Tavid, and Cole." He nodded at the ex-Regs. Three of them didn't move at all. They just stood looking at the far wall like they were on guard. The fourth looked my way and nodded.

"Where are the other ex-Regs?" I asked. Ten had come with us after I freed them from their V-chips, if I remembered correctly.

"The rest are on active duty with other Rez squadrons."

Adrien turned to the stocky boy who'd burned Xona. "This is Rand. You saw his power in action."

Rand grinned.

"And I'm Ginni," said the frizzy-haired girl. "We're all so excited to meet you and welcome you to the team!" She came forward and gave me a huge hug. I patted her back awkwardly. I'd never really been in such close proximity to anyone except Adrien.

"Uh, hi."

City snorted in the background, and Ginni pulled back.

"Ginni can locate people anywhere on earth," Adrien said, smiling. "Down to a few feet."

"Oh," I smiled. "Adrien told me about you."

"He did?" A grin split her face.

"Now that you're actually here maybe we can finally see some action," Rand said, rubbing his hands together.

Ginni leaned in. "Can you really do everything they say you can? Juan told us you ripped metal-reinforced doors out of the wall. Is that true?"

"Um, yeah."

"Telekinesis is such an awesome power. And one day you're gonna be the leader of the Rez," Ginni shook her head slightly, looking awestruck. "To think, I get to be on the same task force as you."

"She's not a leader yet," City said. "Everyone on the task force is of equal rank." She looked at me sourly. "Except some of us have actually trained for years and been on missions."

"Aw, don't get your tunic in a twist, City," Rand said.

City's hands balled into fists. "I'm not getting anything in a twist. I'm just telling it like it is."

"Okay, guys," Adrien intervened. "Everybody out. Let's let Zoe get some rest now."

He ran a hand through his hair after they all left. "I'm sorry about how they acted. They can be a lot to handle all at once."

My skin prickled up at the thought of so many people with such intense expectations of me. I ran my hands over my arms rapidly. "Everyone here knows what I'm expected to do. How can I possibly live up to that? It's too much pressure."

"I know, I'm sorry. But news travels quickly around here. And it's been so long since we've had good news," Adrien added. "People latch on to hope wherever they can find it."

I suddenly felt bad for my outburst. They needed me, not just because I was supposed to help them win, but also because simply believing in me was helping them stay strong.

"Do you want to go get some more sleep?" he asked. "I can show you to your dorm room. Or we can go grab some food if you're hungry."

I cringed at the thought of the protein mix. "No," I took Adrien's hand. "Is there somewhere we can go to be alone and get away from everything?"

"Hmm," he drummed his fingers on his thigh. "Jilia will be back after she takes care of Xona's hand. But everyone else is at lunch, then they'll have class after. We could go to your dorm room."

I nodded. He led me out of the Med Center and down the hallway, but, instead of continuing down the way we'd come, he took a hallway that forked off to the right. At the end of the hallway were several doors. He stopped at one and pressed on the panel to open it. The lights turned on as we walked in.

The room was about twice the size of my old room back in the Community, but there were four beds built into the wall like shelves, two high. A curtain ran along the length of each, for privacy I assumed. A long metal table with four chairs took up the far wall of the room.

"Looks like you've got your choice of beds," Adrien said. "Ginni's been living here alone. I'm sure she'll be beyond thrilled at having you and Xona for roommates."

I nodded. Ginni seemed nice, but I wasn't so sure how I felt about rooming with Xona. She was so hostile. "As long as Jilia takes away Xona's weapons."

Adrien laughed.

I pushed back the curtain and sat down on the other bottom bed beside Ginni's. Adrien sat beside me. But suddenly, I didn't know what to say. A couple nights ago everything had seemed so simple. Adrien and I were finally together again, and that was all that had mattered.

"What now?" I asked, turning to Adrien and searching his eyes.

I'd meant it in the larger sense, but he seemed to take me literally. "Well, we could read for a few hours." He pointed at one of the tablets on the table. "Your tablet should be loaded with the texts for our Humanities class."

I was quiet a moment.

"I could help you catch up. I mean, I know you could read it on your own, I thought it just might be nice—" He looked down.

"No, that's really sweet." I put my hand on his, and wished once again that we weren't separated by my suit. What I really wanted was to curl up into his chest so he could stroke my hair and kiss me. But settling in beside him and listening to him read was a close second. "I'd like that."

He grabbed a tablet from the table. Then we arranged some pillows behind our backs against the wall and he started to read. I felt all my muscles relax at the sound of his voice.

The text was strange, about a man in ancient times, even before the Old World. A king received a vision from an oracle that his son would kill him and marry his wife, the boy's own mother. The king decided to abandon the boy out on the rocks to die as a baby, so he wouldn't grow up and do what the vision had said. But someone rescued the boy, and it all happened exactly as predicted anyway.

As odd as the story was, I was fascinated. I'd only ever read history texts before. We didn't have stories in the Community. It was so interesting to hear the tale unfold through the different characters.

Better than the drama of the story, though, was hearing Adrien as he read. It seemed I could never get enough of looking at his face or listening to him. After everything that had happened over the past few days, it was calming to lose myself in the lilting cadence of his voice. I settled my head against his shoulder as he read.

After a couple of hours, Adrien finally put the tablet down.

"So, the stranger Oedipus killed for insulting him on the road was actually his father?" I asked. "And the queen he married after ridding the city of the Sphinx turned out to be his *mother*?"

Adrien didn't look up at me. He just stared down at the tablet, his eyebrows drawn.

"It's a disturbing story," I said, thinking that's why he looked sad. "I wonder if people were all like that in the Old World before the V-chip. Killing strangers on the road and gouging their own eyes out." I shuddered. "There was so much violence before the V-chips." Then I thought about the Chancellor, the Uppers, and the Rez fighters here at the Foundation. It seemed no one without the V-chip could stay peaceful for long. Maybe that was the price of having emotion, that the bad always came along with the good.

Adrien didn't respond. He seemed preoccupied, and after a few moments of silence, he looked up. "Do you think the oracle knew what was going to happen?"

"What do you mean?" I asked, surprised by the question.

"When he told the king what his son was going to do when he grew up. Do you think the oracle knew that it was his words that would set it all in motion?"

"I don't know," I said slowly.

"None of it would have happened if the stupid oracle had kept his mouth shut. The baby wouldn't have been put out on the rocks and he would have grown up knowing who his dad and mom were, and they'd all still be alive and sane."

When he looked back up at me, I could see tears rimming his eyes.

"Adrien, what's going on?" I tried to take his hand, but he pulled away.

"I gotta go." He stood up abruptly.

"Adrien, wait," I stood up too. "Are you okay?"

"I'm fine," he said. He turned his head away. He knew I

could read him better than anyone else, and he didn't want me to see his face.

"I'm just tired. I'm gonna go get some sleep." He started toward the door.

"Wait," I said, pleading. "Tell me what's wrong."

He paused but didn't turn around. "I don't think I should," he finally said, his voice rough. "Look at what happened in the play. Telling people about things—" His back slumped. "It can only cause more problems. It can get people killed."

"Adrien, it's *me*. I'm not just people. I'm your . . ." I reached out and put a hand on his shoulder, trying to figure out how to say what I meant. "I love you."

He finally turned toward me, but his eyes were still trained on the ground. "I love you too," he said. "That's why I can't talk to you about this."

He was out of the room before I could say anything back. I stomped on the ground in frustration. I wanted to run after him and demand he tell me what was wrong, but he obviously didn't want to. Maybe it wouldn't be right to push him.

I thought about the shadows under his eyes, the way his ribs poked out through his shirt sometimes. Something had been weighing on him for a while now. I realized now it wasn't only guilt I saw in his eyes sometimes. It was fear.

Which brought up the most worrisome question of all. What did Adrien see in his visions that made him so afraid?

Chapter 9

"I'M SO EXCITED we're going to be roommates," Ginni said, almost bouncing where she stood. It was like the girl had invisible springs attached to the balls of her feet. She laced her arm through mine as I looked blearily at the clock on the wall. She and Xona had let me sleep in while they went to morning classes but had come to get me for lunch. I felt like I could sleep another twelve hours. But my stomach grumbled, and I was hungry enough that I could swallow down a whole bowlful of protein goop, maybe even two.

"And I know we're going to be best friends, just like in the books I love to read. Come on, we're already late for lunch!"

Xona looked down at Ginni and let out a heavy sigh. "Wish we could all have our own rooms," she said under her breath.

As we neared the Caf, I heard the noise of voices filtering out into the hall. A loud bark of laughter made me blink in surprise. A place where people could laugh and talk without having to hide emotion. It was so foreign. And loud.

We turned in the next doorway and I looked down at my tight-fitting suit self-consciously. I'd gone through the wash-down chamber and changed into a fresh suit last night before bed, so at least I was clean.

93

Xona strode confidently into the room, scanning the crowd methodically. A quick headcount showed about thirty people already inside. I recognized Rand, City, and Juan sitting at the center table and the four ex-Regs sitting together in the back. Several of the other tables were crowded with adults wearing the gray Rez fighter uniform. The room was bigger than the Med Center, but all the tables and chairs were crammed tightly together to accommodate so many people at once. A long counter with kitchen implements ran along the far wall and, beside it, a cabinet with heat lamps and several steaming trays of food.

I looked back at the main table and felt my eyes widen when I realized who the girl sitting between City and Juan was. Molla. Her red hair was shorter and her face pudgier, but it was her.

"Oh look," City said. "The plebe and the savior have finally made it to lunch." Molla's eyes narrowed when she looked up and saw me.

Xona walked over to City, her fists clenched. "Wanna call me that again to my face, Filicity?"

"The name's City," she said, eyes flashing annoyance for a brief moment before she smiled sweetly. "And your name is plebe. From the word plebeian. As in, not special. As in, should be scrubbing the floors for her betters, not eating breakfast with us."

Xona didn't say anything back, she just reared back her fist so quick I barely realized what was happening. But before she could connect with City's jaw, Rand jumped up from where he was sitting by City and grabbed Xona's arms.

"Ladies, ladies, not here. Save it for the training room floor."
Juan had stood up as well, looking upset.

"No one calls me that and gets away with it." Xona struggled angrily to get loose from Rand's hold, but he was twice her size. "Let go of me."

City leaned in closer. "As if you could do anything to me. I'd drop you at ten feet with the electricity from my little finger."

"Only because you glitchers are cheaters. In a fair fight I'd—"

"I told you she had a prejudice against us," City cut in, then looked at me, her eyes slits. "You should watch out, savior, sleeping in the same room as this one. She'll try to slit your throat in your sleep."

Xona glared, but remained silent.

"Ice it already, City." Rand said, his arms still tight around Xona. Xona let out a growl and jabbed him hard in the ribs. In his moment of surprise, she dropped down and slipped out of his grasp, ready to spring into action.

"Come on, Molla," City said, standing with a fake yawn. "Let's get out of here before the boredom kills me."

Molla stood up, and I barely managed to stop myself from gasping out loud. Her round stomach had been hidden under the table before. I hadn't seen her in months, but now her stomach protruded and she struggled a little getting to her feet. She pushed past me, and I couldn't help staring after her as she left. Max's baby, growing inside her.

Out from under the V-chip control, I thought I'd learned all about emotion. But what had just happened was totally foreign to me, like I'd been dropped in on a game where I didn't know any of the rules. I could barely make out one emotion on someone's face before another had replaced it.

Xona grabbed her food quickly, then sat down at an empty table. Adrien came in behind me. I wanted to ask him more about what had gotten him so upset when we'd read together yesterday, but he was smiling and he leaned down and whispered in my ear, "I know you want the air-filtration system to be ready as soon as possible, but I gotta say, I'll miss the suit."

I blushed and smacked him in the shoulder.

"Just telling the truth." His grin was infectious and I tried to forget about his dark mood yesterday. He seemed fine now. He directed me to the steaming trays of food and pointed out a small circular pot behind the others. The familiar creamy grayish concoction bubbled inside.

"Jilia says to keep eating the protein supplement until we can steal some rations from the Community circuit that we know will be allergen safe."

"Yum." I slopped a large spoonful of the goo into a hard plastic cup, looking over longingly as Adrien filled his plate with meat and steamed broccoli. I looked back down at the shapeless gruel filling my cup and sighed.

We joined Xona's table, where Ginni was now chattering nonstop. Xona didn't look like she was listening. She was too busy eyeing the ex-Regs in the back of the room.

Ginni brightened when she saw Adrien and me coming to sit. "Has Adrien told you about all your classes?"

"Not much." I sat down and hooked up the straw to my

face mask. I took several quick swallows, grimacing only slightly at the taste. "Just that the day will be split between training and school."

"Well, really, there's a lot more training than actual school," Ginni said. "The General keeps saying she needs as many glitchers as soldiers as soon as possible. Everything's been so bad lately, she can't seem to replenish the ranks of normal Rez soldiers fast enough."

I swallowed hard, the reality of the situation settling in. I'd always known it was a war, but it was becoming more and more real to me how many young glitchers and Rez fighters were losing their lives fighting against the Chancellor and the Community.

"How long have you all been here?" I asked. "Out of the Community, I mean."

"I was living in one of the few aboveground cities when the Rez rescued me a year ago," Ginni said. "City and Rand are from the south part of the Sector and caused such a commotion when their powers kicked in that I'm amazed we managed to rescue them before the Community or the Chancellor got to them first. We all stayed in Rez camps till enough of the Foundation was finished a couple months ago, and then we moved in here to study and train."

"So what classes do we have?" I asked.

"Well," Ginni lit up again. I had a feeling nothing made her happier than being asked questions. "First is physical training with Xona's brother. He's so handsome."

Xona finally turned her eyes away from the ex-Regs. "Ugh, you did not just say that. Besides, Tyryn's twenty-two."

"Well in four short months I'll be seventeen." Ginni leaned in. "And it's not like there's a lot of other options around here, you know?"

Xona rolled her eyes, then went back to watching the ex-Regs. At least she wasn't being outright hostile toward us anymore. I had a feeling Ginni was partially responsible for that. You couldn't be around the bubbly girl for too long and keep thinking that all glitchers were dangerous or inhuman.

"Anyway," Ginni went on, "in his class we work out and have weapons and combat training. The next class in the morning is Humanities with Professor Henry."

"That's the class we've been reading stories for, right?" I looked at Adrien.

He nodded. "We read literature and study art and history."

Xona scoffed. "I agree with the General. What use is art when you're in a firefight?"

"It's important," Adrien said. "It reminds us what we're fighting for—the ability to think and feel and create."

Xona just stared at him. "We're fighting to stay alive. Plain and simple."

I looked down at the cup of goop on the table in front of me. I took another couple of slurps from the straw, then pulled back with a grimace. "Ugh, it's even worse when it's cooled off."

"I can help." I looked up to see Rand standing over me, Juan by his side.

Before I could respond, Rand put his hand on the outside of my cup and the protein concoction bubbled. But then the whole cup started to melt and become misshapen.

"Crackin' hell, Rand" Adrien jumped and pushed the cup

away from me with a napkin. "Be careful. You're gonna burn her."

Rand removed his finger. "Oops," he said. He flashed a grin at Ginni and me and sat down. "Hard to turn it down sometimes. Can't contain the Rand, after all."

Ginni smiled and tossed a napkin at his face.

"So wait, your power," I asked, watching with fascination as the bubbling finally stopped, "it doesn't work only with metal?"

Rand leaned in and smiled conspiratorially. "I can heat up just about anything."

Ginni giggled. Xona rolled her eyes.

"Let's not forget the incident where you melted the central truss in the west tunnel and trapped us for three hours until they dug us out," Adrien said.

"Aw, man, why you gotta bring that up?"

"That's why we have glitcher training every afternoon," Ginni said. "To help us learn to control our powers. And speaking of," she nodded to the clock on the wall. "We gotta go." She ate a few more quick bites and then stood up with her tray. I'd gotten enough of the protein mix down before Rand melted the cup that I was full, too.

"Who teaches it?" I asked, standing up.

"Now that Jilia's here, she and my mom take turns teaching," Adrien said. "But I think it's Jilia today."

Ginni clapped her hands together. "Oh good, I've missed training with Jilia! She used to train us when we were at the camps before the Foundation was finished."

"Aww," Rand said mournfully, "I thought I was done with that meditation junk for good."

We headed down the hallway past the Med Center to a small room. Cushions were set up in a circle on the ground. I looked around in confusion.

"Where are the desks and chairs?" I whispered to Adrien.

He laughed. "That's not Jilia's style. We sit on the ground. You'll see."

Adrien settled on a pillow and gestured for me to do the same. Molla came in a few minutes later and sat beside City. Ginni, who sat on the other side of me, leaned in and whispered, "Molla's not on any task force because of the baby. But Jilia said it'd be good for her to still come and meditate with us when she can."

I stared at Ginni. She seemed to know everything about everyone. It made me wonder what she told others about me.

Finally, Jilia came in. After everyone had settled in, she began.

"My job is to help train you in the study of your own minds, so you can control your powers when it counts." Jilia walked around the circle. "Studying the mind is the key to controlling anger, joy, all your emotions. The same parts of the brain are linked to glitcher Gifts, so controlling and understanding your emotions will help you do the same with your Gifts."

My back straightened at her words. This was what I was here for. Maybe I'd finally be able to get my powers under control.

"We'll begin with twenty minutes of silent meditation when I ring the bell," she said. She held up a small bronze bell. "Try to empty your mind and let all your worries and hopes and fears drift away. A wise man called Dogen once said that to study meditation is to study the self. To study the self is to forget the self. And to forget the self is to be connected to all things."

"Aw, Doc," Rand complained, his long muscled legs folded awkwardly on the cushion. "Can't we skip to the fun stuff? Like melting that bell and making it into something useful?"

"I've missed you too, Rand," Jilia said with a smile. "Your complaints, as always, are noted. I'll sound the bell now. Juan, will you begin playing as well?"

I looked up in surprise to see that Juan was sitting on a chair in the corner of the room holding a strange contraption that rested on the ground with a long stringed neck. One of Juan's hands hovered over the strings, and the other held a long slim stick with a ribbon strung along its length.

"Juan's cello music will help us all relax and connect to our emotions. Empty your mind and try to be at one with the present."

Doc positioned herself back on her own cushion and rang the bell. Almost simultaneously Juan put the ribboned stick to the strings, and the most aching sound moaned out.

My eyes widened. Music. I'd heard *of* it but had never actually heard it. When I was still a drone in the Community, they used to play long tones over the Link during Scheduled Subject Downtime, but it was nothing like this. After a few moments of listening, entranced, the beauty of the sound made my chest expand outward.

The buzzing in my mind seemed to vibrate in response to the rising notes of the instrument. It was both scary and exhilarating to feel the power build so quickly. I knew Juan could affect moods with his music—maybe this was finally the key to gaining control.

My power responded. I felt the shape of the entire room and everyone in it inside my mind. Nine heartbeats, no, ten. A small fluttering one. The baby. I could feel Molla's baby. My breath caught.

Then instead of one long weeping note after another, Juan put the ribbon to two strings at once in harmony. The music swept me up beyond the room where we were all sitting. I was disoriented by how quickly it expanded.

Suddenly I could feel everything, not just the shape of the room or the hallway outside. I zoomed outward like a lens readjusting. I could see the entire compound. The two main hallways of the Foundation ran like little tubes, with rooms between and branching out to the sides. I could feel the level below ours too, and the main elevator that led up to the air-transport deck. One second I could sense the complex components that made up the engine of the transport and smell the oiled metal, then the next moment I'd zoomed out again even farther this time.

It was going too fast. I was starting to feel dizzy. Quick as the moment it took for another breath in, I could feel the shape of the whole mountain above us, the canyon stretching out beside it, and the mountain range beyond.

And then I was hurtled into the sky.

Panic spiked through me. I wasn't in control. Not at all. I was being dragged outward helplessly into the endless sky. No shape, no contour. It just went on and on forever. The sky had always terrified me, and now I spun recklessly through it with no tether holding me to the earth. I couldn't sense my own body anymore at all. I was going to get lost.

It was exhilarating and terrifying.

I had to pull it back, had to get control. The instrument hit a high, vibrating note that thrummed straight through me. I tried to hold on to the sound to pull myself back. I quivered with the note and tried to trace it back to the source, back to the center of the rippling vibration.

Suddenly the quiet music was ruptured and I was drawn back into my body so quickly it felt like I'd been ripped in two—part of myself still floating somewhere above in the sky, the other half sitting in a room under the mountain. I blinked hard. I was back in the room, and it was all of me, my mind as well as my body. But the same moment, the cello vibrated and burst into pieces in Juan's hands. Everybody screamed and tried to shield themselves.

Juan's beautiful instrument was gone, replaced by a cloud of dust that filled the air and filtered down like ash above our heads. Silently, all heads turned in my direction, their mouths forming the same perfect O.

"I'm so sorry!" I said, stumbling to my feet, still disoriented by being back inside my body. It felt too small, like my skin was on too tight.

Juan coughed a few times and wiped the dust out of his eyes. "I should have seen that coming," he said. "I could feel the intensity coming off you in waves."

"I'm so sorry," I babbled again, tripping over my own words. I hurried over to his side. "It was just that the music was so beautiful and I lost control of my telek, I didn't know where I was—"

"It's okay, Zoe," Juan said. He tried to smile, but I could see he was upset.

"Everyone's fine," Jilia announced. "Lights up," she said

and the lights slowly brightened around us. The dust that had been Juan's cello covered the floor. A couple of people coughed.

"She ruined your cello!" Molla said, rising to her feet and speaking up for the first time since I'd come to the compound. "Just like she ruins everything else!" Her high-pitched voice echoed around the small space. "She's dangerous. What if that—" she pointed at Juan's ruined instrument, "had been one of us?" She put a hand on her stomach, took one more searing look at me, then stomped out of the room.

Rand let out a low whistle after she left. Everyone else was staring at me. Once again I felt the weight of all their expectations and, even more crushing, their disappointment. Adrien steadied my arm as I stood there.

"I'm sorry," I said again, feeling that empty space at the bottom of my stomach widen. I'd thought today was a new start, that maybe I'd be able to finally get control. But Molla was right. Here I was again, ruining everything I touched.

"Well," Rand broke the stunned silence, dusting himself off and cracking a grin. "At least we know if the Chancellor tries to kill us with stringed instruments, Zoe's got us covered."

Chapter 10

I SCOOTED A LITTLE CLOSER to Adrien as we watched Tyryn and Rand demonstrating some attack moves. It was four days later and the air-filtration system had finally gotten finished this morning. I'd been able to get out of the suit and change into a normal tunic. I took Adrien's hand, marveling at how amazing it was to be able to touch his skin again.

Tyryn aimed a swift punch, but Rand's forearm shot up and blocked it.

"Good," Tyryn murmured, then turned to the rest of us sitting in a circle in the training center. "It's all about repetition and building muscle memory, so that in a fight it just comes naturally and your reflexes are lightning quick."

I was trying to pay attention to the lesson, but I kept wishing Adrien and I could have stolen away somewhere to kiss for hours. Adrien glanced over at me and shared a secret grin as if he knew exactly what I was thinking about. We'd only been able to share one quick kiss before class and I could still feel the heat of it on my lips.

"This is ridiculous," City said, standing up. "I can electrify anything in a fifty-foot radius. I'm never going to need to know this."

Rand, who hadn't sat down yet, crept up behind City while she spoke. In a blink, he'd swept her legs out from under her and had her back against the padded floor. "Oh yeah?" he said with a sideways grin, one hand a little below her neck, holding her firmly down.

She let out an infuriated sound and tried to get up, but Rand easily kept her trapped. Then her face turned to a sweet smile. She raised her hand and touched a pinky to Rand's forehead. I didn't see the spark, but he jumped off her, swearing loudly.

"Crackin' hell, Citz!"

She smiled and stood up, smoothing down her hair in the same motion. "My point exactly."

"Enough," Tyron barked. "Filicity, take your seat."

Rand grinned.

"You too, Rand. That kind of cockiness can get you killed in a fight. You can't always see the threat before it's on you." He walked back and forth, making eye contact with each of us. "The Chancellor is building her own army of glitchers, and you can bet they'll fight dirty. You have to be smarter. You have to be stronger. And most of all, you have to work as a team."

"But it's not just glitchers we'll be up against," Xona said. "We have to learn how to take down Regs." She glanced over her shoulder at the four ex-Regs who stood silently along the wall.

"That's why we will also be spending an extensive amount of time with weapons training," Tyryn said. "There are a few ways to disable a Reg." He clicked on a 3-D projection cube at his feet. The illuminated projection of a Reg filled the space, taller and bulkier than Tyryn.

Out of the corner of my eye, I saw one of the ex-Regs shuffle uncomfortably. The sandy-haired boy, Cole.

"But how do you kill it?" Xona's voice cut across the space.

"There are a few weak points in a Reg's armor, but a kill shot is next to impossible." Tyryn waved his hand and the illuminated Reg swiveled around. "Aim at the joints, especially the knee caps. If you're lucky enough for a Reg to turn its back to you, aim at the small of its back, right here at the waist." Tyryn shone a laser at a small area to indicate where he meant. "The armor here is thinner, to allow full dexterity of movement. This is the one place that, with repeated fire with the highest velocity laser weapon, a Reg can be killed."

"Stop it!"

We all turned at the sound. Cole stepped forward. Usually the ex-Regs' faces were completely placid, but Cole looked visibly angry. Heat flushed his cheeks.

"We shouldn't be training to kill Regs," he said. "We should be trying to save them."

Xona let out a disgusted noise. "The only safe Reg is a dead one. Look at its arm—it was made for killing."

Cole dropped his arm, hiding the double-barreled weapons embedded in it behind his back as if he was self-conscious.

"It's not our fault," he said, his face flushed. I was shocked to see an ex-Reg displaying so much emotion. "You have no idea what it was like when our V-chips were destroyed. We woke up to find that our lives had been stolen from us and that hardware invaded every inch of our bodies. But underneath all this," he pointed to the metal plate on his chest, "is still something that deserves saving. We deserve as much of a chance at a normal life as you do."

"You could only be rescued because you were young enough to handle the destruction of your V-chip architecture." Tyryn's voice was calm, gentle even. "Unfortunately, that's not possible for full-grown adult Regs. We can't save them. In a fight, they'll be coming at us to kill. Deactivating them is the only option, getting a kill shot if possible." He continued his presentation with the laser on the 3-D model. "Now, like I was saying, if you hit here at just the right angle—"

Heavy footsteps interrupted him. Cole strode from the room, slamming the door button with his heavy fist and stomping through it when it opened.

"Good riddance," Xona said under her breath.

I looked back and forth between the door and Xona, then over my shoulder at the three other ex-Regs. They didn't looked fazed by Cole's anger. Their blank expressions gave me a chill.

"Now line up," Tyryn said, ignoring the interruption. "You'll each take turns with the laser-round and continuous-fire-stream weapons."

Adrien wasn't at dinner that night, but as we were finishing, he sent me a message over the com in my arm panel.

Ginni held her hands to her chest. "That's so romantic. I wish I had a boy to send me messages to meet in the middle of the night." She sighed dramatically.

"It's seven o'clock," Xona said. "That's hardly the middle of the night."

"Well that part doesn't matter. All that's important is that they can have some time alone." She lifted her eyebrows significantly at Xona and leaned in. "They haven't had a chance to be alone since she's been out of the suit."

"I am sitting right here, you know."

"Oops, I'm getting carried away again." She looked down and put her hands in her lap. "Professor Henry warned me not to do that."

I looked over at Xona, wondering if she had any idea what Ginni was talking about now, but she shrugged. I looked at the message again.

"Do you guys know where the security hub is?"

"Security hub?" Ginni asked. She looked at Xona with a frown. "I've never heard of it. How have I never heard of it?"

"Oh never mind," I said, looking at my arm panel. "He sent directions."

Ginni smiled again. "If he's telling you to meet him in some part of the Foundation we've never heard of, it's definitely because he wants to be alone with you!" She reached out and took my hand. "Promise you'll tell me all about it? Best friends share all their secrets."

Considering how Ginni usually handled secrets, I wasn't too excited about sharing mine, but I still returned her smile.

As I walked down the hallway, I couldn't help getting swept up in Ginni's giddy enthusiasm. *He wants to be alone with you.* My face broke into a grin at the thought. I looked at the directions lighting up my forearm and hurried down the main hallway, then cut across to the east wing by the training center.

Right before the boys' dorm rooms was a door labeled To SUBLEVEL. I pressed my thumb against the panel at the side and it slid open, revealing a stairwell leading down. Of course. If there was a room Ginni didn't know about, it had to be in the military level of the Foundation.

I went down the stairs and followed a short hallway until I came to the door Adrien had indicated. I stepped into a room with a wall covered in projected monitors, floor to ceiling. There was a bed in one corner, and Adrien sat in the middle of the room at a console desk that curved in a large C around several chairs. A boy I'd never seen before sat beside him.

My heart sank. We weren't going to be alone after all.

Adrien jumped to his feet when he saw me. "Zoe, I'm so glad you're here. This is Simin," he gestured to the other boy. Simin was dark-haired, with big round cheeks. He didn't look up when Adrien introduced him.

"Simin." Adrien nudged the boy in his shoulder.

"No point," Simin grumbled. "She'll just forget."

"You know what the Professor says. Repeated exposure could help you stick longer in people's memories."

Adrien turned back to me. "Simin's the glitcher whose power keeps the Foundation invisible. I think maybe I told you about him before?"

I frowned. It seemed like I had heard something like that, but I couldn't for the life of me remember the specifics.

"Did I catch you in the middle of dinner?" Adrien asked.

I shook my head. "No, I was just chatting with Xona and Ginni."

"Ginni?" Simin finally looked up at me. He seemed to be about our age. "Did she mention me?"

"No, she'd never heard of this place. Which surprised me, since Ginni seems to know everything and everyone."

Simin looked down, and I could see the disappointment clearly on his face. "Not everyone."

"Simin's a top-notch techer," Adrien said, patting his shoulder. "He's been helping me with something. It's about your older brother, Daavd."

I felt my eyes widen. That was the last thing I'd expected. Unbidden images from my old nightmares flashed in my mind. My brother running in a forest. Swarms of Regulators charging through the trees after him. Him on the ground, broken, his eyes frozen on me, his little sister who'd raised the alarm. I swallowed hard.

"What about Daavd?"

"We've been hacking into the Community subject records for known glitchers." Adrien gestured for me to sit on the empty seat beside him. "Mostly we're looking for information on the glitchers we suspect the Chancellor is trying to recruit and the ones she might already have under her power. But we've been practicing our hack codes on older records that are less guarded and won't raise alarms in their systems. So I thought I'd look into Daavd's files . . ."

He started tapping on the console in front of him and opening several directories in the screens on the wall. He clicked through a few more screens then pointed. "The report says they were never able to discover how your brother got past Regulators, much less how he got you to go with him."

He turned to me. "At first we thought maybe he was able to hack their security systems, but then Simin came up with a different theory. What if Daavd's power was something similar to what the Chancellor can do?"

I shook my head. I might not remember him, but Daavd was my brother. There was no way he could be anything like the Chancellor.

But Adrien persisted. "Think about it, Zoe, why didn't you turn your brother in much sooner than you did when he escaped with you as a child? Your first instinct under V-chip control would have been to report him to the Regulators, but you went along with him quietly. What if he could compel you to do what he wanted?"

"But then why didn't it work?"

"Well," Adrien's voice had turned softer. He knew how much guilt I still felt about it all. "Maybe he had trouble with his Gift like you do, and it didn't always work right. Just an instant of his losing control over you would have been enough time for you to call out to the Regulators and get him killed."

"But the Chancellor has the same power." A horrible thought struck me. "Are you saying that we're somehow related to her?"

"No, no," Adrien waved a hand. "Not at all. We just think that Daavd's power is similar to hers and that the small dose of your early exposure to his power is why you can resist her now. There's something unique about your body chemistry. It seems to work like your allergies do."

Adrien turned to Simin. "You want to explain this part? You're the one who made the connection."

Adrien pushed his chair back a little so I could see across him to where Simin sat.

"So we know your extreme allergic reaction to Surface allergens is due to your earlier exposure as a child," Simin said. He clicked through his console while he talked and didn't look up at me. He sounded bored, or maybe he just wasn't comfortable being around other people. "Your body created antibodies against a specific allergen the first time you were exposed, so the next time you encountered it, your mast cells went crazy, releasing histamines to protect against what they registered as a dangerous substance. This sent you into anaphylactic shock."

I shuddered. He recounted it so scientifically, but I remembered the horror only too well. Gasping for air, my throat swelling shut.

"But what does that have to do with why the Chancellor's power doesn't work on me?"

"Histamine-releasing neurons are also found in the brain," Simin continued. "Neural interaction between the hypothalamus and amygdala are at the heart of what makes glitcher powers possible. If your unique immunological response triggered a similar release of histamines in the hypothalmus due to childhood exposure to glitcher compulsion, you could have built up protection against that particular kind of power."

I blinked rapidly, trying to follow his complex explanation.

"But instead of making you sick like your allergies do, your mind is protecting you from a real threat." He finally looked up at me. "It's not a perfect correlation, but you could think of it like an immunization. An early dosage built up an immunity to the disease. It was only possible through the combination of your unique body chemistry and your chance exposure as a child."

"It explains why you're the only person her compulsion doesn't work on, but why every other glitcher power still affects you," Adrien said.

I looked between the two boys uncertainly.

"Zoe," he took my hand. "I know this doesn't make up for what happened. Nothing can change that. But your brother's death could be the reason we're alive. Because of him, you're the one person with the ability to fight the Chancellor. You save lives. You can save all of us. Because of him."

I couldn't breathe. I pulled my hand away from his. "If I had the choice, I'd rather have Daavd back."

"But you weren't given a choice," he said, his voice gentle. "And I'm so, so sorry about that."

Tears welled up and my whole upper body began to quiver. Xona had said her mom believed that good things can come from the bad, that things always work out for a reason. But it seemed so wrong to be glad that my brother had died as part of some twisted web of fate so that I could fight against the Chancellor. Adrien had obviously meant it as a comforting thought, but I didn't want to believe the world worked like that. And still, any way I looked at it, Daavd died because of me. A high-pitched buzzing sounded in my ears. I knew the feeling well.

"Oh no," I said, blinking my tears away and looking at my shaking forearm.

Adrien took my hand in his, then his eyes flashed back up

at mine. "Zoe, your emotions are triggering your telek. Can you calm down and get yourself under control?"

I tried to take several deep breaths, but all I could see was my brother's bloody face. The shaking got worse. I could feel the power building up inside me, begging to get out.

Adrien put his hands on both sides of my face and looked straight into my eyes. "Zoe. You need to Link yourself. Right now."

I whispered the words to reconnect myself. Color leached from the room. And with it, I felt my tumultuous emotions calm and dissipate too. The sliding door of the Link came down, separating me from my fears and anxieties, and replacing them with numb calm.

Simin stiffened in his chair.

"It's all right," Adrien said. "Her powers are under control now."

"No, it's not that," Simin said, grabbing a small device from a shelf under the console and sticking it in his ear. He pointed at one of the monitors.

"What is it?" Adrien asked.

Simin raised a hand to silence him, but, after a few minutes of giving directions over the com, he turned to us.

"It's the General. She's coming in. With a lot of wounded soldiers."

Chapter 11

ADRIEN'S FACE WENT ASHEN at Simin's words. He headed directly to the Med Center where Jilia was already prepping beds. I followed.

He had told me I should go to my dorm room, but I stayed behind anyway. One look at Adrien's tense face helped me fight the numbing Link enough for one clear thought of my own to shine through the fog: I didn't want to leave him when he looked like that. At the same time, I didn't dare un-Link myself. I couldn't risk adding to the crisis by losing control of my power.

I pressed myself against the wall as Rez fighters came stumbling in with a loud chorus of shuffling boots, moans, and shouted instructions. Half a dozen wounded fighters were carried in and deposited onto the waiting beds. All of them bled from one place or another. The Link grayed color as much as emotion, but I could make out the dark stains on clothes and the floor, and the gashes on their skin. Adrien helped them all get situated. The cold readouts of the Link informed me of the size and breadth of each wound. One man's leg looked like it had been blown completely off from the shin down. Another's chest was half caved in, and Jilia laid her hands on him immediately. After a few moments though, her face fell and she cursed and moved on to another.

Adrien's face reflected the horror I couldn't feel.

In the chaos, a woman with sharp cheekbones and a hard mouth strode into the room. She wore the dark gray uniform of the Rez fighters. Her hands were stained with blood, but I couldn't tell if it was hers. Professor Henry followed on her heels. "Are you sure you're okay, Rosalina?" She must be the General.

"What happened?" Adrien asked.

The General ignored him and walked over to Jilia. "How are they?"

"I'm almost done triaging," Jilia murmured, pressing on the abdomen of a woman Rez fighter. The woman winced but didn't cry out. "We lost Tirpte. Jenald might need a bionic replacement." Jilia lifted her hands and finally looked at the General. "But I think the others will make it."

The General breathed out and closed her eyes. "We lost four more in the field. They were ready for us. There were only two cell commanders who knew we were coming." She rubbed her forehead. "Chancellor Bright must have gotten to them."

The Professor's eyes widened. "Then all the cells in the northern quadrant might have been cracked."

The General slammed her palm against a tray of instruments. "She knows our every move before we make it. And she's being considered next in line to become Chancellor Supreme of Sector 6. If she manages it . . ." Her jaw tensed. "We can't let it come to that."

"Why were you in Central City?" Adrien asked. His voice was hard, almost accusatory.

The General's eyes sliced over at him and something passed between them I couldn't read. Her mouth tightened and a vein in her forehead stood out. "That's none of your concern." She glanced over at me. "No one should be in here except medical personnel. Leave now."

Adrien pushed off from the wall and I followed him. He didn't say anything once we got into the hallway, but he stopped and leaned over, putting his hands on his knees and breathing hard.

In the back of my mind, I felt a tugging thought that I should be doing something. But I didn't know what.

"You should go to your dorm room," he said, standing up and raking a hand hard through his hair. His facial features were contorted. The three long tones of Scheduled Subject Downtime sounded over the Link. Numbed by the soothing sounds, I moved my feet forward and shuffled obediently toward my dorm.

I paused and looked back before I turned the corner. Adrien was standing in the same place, his eyes wet as he looked down at the stains on his hands.

The next morning, Ginni told me to un-Link as per our usual morning routine, and immediately everything that had happened the night before rushed in again. The bloody soldiers. The General's anger. And Adrien's face when I left him.

"How are the soldiers who came in last night?" I asked Ginni, trusting that she'd have the latest news.

"One died, but the rest are going to be okay."

I showered and dressed quickly, braiding my long dark hair while it was still wet. I hurried along to breakfast before Xona and Ginni were ready, hoping Adrien might be there. He'd been so obviously hurting last night, and I'd left him there. Just walked away. The Link had turned me into an unfeeling monster. I had to see him and try to make it right.

But other than the early-rising Rez fighters, the Caf was empty.

"He eats breakfast with his mom sometimes," Ginni said as we dumped our trays half an hour later.

But Adrien wasn't in our morning training session either. I came up to Ginni after class, wringing my hands anxiously. "Can you . . . ?"

"Use my power?" she finished. She nodded and closed her eyes for a second, then opened them again. "He's in the east bathroom."

"Thanks."

I hurried to the east bathroom and pushed the sliding door open gently. I heard the rush of running sink water and opened the door all the way.

Adrien was at the sink, splashing his face over and over. He'd half soaked his tunic, but he kept cupping water in his hands and throwing it onto his face, slapping his cheeks hard every time. He finally stopped, his hands braced on either side of the sink, a line of muscle forming on his cheek where he gritted his teeth. He stared at himself in the mirror.

His face looked pinched with pain. His shoulder blades jutted out next to the taut muscles on his back.

Seeing him like this shocked all the questions right out of

me. I felt a hitch in my chest as I watched. I'd never seen him like this before. He was always so ready with a smile for me or a joke for Rand and Juan at the Caf table.

"How long?" he whispered, his voice low and guttural. At first I thought he was talking to me, but then I realized he was questioning his reflection.

"Adrien?" I asked, finally stepping inside.

He looked up and his mouth dropped open in surprise when he saw me in the mirror. He spun around, rubbing his forearm over his dripping face and pasting on a quick smile.

"Hey," he said, then looked away and cleared his throat.

"What's going on?" I stepped closer.

"Nothing." He grabbed a few towels from the dispenser on the wall and started cleaning up the water he'd splashed all over the sink.

I came closer and put my hand on top of his to stop him from scrubbing the sink so hard. "What did you mean when you asked, 'How long?'"

He flinched, but covered it quickly with a smile.

"I'm so sorry I left you like that last night," I said. "Are you upset about the soldiers? Or did you have a new vision?"

He closed his eyes and breathed out in frustration. "I can't tell you."

"Why not?"

"Last time I told you about the future," his words came out harsh, "it caused you so much stress you had a nightmare and lost control of your power."

My mouth dropped open. "That wasn't your fault!"

"Remember that story we read about Oedipus, and how the oracle started it all?" He turned to me, his voice heated. "I feel like it's the same with me. Whenever I tell people my visions, bad things follow. Those soldiers last night . . ." The smiling mask had dropped away and every ounce of grief and pain was clear in his eyes. "I told Taylor about a vision I had, and that's why they were in Central City in the first place. It's because of me those soldiers died."

"Adrien—"

"The things I've seen . . ." He shook his head. "I've tried so many times to change things, and every time I fail. I thought maybe I just didn't have enough power to stop them, so I started sharing all my visions with the General. Even one vision I should have *never* told her." His shoulders slumped in defeat. "Knowing the future changes a person. It makes you desperate, or reckless."

He looked at the mirror again, his haunted eyes reflecting back. "Or hopeless. I've learned my lesson now. You can't stop what's coming for you. What's the point of even trying?"

"Oh, Adrien," I murmured, pulling him into my arms, ignoring his soaked tunic and holding him as tightly as I could. I listened to his heartbeat through the damp cloth. "Shhh, it's okay," I whispered. "It's gonna be okay." I patted his back.

I pulled his head down and kissed his forehead, wanting to comfort him any way I could. I kissed down to his ear, then to his cheek, tasting salt on my lips from his tears. I kept moving, slow gentle brushes of my mouth all the way down his face.

"It's gonna be okay," I whispered again. He stood still in my arms, not moving as I hovered, inches from his lips. He stared at me, his eyes dark. Then he cupped the back of my head and pulled me into him for one deep, hungry kiss. A sizzle of lightning sparked all through my body.

All the anguish and intensity that had been in his voice a moment ago was now transformed into his touch. I gasped as his tongue trailed down my neck and pulled his head back up roughly with my hands so I could kiss his full lips again.

He twirled me until his body pinned me against the wall. One of my legs hitched up around his hips, pulling him closer. He gripped the fabric of my tunic in his fists and a low growl escaped from the back of his throat. I was all lips and nerve endings and a body pressing against his.

I arched up into him, barely hearing the buzzing in my ears go from a slight hum to a raging vibration.

Until the mirror behind him exploded into a thousand pieces, the shards blowing outward.

Chapter 12

I'D BEEN TRAINING with Adrien's mom for the last week—and had the bruises to prove it. But I deserved it. It had taken two hours for Jilia to get all the bits of mirror glass out of Adrien's back. The look Sophia had given me when she came in to see him had cut sharper than the glass splinters embedded in my arm. She had pulled me aside and said she'd arranged for me to train with her every afternoon until I could get my power under control.

It felt like all I did was train now, morning till night. Mornings with Tyryn, then I usually skipped lunch to spend an hour meditating with Jilia, followed by afternoons with Sophia. And still, other than a few rare moments here and there where I'd felt right on the cusp of calling my power voluntarily, I wasn't any closer to controlling it.

"Your power is linked to your emotions," Sophia said, lifting the pellet gun at me again. "But obviously meditation isn't working," she continued. "So let's try getting you angry."

I tried to prepare this time, to gather my telek, but before I could even try to focus on the dim buzzing in my ears, a rubber pellet smacked me in the forehead.

"Why didn't you deflect that?" Sophia asked, her gray-blond dreadlocks flying behind her as she spun around.

"I'm trying," I said through gritted teeth.

She raised the pellet gun in response. "General Taylor doesn't need you to try. She needs you to *do*. She had this place rebuilt to accommodate you because she needs your power to work. She needs you to be a weapon."

"I don't see how shooting me in the face is supposed to help me focus—"

Two pellet rounds smacked into my ribs.

"Hey!" I shouted. "I wasn't even ready."

She sneered. "You think in a fight, a Reg will stop so you can have a moment to get ready?" Another bullet flew toward me. I held up my hands to deflect it, but it just smacked into my pinky finger.

"Ow!" I cradled my finger and looked up at the woman, so frustrated I could scream. We'd already been at this for half an hour, and I was sure I was going to have small pellet-sized bruises up and down my body. I bet she couldn't wait to volunteer for this task. I could almost feel the satisfaction radiating off her. My hands started to shake. I looked down at them in dismay. This was exactly what I didn't want to happen. I didn't want to lose control with Adrien's mom. It would just be that much more ammunition for her hatred of me.

I held up my tremoring arm. "Maybe we should stop for a little bit."

Sophia ignored me, not lowering her weapon. "I told Adrien that he should stay away from you. That you are dangerous."

"I'd never hurt him."

"Oh really?" Her eyebrows raised.

"The mirror was an accident," I mumbled, looking down.

"What if these were real bullets? When you're out there running missions, you need to be able to take care of yourself. My son is strong and smart, but he'd jump in front of a laser weapon to try and save you. Are you going to let him get killed because of you?"

"No." The buzzing got louder in my ears, but I tried to tamp it down. It was coming on too quickly. I knew I was supposed to be trying to access the power, but the truth was, I was terrified of it. Sophia was right. All I did was get people hurt. And our training sessions weren't helping much.

Whenever I walked into the Caf these days, talk quieted at all the tables. Furtive eyes glanced at me, and then quickly darted away. I could tell they'd all heard about what had happened with the mirror, and Ginni had probably filled everyone else in about my repeated failures at the glitcher training sessions. This morning several of the Rez fighters had stared at me in open hostility, making my cheeks flame in embarrassment and shame. They'd all expected me to be this powerful leader. I was supposed to be a sign of hope, a secret weapon against the Chancellor.

But I was none of those things. My torso started shaking with frustration at my repeated failure.

I tried to calm down and take deep breaths, following Jilia's instructions. But all I really wanted to do was run out of the room and go Link myself.

The tremors got worse.

"We've got to take a break," I said, trying to keep my voice even.

"Are you angry yet?" she yelled. "You can feel your power, can't you? Now try to harness it. Control it, don't let it control you."

I looked down at my shaking arm in dismay. Yes, I could feel the power. Maybe Sophia's way, as much as I disliked it, was the path to finally getting control. Now, if I could just direct it the way that I wanted to this time. . . . I gritted my teeth together and tried to remember the breathing methods from meditation class. Deep breath in, deep breath out. I could do this. No one else had to get hurt because of me.

The shaking started to subside a tiny bit, and when I closed my eyes I could feel the shape of the room around me. It was almost like there was a 3-D projection cube of the whole room in my head. I could feel the objects filling the space and sense Sophia's movement without even looking.

Then Sophia launched another pellet at me and my eyes popped back open.

"If you would wait a second—" I started.

Another pellet thumped into my side.

"Just let me get—"

Another pellet.

"Stop it!" I yelled, all my frustration bubbling up and over.

Sophia flew backward six feet into the wall and then crumpled to the ground. I rushed over to her. "Are you okay?"

There was a thin layer of padding covering the training room wall, but I knew it was solid rock beyond. I felt sick at the thought of having hurt someone else, even her. Her hair was tossed in her face. I pushed the thick strands aside. "Are you okay?" I asked again anxiously.

She let out a pained groan but sat up, rubbing her shoulder.

"I'm so sorry," I said, and reached to help her up. "I didn't mean to—"

"Exactly." Her voice was cutting. "You didn't use it on purpose. You can't control it." She jerked her hand back from me and slowly got to her feet. She picked up the pellet gun from where she'd dropped it and shoved it at my chest.

"Your telekinesis is extremely powerful, but if you don't get it under control, and soon, all it makes you is dangerous. I don't have visions often like my son, but I've seen enough. Without control, you are a ticking time bomb. I don't want Adrien around the next time you go off." Her eyes were hard as steel, and she paused to enunciate every word. "Stay away from my son."

"Did you and Adrien get in a fight?" Ginni asked.

Ginni and I were sitting at the long table in the corner of our dorm room. Her half of the desk was covered in different colored fabrics and a small machine that seamed the pieces together with thread. My side of the table was empty except for my tablet. Even though I'd been sitting and staring at the screen for an hour, I couldn't remember a thing I'd read. I'd been like this all week. I couldn't seem to concentrate on anything.

"What?" I asked, looking up.

"Well you two haven't been sitting together as much lately, and you always leave class early without waiting to walk with him. Are you mad at him or something?"

I hadn't meant to be so obvious in avoiding him. "Do you think he thinks I'm mad at him?" He hadn't said anything.

But then, we hadn't really talked since the mirror incident, and that was almost two weeks ago. We'd say hi and joke around in the Caf. But we hadn't had a real conversation, the kind that went below the surface, in a long time.

"Are you?" Ginni pressed.

"No, I just . . ."

I just felt helpless when it came to my powers and I was afraid of hurting him again. Part of me wanted to com him and ask if we could meet somewhere alone, but then his mother's words would echo in my mind. *Stay away from my son.*

I didn't want it to be true, but Sophia was right. Strong emotions made my power unpredictable, and being alone with Adrien was always inherently emotional. As much as I wanted his arms around me, how could I willingly put him in harm's way?

Before I could think of what to say to Ginni, Xona burst in.

"Looks like I'll be joining you for meditation during lunch tomorrow," Xona said, tossing her tablet case roughly on the ground and then flopping onto Ginni's bottom bunk. "I got sentenced to extra sessions all week."

"What happened?" Ginni dropped the two squares of fabric she was holding.

"I caught that ex-Reg Cole following me on my way to a private training session. It's not the first time either."

Ginni looked at me, a secret smile playing on her face. She got that look whenever one of us started talking about a boy at the Foundation. She'd always nudge me with an elbow or nod and wink. It probably had something to do with the books she was always reading. She'd pause periodically to look up from the words, clutching her reading tablet to her chest and sighing loudly.

"And . . . ?" Ginni prompted.

Xona smirked, leaning back to lazily entwine her fingers behind her head. "And I gave him a quick elbow to the throat. Now he knows better."

Ginni gasped.

"City saw me do it and reported straight to Jilia. So, anger management meditation it is."

"But what if he was following you because he likes you?" Ginni asked. "Maybe he just wanted to talk."

Xona glared at her, all traces of humor gone from her face. "Don't try to turn ex-Regs into romantic heroes like in your books. They're killers. That's all they know how to do."

"Well it's not like we have a lot of options." Ginni's face soured. "Adrien's with Zoe. All the other students are too young. Which only leaves Rand."

Xona scrunched up her nose. "Oh honey, you can do better than Rand."

Ginni looked down at her sewing again. "He seems to like City anyway. They're always flirting."

"Rand flirts with everybody," Xona said.

"You should give Cole a chance," I said to Xona. "He's not like the other Regs. He even smiled at me when I knocked him over during training." Sophia had brought him in to train with me after I'd thrown her against the wall a second time. She figured an ex-Reg could take the hits better.

"Are you finally getting control of your power?" Ginni asked excitedly.

"Sort of." I sighed. "I can call it up sometimes, but usually only when Sophia gets me mad. And then I never direct it the way I'm supposed to. I just knock things over. I might as well not have the power at all."

"Well as long as you're banging up a Reg, it sounds great to me," Xona said.

"And it does sound like you're getting somewhere," Ginni said, with a comforting smile.

"Maybe." It wasn't exactly progress, but maybe it was something after all. I hadn't had any more seizures because I was releasing my power regularly. I still had to be Linked when I slept, but that wasn't so bad.

"So do you think they'll let you go on a mission soon?" Ginni asked. She averted her eyes and flattened the fabric on the table.

Xona looked over at Ginni curiously. "Why? What do you know?"

Ginni bit her lip. "Well, I might have heard something about it is all. Word is that General Taylor is prepping for another big mission."

"I heard a rumor about it too." Xona sat up straighter. "Tyryn let me borrow some practice weapons, and I've been training every minute the center is free." She popped two shiny weapons out of her holster.

"Not that he'll let you take any ammunition outside the training room," Ginni reminded her.

"Well, some live rounds might have accidentally fallen into my bag in the equipment room."

"Xona!" Ginni sounded appalled.

"What? I'm the only non-glitcher on the team. When we get into battle I can't hocus-pocus my way out of it. I need these beauties," she patted her weapons affectionately. "But about the mission. Tyryn wouldn't tell me any details. What have you heard?" She looked back at Ginni.

"Well, I might have overheard that the General is planning to pit us against the Chancellor's group of glitchers."

Xona let out a low whistle.

"I wonder what kinds of powers they'll have," Ginni said. "What do you think, Zoe?"

She turned to me and I felt like shrinking down in my chair. I was sure the General was well aware of my lack of progress. Sophia would have made sure of it. If the General was planning a mission, she wasn't going to take me.

"I don't know," I mumbled. But then I really considered the question. If we were going up against the Chancellor's glitchers, would that include Max?

"Ginni—" I sat up suddenly. Why hadn't I thought of it before? "You can locate anyone in the world, right?"

She looked up in surprise. "Yeah."

I grabbed her hand. "Can you find my friend Max?"

"I'm sorry, Zoe. Molla's already asked." Ginni's eyebrows drew together. "Whatever it is about being a shape-shifter, it makes him invisible to me. He can fool anyone into seeing him as someone else, and it fools my power, too."

"Oh," I said, feeling a mixture of relief and disappointment. I tried to picture him escaping the Chancellor and running off on his own, impersonating an Upper somewhere and living the luxurious life he'd always wanted. But I knew it was unlikely. He'd gone back to the Chancellor. She wouldn't have trusted him again and would be sure to keep him under constant control with her compulsion power.

"I don't see why you or Molla even care," Xona said. "He chose to join the Chancellor. He helped her."

"It's more complicated than that," I said. "He made some really bad choices. The Chancellor got to him right when he was new to glitching. He thought working for her would keep us safe. He didn't realize what she was planning—"

"Yeah, maybe," Xona scoffed, "but then he stayed behind when he had the chance to escape. After he knew how evil she was."

I opened my mouth, but then closed it again. I couldn't deny she was right. Max had done some horrible things. But I truly believed he'd started out with good intentions, and I wasn't blameless either. If I deserved a chance at redemption, after what I'd done to my older brother, didn't Max? After all, no one had *died* because of him.

And he'd only stayed behind with the Chancellor because he couldn't bear to come with me. I didn't know how to explain that, if circumstances had been different, I was sure Max could have been a much better person. Or how, in spite of everything, I still considered him family. "I've got to believe there's still some good in him."

Xona smirked. "I knew it. You really do think you can save everyone." She turned to me, her face dark. "Look, you've been protected in one bubble or another your whole life. You haven't seen what's really going on out there. But I have. Trust me, sooner or later you're going to find out that not everyone makes the right choice when it matters most. Not everyone is worth saving."

I felt my face heat up. "Who are you to decide who's worth saving and who's not?"

"I don't really care who we save and who we don't." She leaned in. "I just want to kill as many Regs as I can and, maybe if I'm lucky, take out some Uppers too. I want to make them all pay." She spun one of the guns around her finger and then resheathed it.

Ginni had been ignoring our conversation and kept pushing material through her machine, but she stood up and dramatically twirled the fabric in a circle. "All done. It's called a skirt!" she exclaimed. The skirt was patchwork, made from odd-shaped squares of old Community uniforms, some ex-Reg coverall blue, browns from the service worker uniforms, even the surgeon's reds. "Isn't it pretty?"

Xona touched the cloth skeptically. "Looks like it'd be hard to run in."

This time it was Ginni who rolled her eyes. "It's not for running. It's for looking pretty." She grabbed the skirt back from Xona.

"Who you trying to look pretty for anyway?" Xona asked.

Ginni turned to us, mouth open like she planned on mentioning something or someone. But then she paused and frowned. "I can't remember."

Chapter 13

"GOOD AFTERNOON LADIES," Jilia said, settling herself down in front of us.

I sat down on the cushion while she put a box on the ground beside her. Xona leaned over and opened it. A cluster of little clear balls lay inside.

"What are those?" I asked.

"Marbles," Xona said. "I used to play with them when I was a kid."

"I wanted to try something a little more tactile for Zoe to focus on while we meditate. But the same practices apply to non-glitchers, so it will be useful for you as well, Xona."

"Okay," I said, but I wasn't convinced. Nothing had worked so far.

"First, Zoe, I want you to think about some memory that brings up strong emotions."

I looked over at Xona, then down at the ground again. "Um, that might not be . . . safe."

"It will be fine," Jilia said, her voice calm and soothing. "You won't hurt us. You can always Link yourself if you feel like you're going to lose control. That's been part of the problem, I think. You're so afraid of losing control that you never allow yourself enough leeway to access and explore your power. Being locked up in the research lab for all those months only exacerbated the problem right when your power was expanding and you needed to be experimenting most. We've got to break those habits. So try to abandon your fears. This is a safe place. Just remember you can Link yourself the moment you feel your power getting out of control. Think of that like a safety switch."

I nodded, uncertain. What she said made sense, but I'd been afraid of my power for so long . . .

"Close your eyes and think of a powerful emotional memory. As soon as you feel the power start to build, let me know."

I closed my eyes and sifted through my memories. Well, getting mad at Adrien's mom usually worked to get me upset. I thought about our latest session yesterday and how she'd said that I would always fail the people I loved most. A slight buzzing did begin to build in my ears at the thought. But then I shook the memory off. No. I didn't want to draw on negative emotions if I could avoid it.

Instead, I switched to another memory. Of Adrien and me alone in my room back in the Community, when he'd tried to explain what love was. He'd called it a miracle that, in a world so broken and painful, love could still exist.

I still remembered the tenor of his voice and the intensity of his gaze as he'd spoken. *Love shouldn't exist but it does. It's the biggest anomaly, some might say the biggest defect, of the whole human race. But it's the most beautiful anomaly. I understand that now. And I would give up anything for you . . . Because I love you.*

And then I'd said it back to him and we'd kissed until I felt like I was soaring right up and out of my body. So much had happened since then, but my love for him was the one thing that had remained constant. I felt warm just thinking about it, and a soft buzz rose in my ears.

But then, without meaning to, the scene switched to our kiss in the bathroom, right before I'd lost control and shattered the mirror. There had been passion in that kiss too. More than that—desperation. Tied up in the memory was fear about how upset Adrien had been and worry about what he saw in the future that had him so scared. I thought of the haunted look in his eyes. The buzzing in my ears suddenly became a loud drone and my hand started to tremble.

I gritted my teeth as the tremors worsened. My first instinct was to choke off the emotions or Link myself. Instead I let myself linger in the memory of our kiss. It wasn't the purely happy memory I'd wanted, but maybe the strongest emotions were always a complex mix of good and bad. I replayed the feel of Adrien's hands on my body, pulling me into him and kissing me like he was a starving man and I was a full course meal. I let the mixture of desire and desperation resonate throughout my body. The buzzing came to a fever pitch in my ears. "Okay," I finally whispered, my voice trembling. "I can feel it."

"Good," Jilia murmured. "Now I want you to try to channel that energy into the box of marbles in front of you. Visualize yourself and all that emotion you feel as being contained in the marble. Make it a single thought to focus your energy. Think: I am that. Repeat the phrase with your breaths in and out. Like this. I," she breathed in, "am that," she said after her breath out.

"I'll try," I said. I closed my eyes. The shaking in my hands was getting worse. I should Link myself so I didn't hurt anybody. I tightened my jaw against the thought. No, I wouldn't give up before I'd even tried. I knew from training with Sophia that I had a little bit longer before I lost control. I'd wait until the last moment to Link myself if I had to.

I am that, I repeated internally. I am that.

"Do not think of any moment beyond the present." Jilia's voice was sonorous. "There is only now. Anything can happen next, but what happens next is not important. What is important is now, inhabiting this space. There is no separate you. You are connected to all things. You are the marble."

The power bubbled up inside of me, but for once, maybe the first time ever, I felt completely present with it and was not afraid. The mental projection cube rose up in my mind and I felt the shapes of the marbles in the box. There was one sitting on top of all the others, and I zeroed in my focus. I am *that*.

The marble started to vibrate, shaking and knocking against the other marbles with a slight tinkling sound. Even though I wasn't touching it physically, I could feel its surface texture. It was so smooth, but as I zoomed in closer and closer, I could feel the tiny imperfections, the slight indentations and pockets of air in the glass.

"Good," Jilia murmured. "Now lift the marble up."

I felt the power inside me boiling over, tingling in my fingertips. For a second I worried. What if I lost control? Then I gritted my teeth and pushed the fear away.

I focused only on my power extending outward past my skin and covering the marble.

I am that.

The marble lifted up into the air. Then I lifted another and another until all of the small spheres hovered in the air. I raised them up a foot, then two.

I opened my eyes to look at them. Xona was watching in stunned fascination, but I ignored her.

The marbles formed a circle in the air. I spun them like a giant wheel. The glass glinted in the light with each rotation and I kept it spinning faster and faster until all I could see were brief flashes of light. And for the first time for as long as I could remember, I felt completely at peace.

Then several things happened at once.

Cole charged into the room with a loud roar. There was a sharp knife raised in his hand.

Xona's head jerked up and she immediately pulled out two weapons, one from her ankle and another from her hip.

Jilia screamed at them both to stop.

I watched, detached almost, as the components of a disaster fell into place in front of me. I raised my arms and gulped in the room with my power. Everyone in the room was within my mind's projection cube now and I could manipulate them as easily as I could the marbles. I wasn't afraid.

"Stop," I whispered, and they did. Cole had leapt up into the air, knife raised. He froze there, three feet above the ground, and I held him perfectly immobile with my telek. Xona's hand likewise stopped in place.

"Let me go, Zoe," she shouted. "I can take him!"

But I ignored her. The spinning marbles stopped, hovering around me in a giant sphere. I held everything perfectly still.

In the next breath I pulled the weapons out of Cole's and Xona's hands and placed them gently against the wall. I lifted

Cole up almost to the ceiling, and then over to the doorway, far away from Xona.

And then Sophia stepped from the shadow of the hallway into the room. "Good. You passed the test. You're ready."

Suddenly my control faltered. I lowered Cole back to the ground quickly before I lost it. The marbles dropped to the ground, bouncing on the hard floor with small clinking noises.

Anger quickly replaced the sense of peace I'd just felt. "It was all a test? What if I'd failed! Xona could have killed Cole."

Sophia frowned. "She shouldn't have loaded weapons."

Xona let out a disgusted noise and kicked her cushion to the wall before pushing past Sophia to leave.

Sophia turned back to me, her cool eyes meeting my glare. "Come with me. It's time to see the General."

Chapter 14

GENERAL TAYLOR STOOD at the front of the Caf. She'd
called a meeting with my whole task force. Well, everyone
except Xona. When I'd come down the hallway earlier Xona
had been arguing with Tyryn about why she should be able to
go with us. But only Tyryn was in the room now, so I guess
she'd lost the fight.

The General paced the front of the room until everyone
had gathered and was seated. "I've called you all here to dis-
cuss an important mission. One that only this particular task
force can perform, now that all of your members are ready."
She glanced over at me, and I felt my face redden. Had she
been waiting for me to get control of my powers before she
okayed the mission?

City's eyes lit up and she grinned at Rand.

"Bright travels all over the Sector as Underchancellor of
Defense," Taylor continued. "We've been able to map each
place she goes, thanks to Ginni."

Ginni blushed at the acknowledgment and looked down.

"For the most part we can correlate each location to her
official activities and duties. However, there is one building
that remains unaccounted for, one that doesn't officially exist

on the Uppers' property registration database. I believe it is Bright's version of our Foundation. We know of ten individuals staying regularly at the facility, and several of them had been on our glitcher watch lists. We were planning on sending Rez units into the Community to collect them, but Bright got to them first."

I shivered, imagining how different my life would have been if the Chancellor had gotten to me in the Community before Adrien had.

"Bright has been tracking our spies and using her compulsion on them to make them double agents, cracking at least half a dozen other Rez cells the agents were in contact with. In short," she put her hands down on the nearest table and leaned in, "Bright is winning. This is our first opportunity in a long time to deal her a huge blow."

Rand grinned and turned to high-five Eli, the ex-Reg sitting next to him. Eli didn't budge or react at all. Taylor paused, narrowing her eyes at Rand until he lowered his hand and sank back into his seat.

"But wait," City interrupted. "If Ginni can locate Bright wherever she goes, then why don't we just bomb her in the air or something? We've got the weapons tech, right?"

Taylor shook her head. "We've tried that already, twice. Both times, the missiles were shot out of the air in spite of Henk's cloaking tech. We don't know why. The larger transport vehicles utilizing the cloaking mechanisms are never detected. We suspect that a glitcher Gift is involved somehow. That is why we must choose stealth and strike while the Chancellor is absent. Our task is twofold on this mission: infiltrate and retrieve. There will be glitchers under the Chancellor's command, and there will be Regulators on guard."

Her eagle eyes locked on mine. "Zoel, you will first disable any Regulators on-site. Then Adrien will hack the system to get past their security and get us in."

"Excuse me, General Taylor," I broke in. "When you say disable, do you mean—"

Taylor stared at me a moment as if she was unused to interruptions. "You need to neutralize the threat. Deactivate them."

"But," I sputtered, almost standing up. "I can't just kill them." I thought about the ex-Regs on our own team and how easily they could have been the ones guarding the Chancellor. They wouldn't have had a choice.

Taylor's face was hard. "Believe me, I would love to send my Rez fighters to do the job. But you are the one with the invisible powers that can reach through walls and snap necks. Not to mention we don't have solid intelligence on the nature of the glitcher powers we're up against once we're inside. It's one of the reasons I put off this mission until you were ready."

Well that answered that question. "But I—"

Taylor's nostrils flared. "We are fighting a war here. We all must play our part." She swept her arm. "Look around you. This is the Rez's finest, most expensive facility, and even here you can see we've had to fight for every inch we have. In war, it's either them or us. It's as simple as that."

I felt all the eyes in the room on me.

"Rose, they're just children," the Professor spoke up.

"They are soldiers," Taylor said sharply. She took a breath and calmed herself, though it looked like it took some effort.

"Now as for the rest of you," she pulled back and gestured to the Professor. His brow was still furrowed, but he came forward and clicked on a projection cube in the center of our table. A squat building rotated in the illuminated space. We all pushed closer as the Professor touched the apex to expand and enlarge the image.

"We enter here." Taylor pointed to one side of the floating image and spun it so we had a clear view of the back loading dock.

"Rand, City, and a detachment of Rez fighters will retrieve the glitchers who are held in locked cells here." She touched the 3-D image again to show the hallway that split like a T from the dock. She pointed down the hallway that led to the left. The model animated, moving like a camera on a trolley down several long hallways until it opened to a larger circular room at the end.

"The cell doors are here. Rand can melt through the doors to get to the glitchers."

Rand grinned again and rubbed his hands together.

"The team of Rez fighters will tranq each glitcher as soon as Rand gets a hole opened. The Chancellor won't be there to use her compulsion power, but there's always a chance some of them may be working for her voluntarily. That's where you come in, Filicity."

City sat up straighter in her seat while Taylor continued, an excited flicker of blue electric current shooting across her palm.

"We don't know what we could be facing, so we want to knock them out before there's even a chance for them to start using their powers against us. Filicity is the backup in case something goes wrong with the tranqs. Sophia informs me you've recently been able to manipulate your electricity to an amperage that will only stun, not kill, is that correct?"

City nodded. "No problem."

"Good. We want, if possible, to take all the glitchers alive. Then we not only deprive the Chancellor of her weapons but gain more for ourselves."

I frowned at glitchers being referred to as weapons. Was that really how General Taylor thought of us?

She clicked the image again so that it zoomed back out. "There is a secondary objective. Adrien, Zoel, and I will head this direction to retrieve an object located on-site." The camera started again, this time following the hallway leading right and then dropping five stories down an elevator shaft.

"At the bottom of the elevator, there are three barrier doors that not even our best tech hackers would be able to crack in a timely manner. Zoel, this is your second task. I'll need you to open them with your power. Disrupting the first door will signal a breech," Taylor continued, "but the Regs on-site will be deactivated. The response time for an external security team is sixteen minutes. We should have plenty of time to complete the mission and be out before their reinforcements arrive. This mission hinges on it being a quick surgical strike. We hit fast, get what we need, and are out of there in fifteen minutes flat. Understand?"

We all nodded, our group uncharacteristically silent.

"The mission has been planned down to the smallest detail, and you will be well prepared. You have your schematics and detailed instructions downloading onto your arm panels as we speak. Memorize them as we prepare. Ginni," she looked at the frizzy-haired girl, "you are to keep constant watch on the Chancellor's location. After I feel everyone is ready and able to accomplish their personal mission objectives, we'll wait until the Chancellor leaves the site again, and then we'll strike."

All we did was train, eat, and sleep for the next two weeks. As the days passed, my power buzzed to life faster and faster, and the more practiced I became, the further my control seemed to expand. The looks that came my way in the halls and cafeteria now had a hint of respect, or at least were no longer openly hostile. A new energy of anticipation filled the halls.

"Now find the four ex-Regs," Jilia instructed.

I closed my eyes and let the buzzing expand inside me for a moment before sending it outward. I could easily feel out the entire shape of the room, but I pushed beyond it, farther and farther until the entire Foundation was a vibrating projection inside my head. It was a strange sensation; I could sense movement tugging at my scalp and from behind my eyes, like ants crawling in my skull. I tried to ignore it and focus on my objectives.

Moving bodies dotted my mind's projection. One right outside the Med Center had the bulk of an ex-Reg. I paused, then continued exploring down the hallways. There, another one was in the corner of the Caf. The third stood by the wash-down station at the exit, and the fourth . . . where was the fourth?

I passed body after body—too slim, too short—but still

couldn't find the fourth ex-Reg. I breathed deep and pushed out a little farther, up the elevator shaft and all the way to the transport bay. I hadn't gone this far before, and the projection shimmered and faltered in my head, as if it would collapse at any moment. I gritted my teeth and took several moments just to breathe, holding the image still. Two people stood in the transport bay, but one was larger than the other. Definitely an ex-Reg. He was standing beside the largest transport vehicle.

I squeezed my eyes shut tighter, only holding on to the four ex-Regs and letting some of the other details of the rooms go. These were my targets. I pushed past their skin, through the metal and muscle and all the way to their spines. I counted down the notched vertebrae from the top to the C2. Jilia had assured me spinal reattachment was an easy surgery. I was glad to have found an alternative to killing the Regs. Even Taylor had reluctantly approved.

I stayed there a moment, holding the four spines with my mind before pulling back out of their bodies to the hardened plaster poles they held in their hands. I snapped all four poles at the same time, feeling them clatter to the floor beside the ex-Regs. I finally breathed out and pulled back.

I'd learned to sever my telek connection gradually, since doing it too quickly left me dizzy and nauseated. I slowly worked my way back, letting each room dissolve in my mind's projection cube until I was back in my own body, looking out of my own eyes.

I felt Taylor's narrowed gaze on me. "It's done."

"Good," she said. "Let's keep going, to make sure your stamina can hold up. Can you continue?"

I swallowed. The truth was I felt light-headed and tired, but I didn't want to admit it. "Be honest, Zoe," said Jilia gently. "It won't help anyone if you get on-site and aren't able to perform."

"I can keep going."

"Good," Taylor said. "Get into your suit; I'll meet you in the transport bay." She spun on her heel and left without another word.

I changed and took the elevator up. The bay was a low, wide space, with steel struts crisscrossed over our heads and down the walls. It was open to the Surface on one side, an uneven rectangle of light so bright I had to look away. I tugged nervously on my glove and took one more glance back at the green beyond the opening. I shivered despite the warmth of the suit.

General Taylor stood off to the side with Rand and one of the ex-Regs. A mountainous jumble of metal was beside Rand, melted beyond recognition. Parts burned orange around the edges. The ex-Reg, Eli, reached forward with a coolant tank. He released the top valve and liquid sprayed over the melted slag. Steam billowed off in clouds, but it didn't injure the ex-Reg's metal reinforced hands.

I came forward, familiar with the routine. Since we didn't have spare giant metal doors lying around, Taylor had us train with a pile of steel left over from construction on the Foundation. Rand melted down more metal into the heap each day, making it heavier and heavier. By the time I reached them, the steam was gone, and only a swath of glistening icy coolant was left behind on the surface.

"Lift it," Taylor said, a bit unnecessarily. I'd been doing this all week; I knew the drill. I closed my eyes and let the telek expand again. Almost immediately the transport bay filled the projection cube in my mind. I surrounded the slab of metal with my telek.

It was melted solid into the rock underneath, but as I poured more of my energy out, like a web surrounding it, I felt the satisfaction of knowing it didn't matter. Weight didn't matter, gravity didn't matter. It was an object filling a space, and I could move any object as I chose. I knew later I'd feel the exhaustion of having used so much energy. But right now all I felt was the powerful sense of being in control. I'd been afraid my power was too much for a human body, but now that I'd managed control, all I could do was revel in it. My focus was sharp as I imagined molding myself and the rock together into one entity.

I am that.

I lifted the half-ton weight with ease, dropped it down, then lifted it again three times.

When I put it down the last time and opened my eyes, I felt Rand's and Taylor's stares.

"Whoa," Rand said.

Relief and anxiety both reared up in my chest. I'd passed the test and I felt ready, but at the same time, I'd never been truly tested in a mission before. Taylor led us back toward the elevator. I hurried after her, but when we got to the elevator, Adrien stepped out.

"Adrien," I said in surprise. "What are you doing here?" We'd both been so busy with our separate training schedules that I'd barely seen him the past couple weeks.

He smiled. "I hoped I'd catch you. I thought since you

were in your suit already maybe I could show you something."

He looked at the General standing beside me and the edges of his smile drooped a little. "General," he said with a slight nod.

She stiffened, but nodded back before stepping into the elevator.

I stared a moment, watching the General frown as the doors closed behind her. "Sometimes I don't think the General likes glitchers."

"She might not like us," Adrien said, "but she knows she needs us."

He looked down at the clock on his arm panel. "Come on, we've gotta go or we're going to miss it."

The grin was back on his face as he tugged on my arm and led me toward the bright Surface opening. As we got closer, the sunlight almost hurt my eyes, it was so intense. A small wave of anxiety swept over me. I knew I could trust my suit to protect me, but the Surface still filled me with an instinctual fear.

The light cut a sharp line at the end of the tunnel, like a dividing edge between underground and the Surface. I paused at the shadow's edge.

Adrien had walked straight into the light. He held out a hand to me, and finally I reached for it. We stood there, arms stretched out between us for a long moment, one in sunlight, the other shadow, until he tugged me forward.

"Good," he murmured, looking out. "We got here right at sunset."

My eyes widened when I realized we were at the edge of a

cliffside. Brush and tree branches extended overhead and around us to the side, but there was still a clear view of the valley and mountains in the distance.

"Amazing, isn't it?" Adrien whispered. "I thought you might like to remember what beauty looks like. That, out there, that's freedom. Beauty. Life. Everything we're fighting for."

Mountain ranges spilled over each other, cascading down as if they'd been planted there just for the purpose of looking pretty. Peaks one after another, each giving dramatic backdrop to the last. And then there was the sky, full of colors like I'd never seen before. Purples, blues, pinks, and other hues everywhere in between.

I'd never thought of the Surface as beautiful. It was always a scary place, but the scene in front of me made my breath catch in my chest.

"It's incredible," I admitted with surprise. I turned to look at Adrien. The setting sun lit up his blue-green eyes, making them brilliantly translucent against the black of his pupils. He seemed so much lighter than he had been the last time we'd been alone together. Less weighed down. Even the shadows under his eyes didn't seem as deep.

"There was a place like this where Mom and I lived for six months, in a cave up in the mountains. Every morning I'd walk down to this little stream that was half a mile from the cave. Everything was so green. Mom was always tense and on the lookout for flyovers. But I just looked."

His eyes were bright as he talked. "I'd sit for hours underneath one of the thick trees near the cave. All kinds of animals would come up to me after awhile, if I sat still long enough. Squirrels would run right over my legs like I was just part of the tree roots, and I'd get this amazing sense of connection to everything around me. Life calling to life."

He looked down, his smile dimming slightly. "I forgot about it for a while when I was training so hard to become a Rez operative. But you brought it back to me. It's how I felt when I met you too, you know."

"Like what?"

"First when I had visions of you, and then after I met you in person, I felt it even stronger: I thought—here is a soul that calls out to my soul."

I felt a deep, singing happiness at his words. He slipped behind me and tucked his hands around my waist, pulling my back into his chest. His chin nuzzled my neck as we looked out together. The colors shifted as each minute passed and, right when I'd think it couldn't get any more beautiful, another shaft of light would break through and light up the earth with a new color. I was so swept up in the color and sharing it with Adrien that the moment felt magical. Unearthly. Incredibly fiery purple-gold rays shone from the edge of the horizon right as the sun finally dipped down behind the mountains.

"What changed?" I turned to look up at Adrien. I bit my lip hesitantly. I didn't want to ruin the moment, but I couldn't help asking. "You seem different now. Did you have a new vision? Something good?"

"I have had some visions," he said slowly. "They don't always make sense. Some visions seem to contradict others." He stared out at the dimming light. "Then there are things I've seen that *have* to happen if there's any hope for us at all, even if they're bad. I used to worry about it constantly, trying to follow the threads that connect the whole chain of events together. I spent countless sleepless nights trying to understand which visions I might be able to change and which ones I shouldn't and which ones I would make happen by trying to stop them. It was making me sick." He was quiet a moment. "But I had some long talks with the Professor and he's helped remind me of some things I'd lost sight of."

I swallowed. "Like what?"

"Like that the world is far bigger than just me." His face was barely visible in the twilight, his strong cheekbones cutting a sharp shadow. "And I think I'm finally getting it in my head that having visions doesn't make me personally responsible for everything that happens. I'll still try to change what I can, and make happen the visions that need to come true. But I can see that I was spending so much time worrying about the future, I was losing out on the moments I have now."

He looked at me, his voice soft. "Time is more precious than ever. And I want to spend every moment I have with the people I love. I want to spend it with you." He pulled me close, wrapping his arms tightly around me and burying his face at the nape of my neck. "All I want is you," he whispered. His body was so warm against mine, like he'd soaked up the sun and was reflecting it back to me. "All I want is you." He repeated, his voice a low rasp.

Darkness fell around us, and it suddenly wasn't enough to feel the pressure of his arms around me. I wanted to be able to touch him.

As if reading my mind, he pulled away and laced his fingers through mine. He tugged me back through the transport bay to the elevator. We didn't say anything during the ride down.

His words—*All I want is you*—kept pinging around my head. A flush crept up my neck. When I glanced up at him, he was watching me with a heart-thumping intensity. Something in the air had shifted. We were still just holding hands, but even through my glove, the touch felt electric.

The elevator pinged as we arrived back at the Foundation level. Adrien stepped out and gestured to the wash-down rooms. "You go first." His voice was a little higher pitched than normal.

After moving quickly through the wash-down chambers, I hurried into the changing rooms and pulled on a fresh tunic set. I toweled off my hair and let it hang long and damp down my back.

Adrien emerged from the shower right as I came out of the changing room. He'd wrapped a towel around his waist. His chest was sturdy and wide, with the lightest tufting of hair.

He paused, watching me watch him.

The temperature of the room seemed to burn ten degrees hotter. He crossed the space between us and dipped his lips roughly to mine. He cupped my jaw and pulled me in closer.

I became aware of how little cloth was between us. I kissed him deeper and felt the buzzing explode in my ears, but I managed to keep the power inside me. I felt another burst of heat as I realized what that meant. With my newfound control, my power wasn't a barrier between us anymore. We could finally get as close as we wanted to, with nothing to stop us.

I pulled my tunic over my head, leaving only a thin camisole beneath. Adrien paused, eyes widening for a moment before he pulled me back in tight. I kissed him harder, wanting to draw him as close to me as possible now that I could.

Sensation pulsed through my stomach like a sound wave. The intensity of it grew the longer I kissed him. His hands slid down my back, moving slowly from my shoulder blades down to my waist. I pressed my chest to his, letting out a low moan as he kissed from my neck down to my collar bone. I grabbed his head and forced his lips back to mine.

The pulsing heat sizzled inside me, building up and up—

But then suddenly both of our arm coms buzzed loudly at the same time. Adrien pulled away, breathing heavily, and I looked down at my wrist.

I swallowed hard as I read the words on the small readout screen, the moment shattered.

Ginni confirms that Chancellor Bright has left the site. Mission commences in one hour.

Chapter 15

SEVERAL HOURS LATER, our team was poised at the back docking station of the Chancellor's glitcher compound. We'd taken two air transports and then switched into a supply vehicle that the Rez had hijacked. After so much waiting, it was surreal how fast everything was suddenly happening.

Taylor ordered us all to be silent and focus on our role in the mission. I shifted uncomfortably on the bench in the back of the truck. The air transport had been smooth, but this older vehicle still used wheels and it jostled constantly. The whir of oxygen circulating in my face mask seemed unduly loud in the silence.

The vehicle stopped suddenly and I was thrown into City's shoulder. She didn't even give me a glare. She looked as tense as I felt. No one said a word or looked at me, but I could feel the pressure mounting.

We all jumped down from the back of the vehicle onto the docking station. Adrien hurried over to the door and attached a small box. A small console screen projected from the door panel and he started clicking through complicated code.

"Zoel," the General said, touching her earpiece. "Ginni

says there are five Regs on the other side of that wall, and five more throughout the compound. Can you sense them?"

I breathed in and out like I'd trained and let the telek buzzing rise in time with my heartbeat. I felt myself expand outward, beyond the wall. Yes, there were the Regulators stationed at intervals in the hallways. Two of them began moving toward us. They must have been alerted to the supply van's arrival.

Anxiety rose up and panicked thoughts tumbled over one another. What if I couldn't do this when it counted? I thought about their metal reinforced hands crushing Milton's head like an overripe fruit.

I needed to empty my mind, not let these frantic thoughts clog my head. I breathed in and out, focusing on the sound of my breath. The telek expanded outward again. The Regs were moving closer, but I didn't allow myself to worry about what would happen if I failed. I just closed my eyes and let the energy surround each of the ten Regs throughout the compound. I squeezed my eyes tighter as I yanked the vertebrae apart, snapping their spines right at the C2.

The Regs all collapsed where they stood.

I nodded at Adrien. He'd been flicking through pages of code and hacking further and further into the security feed. At my nod, he tapped a few last times. The door slid open sideways with a hiss.

The General motioned forward with one arm. We crossed the threshold and then we were inside. The lights were bright after the heavy cloak of darkness. We all squinted as we piled into the narrow loading dock room while Adrien went to work on the next door.

City paced in a circle by huge crates stacked to the ceiling. She dug her fingers into her palms. She had boasted so often about going on missions before, but I got the feeling those missions had been nothing compared to what we were attempting now, directly attacking a Comm Corp building.

I looked around at everyone else. Half a dozen Rez fighters had joined us when we'd switched transports. They stood still beside the four ex-Regs. Rand rubbed his hands together. A slight tendril of smoke came out from between his fingers.

"Hold it in until you get to the glitcher cells," Taylor snapped.

"Sorry," Rand said, and put his hands at his sides.

"Got it." Adrien motioned forward as the door slid open, revealing a hallway that led in both directions. The hallways were sleek, with smooth, cream-colored walls and black tile on the ground. Halfway down the right fork, I could see two Regs laying on the ground where I'd dropped them.

"Just like we discussed during the debrief," Taylor said. "Detachment A, you head left to release the glitchers. Detachment B, follow me."

Adrien and I headed after Taylor, half the Rez fighters and three ex-Regs following right behind. I looked back once and watched the other team head the opposite direction. Anxiety bubbled up in my chest.

This was it. I'd already accomplished half my job. I tried to feel confident, but my heart still thumped wildly.

We stepped over the two immobile Regs, and I couldn't resist a quick glance down. Their eyes were moving rapidly, but the rest of their bodies were completely still. For a moment I imagined what it must be like for them, their minds still receiving commands in bodies that would no longer respond. I shuddered a little, but then raised my eyes ahead and kept walking. At least they were alive.

The hallway ended at an elevator tube. As we came to it, Adrien swung his bag around and pulled out a slim card. He swiped it in front of the reader and the tube door slid open.

"Half of you stay to keep watch," Taylor gestured to the Rez fighters, "And Tavid." She indicated the tallest ex-Reg. "The rest come with me."

We stepped into the elevator pod, everyone pressing closely together to fit. I looked around and wondered again what exactly we were retrieving.

We dropped swiftly, and the elevator opened again to a narrow entryway space leading to the thick metal door I was supposed to open. Two more Regs lay prone on the ground. I looked down at them, ready to see the blinking eyes, but while one of the Reg's eyes twitched frantically, the other one was completely still. His eyes stared lifelessly ahead. His mouth was open and a line of spittle trailed down his chin. I dropped down and put a hand to his chest, trying to feel if there was a heartbeat or any movement of breath, but there was nothing.

He was dead.

I gasped, feeling a dizzy swirl of emotion. I couldn't stop staring. I'd killed someone. He'd been alive one moment, and gone the next. Because of me. I felt like I was going to be sick.

Taylor stepped out of the elevator behind me and hauled me to my feet. "Focus on the mission." She pointed ahead. "This is the first of the doors you have to open."

When I didn't reply right away, Taylor grabbed my shoulders and pushed my back up against the wall. "You have to focus."

"Hey, stop it," Adrien shouted, putting a hand on Taylor's arm, but she easily pushed him back.

"The survival of the Rez itself depends on what is behind that wall," she said. "Conscience, fear, regret, and any other thought in your head can wait until after this mission is through. Got it?"

I nodded and she let go. I knew she was right. I had to swallow the guilt for now. She and everyone else were depending on me.

She put her arms on my shoulders again. "Open these doors, and then we're out of here. Can you do it?"

I nodded again and closed my eyes. For a second it was hard to grasp my telek. I couldn't feel it anywhere. My thoughts were scattered. I could hear Taylor's impatient huffing and felt Adrien pacing tensely in the background. He was angry at Taylor. I wasn't. I couldn't blame her for expecting me to do my part. The others stood silently.

I breathed. In and out. In and out. No distractions. I could do this. I would do this. I opened my eyes and looked at the thick door. I remembered back to my practice and thought about all the times I'd lifted equal weight with ease. I could not let myself fear. Fear would cripple my control.

Adrien came up beside me and took my hand. It was the anchor I needed. I stopped thinking. A high-pitched whine filled my ears, finally settling into the familiar buzz. My telek was back and at the ready.

I cast it outward and poured myself entirely in.

There. I finally felt the room in my head and with it came a sense of power and control.

Mentally, I lassoed a web around the door and tugged it. With a screeching grind of steel, the door lifted upward on its tracks.

I glimpsed the next metal door as Adrien went rigid beside me. He was having a vision, but there wasn't time to wait for him to finish. Taylor had said this first door would set off an alarm. I had to keep going so we could get out of here as fast as possible. I cast my telek toward the second door.

But then Adrien shouted, "Oh God, it's a trap!"

Chapter 16

IT WAS ONLY because my telek was already active that I sensed the laser barrels drop from the ceiling in front of the metal door.

I screamed in terror and felt the energy leave me without my control. Adrien threw his weight into me, knocking me behind one of the ex-Regs as my power ripped the weapons apart.

"We've got to get everyone out!" Adrien shouted, scrambling off me and pulling me to my feet. The ex-Reg we dove behind had some shrapnel from the laser barrels lodged in his chest, but he moved as if it didn't bother him.

I looked back at the second barrier doors. "But we're so close." Taylor had said the object was vital to the Resistance's survival. "Should we still try to get it?" I turned to General Taylor for orders, but just as I did, she crumpled to the ground.

A blooming red stain spread at her stomach. She gasped as she looked down at it.

A sharp hand-sized piece of metal was lodged in her left side, right below her rib cage. I'd been so clumsy with my telek, I hadn't had time or thought to direct each piece of shrapnel safely away from us.

"Today?" Taylor whispered, looking back up at Adrien. Then she slumped sideways, unconscious.

"Adrien!" I screeched. I dropped down and reached to pull the chunk of metal out of her, but Adrien caught my hand.

"Don't! She'll bleed out for sure if you pull it out."

I clicked my wrist com frantically. "Detachment A, are you there? Taylor's down. We've got to abort. Now."

I waited a second, but the only response was silence with an occasional clicking static.

"What do we do?" I asked.

"Grab Taylor," Adrien said to Cole. The bulky ex-Reg boy picked Taylor up as Adrien swiped the card in front of the elevator tube.

Nothing happened.

"No!" Adrien yelled, slamming the wall. "Power to the elevator must have shut down."

Adrenaline pulsed through me. I turned back to the elevator and pushed the door open the same way I'd done with the security doors.

"Get in!" I yelled, trying not to think in case I lost any of my momentum. The two ex-Regs and the other soldiers piled in, with Adrien and me right behind. I spared one last glance at the metal hatch behind us.

"If they knew we were coming, they'd have moved whatever was there anyway," Adrien said, seeing where I looked. "Get us out of here."

I nodded and closed my eyes. My telek was sharp. I could feel the shape of the tube tunnel above us and our elevator car lodged at the bottom.

I shook my head to get rid of my mounting fear. "No gravity," I whispered, and suddenly the elevator's brake gear had snapped and we were shooting up the tube. Light from the broken door sparked as we went. I only slowed us down as we came to the top floor. The elevator car shook as I tried to hold it steady long enough for everyone to get out. I could feel the edges of my control unraveling.

I exited last and then slipped and fell to my knees.

The floor was slick with blood. I barely held back a scream as I saw the Rez fighters we'd left at the top of the elevator were dead, torn apart by laser fire.

"Oh my God," Adrien said.

Tavid was dead, too. Cole let out a strangled noise when he saw him. He handed Taylor off to one of the Rez fighters who'd come up the elevator with us.

The laser barrels clicked to life above our heads. They must be motion sensitive. I'd been barely able to hold the elevator. I didn't know if I could split my focus enough to disable them. But before I could even rally my telek to try, Cole leapt up, his hydraulic legs hissing as he launched himself toward the weapons. He ripped them off the ceiling before they could fire.

I couldn't stop staring at the dead soldiers. My breath stopped in my chest. This was all wrong. None of this was supposed to happen. It was supposed to be a simple retrieval mission. No one was supposed to die.

A Rez fighter ran down the hall toward us from the entrance. "Someone's trying to remote hack the transport. We need the techer right now."

"Go." I pushed Adrien ahead. "We'll get the others."

He hesitated.

"There's no time. If they hack the transport, none of us are getting out of here."

He nodded and ran after the Rez fighter.

I clicked my wrist com, but still there was no answer from the other group. "Why aren't they answering?" I didn't dare voice my real fear: What if they were already dead?

"Take Taylor back to the transport," I said to the Rez fighters with us, before turning to the ex-Regs. "You two come with me, we've got to help the other group get out."

They nodded and we ran down the hallway. I couldn't hear anything from the other end. No laser fire, no screams. What was happening down there? My legs pumped fast even though I was exhausted from using my telek so much. I'd never done anything as energy-intensive as raising that elevator.

Suddenly the silence became complete. I couldn't even hear my own huffing breath. It was like we'd passed through some invisible wall where all sound was cut off.

I turned to the ex-Regs. "What's going on?" I yelled. My voice made no sound.

The ex-Regs barely even paused. They gestured to one another with what looked like military hand signs and kept running to the end of the hallway. I remembered from the projected schematics that the hallway turned a sharp corner before the last stretch that opened to the circular room where the glitcher cells were. I hurried to move around the corner, but Cole grabbed my arm to hold me back.

He mouthed something I couldn't understand. Eli peered around the corner quickly and then pulled back. He made two sharp forward motions with his arms and then we were running again. Cole and Eli ran side by side in front of me, blocking my sight of what was ahead and shielding me. The hallway seemed to go on forever. All I could see were flashes of light from over their heads. Whatever was going on at the end of it looked like a firefight. I tried to push in between the ex-Regs, but they stayed locked shoulder to shoulder.

Until they were blown backward off their feet. Eli's heavy body landed on my leg and took me down with him. My head cracked on the ground and the building shook as a wave of blue light burst past us. The ex-Regs were quickly on their feet again, and Cole hauled me up as well. I screamed as I tried to stand and looked down. My left ankle hurt like hell when I tried to put weight on it, but at least my suit hadn't ripped. I held on to the wall for support.

A girl surrounded by a bright blue orb blocked the entryway to the room. She had to be a glitcher. Through the undulating blue light, I could see Rand, City, and several others standing on the other side. They were alive. A flurry of relief rushed through me.

The girl's back was turned to us. At first I thought she was one of the glitchers we'd been sent to free, fighting alongside my team. Then I saw a crackling spiral of electricity burst from City's fingertips, aimed at the orb. The electricity hit it, but didn't penetrate. That was when I realized the girl with the orb wasn't helping us at all. She was trapping everyone inside.

Cole and Eli unloaded laser rounds that bounced harmlessly off the glowing shield. The girl turned to look at us. A flash of recognition or relief seemed to pass over her face as she saw me. She made a slight motion with her arms. The momentum of an energy wave built in the orb surrounding her, and released outward in a concentric circle.

I tried to cast my telek to stop it, but I couldn't sense it at all. I couldn't hear the buzzing in my ears either. I had no idea if I even had any energy left, I'd already used it so much tonight. The wave hit me before I could make any sense of it, and I was knocked off my feet again. It dissipated and passed into the walls with a foundation-shaking quake.

I tried to motion to Eli to charge the girl, but he must have misinterpreted me, because he picked me up and ran with me toward her instead. Her eyes were fixated on me as we got closer. I desperately tried to find any thread of telek I could. If I could just cast a web around her, disable her like I had the Regs or stop her heart—anything to drop her so everyone else could get out of here before the next wave of reinforcements arrived. Or worse, the Chancellor herself.

The girl released another wave and I felt the adrenaline surge inside me as I braced for the blow. While the wave hit like a sledgehammer to the chest, Eli stayed on his feet. Everyone else had been blown back again, but Eli kept advancing forward. It was my telek, it must be at least partially working. The girl's eyes widened as we kept pushing forward, even through the next wave she released.

I tried to expand my telek outward to get to her, but I could only barely sense the room in my head. My mental projection cube kept cutting in and out. My body felt flayed by the bursts of blue light. I didn't know how long I could keep this up. When the next wave hit, Eli stumbled backward, dropping me.

Then suddenly the girl in front of us sank to the ground. I scrambled to sit up, looking around.

Stunned, I saw Tyryn standing behind her, holding a tranq gun steady. He must have shot her in the split second after she'd released the orb, before she could build another one. She'd been so distracted watching me, she hadn't even seen him come up behind her. Three tranq rounds stuck out of her neck.

I got to my feet, gritting my teeth against the roaring pain in my ankle, and hobbled into the huge room. We'd gotten here at the end of the fight. Rand, City, and Tyryn were the only ones left standing. The ex-Reg, Wytt, slowly got to his feet, part of his chest plate scorched black.

Bodies were strewn all over the ground. And so much blood. Some wore the gray and green of the Rez fighters. A few others I didn't recognize, but they looked like teenagers. Glitchers, no doubt. Smoke filled the air. Weapon racks on the ceiling were melted and still burned orange. A few molten drops dripped onto the ground below. Clearly Rand's handiwork. Half of the left wall was cut up by laser fire, exposing the steel support beams.

"We've got to go!" I shouted. Still my voice made no sound.

I'd thought the girl with the orb had also been controlling the silence, but she was knocked out, and no more glitchers were standing. At least that we could see. I felt my heartbeat ratchet up a notch. Ginni had said there were ten glitchers here. Three were on the floor, so where were the others?

City and Rand helped a fallen Rez fighter to his feet. I closed my eyes and concentrated, but between my exhaustion and the silence that quieted the buzz I usually used as a guide, my connection to my telek was unsteady. When it cut in again, I felt the whole room in my head. I grabbed it and tried to hold on. For a moment I managed, and expanded farther beyond the wall.

And that's when I felt them. There were people huddled in tiny cells beyond the wall, no bigger than the room I'd been closed in for months at the research lab. The bodies were too small to be Regs. They had to be the Chancellor's other glitchers.

I hesitated for a moment. The girl with the orb was clearly working for the Chancellor voluntarily. But if these glitchers were a danger, wouldn't they have attacked already? I steeled myself. We had failed part of our mission, but we could still accomplish this objective. I had to try.

Adrien appeared beside me. He made wild gestures with his hands and waved at us to follow him. At least that meant the transport must be fixed. He wouldn't have come back otherwise.

I pointed at the wall behind us, putting my palms up and trying to show he needed to stop and give me a second to try to get to the other glitchers. But of course he had no idea what I meant. Adrien shook his head, pulling at my arm to get me to follow him. I tugged away from his grasp, barely managing to stay upright by putting my weight on my un-hurt foot.

Others hurried past us. City and Rand held an unconscious Rez soldier between them. Cole carried a limp girl in his arms; I couldn't see her face to tell who it was. I closed my eyes and bit my lip, straining to concentrate in the chaos.

I felt Eli pick me up, the metal of his recently fired forearm weapons warm against my skin. He started to carry me out of the room in the opposite direction from the glitchers. I didn't waste any energy trying to protest. For a moment, the flicker of the projected room rose in my mind. Before I could lose it again, I quickly latched on and tore the wall away.

I opened my eyes right as Eli and I neared the exit. The small cells across from us were exposed and a few figures slowly rose to their feet. One short, thin boy stepped out and looked straight at me. I waved frantically over Eli's shoulder for the glitchers to follow us, but half of them weren't even looking my way.

The few who did see me ran across the room toward us. A couple of the others saw them and followed. In the cell on the end, I could see a blond boy lying on the ground. He looked unconscious and his legs were bound. My vision bounced with each of Eli's heavy steps, but I squinted to look closer.

And then my heart stopped in my chest.

I knew that rumpled blond hair and the tilt of that nose well.

Max.

I screamed, but still no sound came out.

Eli kept running, taking me farther away. I flailed and beat at his armored chest with my fists, and he finally paused when we reached the entry to the hallway. He looked down at me with no expression on his face.

Then suddenly an explosion rocked the building. Half of the domed room we'd just left collapsed and the walls blew outward. Eli and I were thrown hard into the hallway wall from the blast, but somehow he managed to stay on his feet.

Sound rushed in again, a cacophonic mix of screaming and

the squeal of steel beams cracking overhead. Debris and dust filled the air.

For a moment I blinked in a daze. I had no idea what was happening. Nothing made any sense. There was a painful ringing in my ears. One of the girls who'd escaped the cells lay on the ground right beside me, bloody and unmoving.

"I saw Max!" I shouted. "We have to go back for him!"

I looked over Eli's shoulder. Clouds of dust made it impossible to see, but it was clear that many of the cell rooms had been destroyed in the blast. The glitcher responsible for the silence must have been in one of them.

But Max, where was Max? I wiped at the grime on my face mask and caught only the barest glimpse of him, still lying inside his cell before Adrien shouted, "Get her out."

Eli picked me up and started running again. In the opposite direction from Max. "No!" I shouted into his ear.

"Don't put her down," Adrien yelled over his shoulder. "The General's orders are to protect her. Get her to the transport, now." Eli kept running, his arms around my waist like a vice grip. A few of the escaped glitchers ran just behind us.

"Stop listening to him and put me down! We have to go back!"

I tried to gather my telek so that I could make Eli stop. But just then, the wall on one side of the hallway began to groan and buckle. Part of the building that had already collapsed was pulling down the rest. The groans became screeches.

The ceiling cracked and a pile of concrete and rubble collapsed straight on top of us. I screamed and threw my hands in the air. A huge slab of concrete stopped a mere foot above our heads, caught in my telek web.

Debris sifted down around us. All down the exit tunnel the walls were buckling, creaking under the strain. The rest of the ceiling would come down soon. I threw my telek at it to keep it from collapsing long enough so we could escape. I tried to hold the slab overhead while also reaching back into the circular room to help Max. But the second I tried to split my focus, the ceiling dropped closer.

No, this couldn't happen again. The scene was too familiar, an ex-Reg carrying me away while Max was left behind. I had to save him this time. He'd obviously seen the error of his ways. He wasn't working with the Chancellor anymore. She'd tied him up and left him here.

I strained to turn around.

But right then, the ceiling finally dropped behind us. I couldn't hold it anymore. A glitcher boy who had lagged behind was crushed in front of my eyes.

I screamed in rage and grief, clinging to the last bits of my power to keep the hallway ahead of us clear. I poured every ounce of strength left in my body into the telek, and then when that was gone I pushed harder still. I remembered the image I'd seen in my dream of all the blue lights spilling out of me as I cracked like a smashed glass. It was going to break me, but I didn't care. I had to hold on a moment longer. Just a moment.

The next instant we were out in the night air and my power dropped out completely. I dropped my head in exhaustion against Eli's shoulder as the building behind us shook with a terrifying tremble before it crumbled in on itself. The sound was deafening and dust billowed outward in a thick cloud.

So much had gone wrong. In my exhaustion, I turned to Adrien. He looked distraught, but his eyes lacked the bewilderment and shock showing plainly on the faces of the rest of our disheveled and injured crew. And with a rush of pain and grief, I realized why.

"Did you foresee this?" I asked. He looked away. "DID YOU SEE THIS?"

But then even my voice was gone and the world swirled around me. All I could manage before I passed out was to whisper a name no one could hear: Max.

Chapter 17

I SPENT A WEEK in bed. Jilia had easily healed my fractured ankle, but pushing so hard with my telek had taken its toll on my body. I was absolutely depleted, without enough energy to lift my own head. Ginni helped me to the bathroom a few times a day and brought me food, but otherwise I remained in bed and stayed Linked.

I was afraid of the rush of emotions I knew would come as soon as I disconnected, even though I probably didn't have enough power left in my body to be dangerous for a while. After a few days, when I finally did disconnect myself for a few hours, I was surprised that I felt almost as numb as when Linked. I was left alone to stare at the drawings on my wall and let Max's accusing gaze stare back at me. I had sworn that if I ever got the opportunity, I wouldn't fail to save the people I loved. No matter what.

But I *had* failed. We all had. Ginni said that after the General had been healed, she'd nearly torn up the Med Center in anger. I closed my eyes and I was back in the facility, feeling the blast buckle the ground beneath our feet, watching the ceiling caving in on us. I saw Max lying there tied up before the ceiling collapsed on top of him.

The hours were tortuous as I replayed the scenes in my head, thinking of all the ways I could have done things differently. But I didn't let myself re-Link, except at bedtime. I deserved to feel the pain.

On the sixth day, Adrien pulled back the curtain and sat on the mattress beside me.

I turned my face away to hide it in my pillow. I knew I shouldn't blame him for what happened. I knew his visions were only flickering images of a future he had never been able to change, but I couldn't help it. He should have warned us what was coming. We could have tried to stop it.

He took my shoulders in his hands.

"Jilia says you should try to get up today."

I closed my eyes.

He let go of me, shaking his head. "We did everything we could. I know you want to save everybody, but this is the way it is. It's the way it has to be."

Anger lit through me and I sat up. "How can you say that? Max wasn't just anyone to me. He was my friend. I loved him, in my way." I grabbed my head, feeling a bit dizzy from the sudden movement. "He only stayed with Bright because he couldn't bear coming with me when we escaped the Community. I just always thought someday we'd have a chance to start over."

"What you're feeling is guilt," Adrien said flatly. "Not love."

I stared at him, openmouthed. "Why are you being like this?"

He leaned in, his face dark. "Because anger is what you need to be strong right now, not sadness. Anger will help you get out of this bed."

His words surprised me, but then I realized I was sitting up for the first time in a week. And I wasn't too tired. The buzzing thrum of my power was back, quieter and weaker than usual, but there.

"You're right," my voice was hard, "If I need anger, I have plenty of it. I'm furious with myself. And maybe it's not fair, but I'm furious with you too."

Adrien looked down. "Believe me. You couldn't be any angrier with me than I am with myself. The whole thing was a trap. The Chancellor knew we were coming. And how else could she have known?"

I stared at him, not following.

"Because I told her."

I let out a confused gasp, but he continued, "I couldn't understand why I wasn't getting any visions of this mission. It was so strange. Usually when something big like this happens, I'll get long-term visions well beforehand. But I didn't see anything about this mission, and I've realized why."

He looked at me, anguish clear in his eyes. "It's because I already had those visions, a long time ago. Before we escaped the Community, when the Chancellor used her compulsion on me. She made me tell her my visions and then made me forget. She must have known long ago that we would be coming on this raid. What kills me is that I must have foreseen her setting the trap for us. I gave her the blueprints for exactly what to do." The words poured out of him in a rush. "The only reason we're still alive is because the explosives in the second half of the building malfunctioned."

He'd answered the question I'd screamed in rage at him during the raid. The question I could see had been giving him sleepless nights ever since.

He *hadn't* known this would happen.

He hadn't known, but he blamed himself all the same. And I'd pushed him away, reinforcing that blame. The look on his face bored a hole straight through my chest.

"I'm sorry," I said. I was such an idiot. I took his face in my hands, then leaned in and put my forehead against his. "I'm so sorry. Of course it's not your fault. I shouldn't have accused you."

I kissed his lips, but they were hard and unyielding. After a second he relaxed into me, but then he pulled away again just as quickly. "I've gotta go to training." He paused before leaving. "Will you be in classes today? Even if you don't feel up for training, you could at least come to lunch. Everyone would really like to see you."

I swallowed hard, but nodded. He'd pulled away so quickly. I wasn't sure he'd quite forgiven me yet. I'd assumed the worst of him and hadn't even given him a chance to explain. I didn't deserve his forgiveness. But he was right. I had to get out of bed. I had to keep moving forward somehow, in spite of all that had happened.

When I walked into the Caf, talk quieted and countless pairs of eyes watched me. Some of the Rez fighters immediately looked away again, their faces hard. Others, like the younger glitchers on the other task force watched me with wide eyes. Were they impressed with what they'd heard I'd done or disappointed that I didn't do more? I was supposed to be able to save people, but four Rez fighters and one ex-Reg had died, not to mention the Chancellor's glitchers. One of the Rez fighters put down his spoon as I passed by and outright glared at me. Okay, so disappointment it was.

I looked down and headed toward the serving line. My legs were a little stiff, but otherwise my body felt healed. I tried to forget the eyes following my every move. I piled the colorless goop into a bowl and went to the table, sitting between Adrien and Xona. Rand was gesturing wildly when I sat down.

"—and when the weapons dropped from the ceiling, bam, I unleashed the Rand on them before they could get a single round off."

Xona sat across from him and rubbed her temple. "It's been a week already. Is there any way we'll stop hearing this story by next century?"

"Wait," I said, "I actually want to hear it. I never heard everything that happened with your group."

Rand grinned and settled back in his chair. "So we get into the open chamber at the end of the hall, and all of a sudden none of us can hear anything. That's when I saw the weapons dropping."

He lifted his hands up dramatically like he was reenacting the moment. "And a millisecond later, I'm on it. I've been working on melting stuff without touching it, but usually it's just things within a few feet of me. These weapons were over ten feet high, but I knew if I didn't take them out, we'd all die."

City turned from the other table and looked at Rand. "Oh please. If you hadn't been there I could have easily electrified them."

Rand made a face and waved a hand dismissively. "I didn't see you taking care of it."

She stood and put her hands on her hips. "Probably because

I was busy with the other attackers rushing in. Which I didn't see you doing anything about."

"How many were there?" I asked.

"Five came through the door at us." City dropped down to sit beside Rand. "I don't know if they were all glitchers, some of them had weapons. They got a couple of shots off before I dropped them. And they only managed that because there was this glitcher who could inflict pain."

Rand nodded, looking almost solemn. "It was like a spike straight through my head. All of us were on the ground. I was screaming but couldn't even hear my own voice 'cause of the whole silence thing."

"So what happened?"

City smiled and pointed her forefinger. "I fried him."

"You killed him?" Ginni choked on the mouthful she'd taken.

"Of course I did. He was attacking us."

"It's too bad, though. The General was disappointed we didn't capture him alive," Rand said. "But we do have the orb girl. City's electricity wasn't anything against her."

"I can't believe they brought her back with us," City said.

"You're just bent out of shape because you couldn't take her out," Rand said.

"Well, maybe I'll get another chance." City glowered. "Either way, she's not rooming with me, that's for shuntin' sure."

"She's here?" I asked, stunned. "She's staying in the dorms?"

"Don't look at me," Rand said. "Adrien's the one who had a vision that she needed to be saved."

I looked over at Adrien. His eyes had widened.

"You told them your visions?" I felt a pang of hurt. After everything he'd said about it not being safe to share his visions—

"Nah, Taylor gave it away," Rand said. "City was giving Taylor attitude about bringing the girl back, and Taylor's all like," Rand stiffened his back, imitating the General, "'retrieving the girl was one of the mission objectives.' City figured it out later."

"Is that true?" I turned to Adrien. I knew he'd told some of his visions to Taylor, but I'd assumed that after the wounded Rez fighters had been brought back he'd stopped sharing them.

He shrugged, looking uncomfortable. "I don't want to talk about it."

"So where is she now, anyway?" Rand asked casually. "I got a look at her in the Med Center when I was passing by, and she's kinda cute."

"Really?" City asked, her fists clenched. "You have to hit on every girl in the building, even our enemies?"

Rand grinned rudely at her.

Ginni piped up. "First of all, she has a name. Saminsa. She's been staying in the Med Center. Doc kept her sedated so she wouldn't attack again, and they're explaining to her how the Chancellor's evil and we're the good guys."

"And that worked?" I asked skeptically.

"It did once Doc convinced her that the only way the building could have blown like that was if it had been wired from the inside. The Chancellor was willing to blow up her own people just to get Zoe."

"Me?"

"Yeah," Ginni said. "The Chancellor told all of them to click their transmitter once someone saw you. They didn't know, but it set off the device for the bombs."

"That's horrible," I whispered. "The Chancellor had the girl bring the place down on top of herself. All because she was so desperate to kill me." I pushed my bowl away, afraid I was gonna be sick. I suddenly felt I deserved all those accusing glares. I was a walking target, endangering everyone around me.

"Yeah," Ginni said. "When Saminsa figured all that out, she stopped talking. Hasn't said a word since. But she hasn't tried to kill anyone, so that's a good sign."

City leaned forward. "A good sign? You didn't see what she did. When she made the first orb, it cut Rez fighters in half like they were made of butter."

I shuddered. I'd seen bodies on the floor, but I hadn't looked too closely. If Eli and I had gotten any closer before Tyryn took her down, we would've been killed too.

"It wasn't her fault," I said. I seemed to be saying it a lot lately. But it was still true. All of us were pawns in this game.

"The Chancellor wasn't around," City said. "The girl wasn't under any compulsion. She attacked us all on her own. And she could be biding her time before she does it again."

"The Chancellor took her from the Community, from her home, and filled her head with lies," I said. "As far as Saminsa knew, we were the enemy. Any one of us would have done the same thing in her position."

Ginni seemed to understand. She rested her hand on top of mine. "I heard your friend was in the building when it went down. I'm sorry, that must have been hard."

I swallowed. I wasn't ready to talk about Max yet, but I attempted a smile to show her I appreciated her concern.

"Just keep the girl away from me is all I'm saying," City said.

"She can room with us," Xona said. "Anyone you're that scared of I'm bound to like."

"I'm not scared of her." City exploded off her chair.

"Sure sounds like it."

City's face turned red with anger. "Says the plebe who wasn't even allowed to go on the mission."

Xona shot up out of her chair too. Ginni put a hand on her arm to calm her. Xona shrugged it off and glared at City for another moment. But then she sat down without another word. I was surprised. In the past, she wouldn't have backed down until a punch was thrown. Then again, I'd noticed Xona's attitude had improved a lot lately. I'd been afraid she would be angry or mistrustful of me again after that ridiculous test Sophia had set up, but Xona had just taken it in stride.

"What about the other glitchers? The ones we rescued?" I asked, trying to redirect the conversation.

"A girl and two boys," Ginni said. "The girl's a human lie detector. Awesome, right? And the boys are twins. They're telepathic, but only with each other."

"None of them are very useful to us," City said. "We need glitchers with offensive talents. The General wasn't too happy."

"That's not fair," Ginni said. "Besides, they gave us some good intel on some of the other glitchers the Chancellor has, ones that were too valuable to leave behind in the building to get blown up. Apparently there's this red-haired boy who can make you hallucinate and see things that aren't there. He liked to terrorize the other kids. The twins got all shaky when they talked about him." She shuddered. "It creeped me out just listening to it. I hate powers that can get inside your head."

"The Chancellor's getting more and more powerful," Xona said, frowning. "She'll keep stocking up on glitchers she can use against us."

Xona's words hung ominously for a long moment.

"What happens next?" I asked. "The General didn't get whatever it was she was looking for."

"I don't think even the General knows what to do next right now," Xona said, her voice subdued. "This past week alone, ten Rez cells were cracked. Double agents working for the Rez keep getting found out and imprisoned. It's not safe anywhere except here."

"I heard the floor below ours is flooded with Rez fighters who managed to escape the safe house raids," Ginni said.

"Just soldiers?" I asked. "What about civilians and families?"

"The General doesn't want to open up the Foundation to nonmilitary personnel. We'd go through rations too quickly. She worries about the visibility of every shipment of supplies coming in as it is. But I also heard she does have a plan," Ginni leaned in and dropped her voice to a whisper. "Something big."

"What?" I leaned in too.

"I don't know the details," Ginni said. "But I overheard her arguing with the Professor. She said something about how she was gonna change the world."

"Change the world?" Adrien suddenly leaned in, his green eyes flashing.

"What does that mean?" I asked.

Ginni shrugged. "That's just what she said. That if it was the last thing she did, she was going to change the world."

Chapter 18

"EVERYONE, THIS IS SAMINSA." Jilia stepped into the room and gestured forward to the girl standing behind her. She was a slight little thing, with cropped brown hair and a heart-shaped face.

"Hello!" Ginni said and bounded toward the girl with open arms. The girl flinched back, moving behind Jilia again.

"Don't freak her out," Xona said, jumping down from her bunk.

"Oh," Ginni stopped, visibly trying to rein herself in. "Sorry! I'm just so excited to meet you. Look, there's this empty bunk right over mine. This is Xona by the way," she gestured, "and that's Zoe. Oh," she paused nervously, "I guess you've already met Zoe."

Ginni's face reddened. I imagined she'd just realized exactly where and how I'd met Saminsa. "But—I mean—well now you can be properly introduced!"

Saminsa eyed us warily. From her tense stance, she looked like a cornered animal, ready to attack or flee at any moment.

"It's safe," Jilia said gently. "I promise. You're safe now. No one will force you to do anything anymore."

Saminsa's eyes flicked up at Jilia, but she still stayed silent, her mouth a hard line. She looked slowly between Xona, Ginni, and me. Cautiously, she eased forward and grabbed the bedding out of the bunk above Ginni's and tugged it over near the doorway.

"What's she doing?" Ginni whispered, frowning deeply.

"She's taking up the most tactically advantageous position while in a new territory," Xona said with a smirk, her eyes twinkling with approval. "I wouldn't want to be stuck in a box within an enemy camp either."

"But we aren't enemies!" Ginni exclaimed.

"Guys," I hissed. "Stop talking about her like she's not here." Saminsa looked both terrified and fierce as she dropped the bedding and stood with her back to the wall, her quick eyes flicking back and forth between us all.

"Come on," Jilia said, "I'll show you the bathroom and shower." The girl followed Jilia out.

I went back to the drawing I'd been working on, but I couldn't stop thinking about Saminsa. I could only hope that with time she'd see we weren't the enemy. I looked down at my paper. The Professor had given me colored drawing pencils, and I was trying to figure out the best way to blend the colors together.

Ginni sewed beside me and Xona changed into her training clothes and left. It seemed like she was always working out lately or putting in more hours of weapons training. I'd gathered she was still mad about not being included in the mission and was determined to show her brother she was as capable as any Rez fighter.

My drawing wasn't working. I couldn't seem to make the picture on paper match the image in my head. I put down the purple pencil I'd been using and stared at the door Saminsa had left through. I wondered if she'd get any sleep tonight, or if she'd stay up keeping guard against us.

Ginni chatted on like she always did. "So I heard that Tyryn might be dating one of the new Rez recruits. She's got auburn hair that's so smooth and shiny, I would just die for it. Nothing like mine." She tugged at the ends of her frizzy hair and sighed.

I paused and looked at her. "How do you always know about everything that's going on with people?"

"Oh, you know, I just hear things." She looked away.

"Yeah, but it's more than that." I frowned. "You seem to know things no one else does."

She bit her lip, hesitating before looking back at me. "If I tell you something, will you promise not to hate me?"

I laughed. "Of course."

She looked down at the line of stitches she'd made. "I used to be a Monitor."

My mouth dropped open. "What?"

"The officials at my Academy figured out I'd been glitching from the repeated anomalous incidents flagged in my record. They offered me safety if I spied on the rest of the students for them. So I did." She fidgeted with the edge of the fabric while the words rushed out.

I couldn't help gaping at her in horror. Monitors were specially trained as spies, hidden among the regular population. They were adept at detecting all the subtle clues that someone's V-chip hardware was malfunctioning. After they turned in someone, the subject would be taken away for new hardware installation or, worse, deactivation. An involuntary shiver snaked down my spine. Ginni couldn't be a Monitor. She was too sweet and good.

"Eventually they even had me tracking not only anomalous students but also other Uppers who came through our Academy. I was good at it because of my power. I always knew when a person was somewhere they weren't supposed to be. I'd sneak up close but out of sight and listen to their conversations, then report."

"And you just . . . went along with it? You helped them capture other glitchers like us?"

She squeezed her eyes shut and I immediately felt bad for the accusatory tone of my voice. "When you become a Monitor, they put more tech in your head. Even though I was glitching and safe from the V-chip, I couldn't escape the new hardware."

"Oh Ginni," I put my hand over hers. Here I was again, accusing someone before I'd gotten all the details. "I'm so sorry. I had no idea that was how Monitors worked."

She forced a smile. "Don't be. I'm the one who's sorry. When the Rez rescued me, they tried to disable the extra hardware, but they couldn't completely. I still have the compulsion to spy on people and learn their secrets. The Professor says I can try to fight it, or at least keep the things I learn to myself. But it's hard."

I squeezed her hand and pointed to the hardware portal at the back of my neck. "The Community left its mark on all of us. We're all trying to recover from what has been done to us."

I went to sleep soon after Xona and Saminsa came back. I pulled the heavy curtain to my bed box closed and said the words to Link myself, waiting for the usual calming tones of Scheduled Subject Downtime to play as my thoughts melted away into the Link.

But as my senses dulled, I realized it wasn't the calming tones of Scheduled Subject Downtime playing. I'd Linked right in the middle of the Link News, complete with audio and video reports. The Link did its work, slowly numbing me to my outside senses, shutting me up in the gray of my own mind with no stray sensory data or reactions.

Anomalous activity continues to be on the rise. Families of those reported for anomalous incidents must submit to additional testing.

Footage played of the current Chancellor Supreme of Sector 6, a short gray-haired man. He stood at a podium and spoke. *"We are Humanity Sublime for a reason. We have stamped out the destructive passions that ruled our ancestors. Any and all anomalous activity poses a threat to our peaceful and productive society."*

The vid scene switched. A girl screamed and thrashed on the ground of an Academy cafeteria, held down by Regulators on both sides. All the other students watched passively, faces mute of any emotion at the scene playing out before them. The girl looked like she was about fourteen. Her blond hair fell out of the careful clip and her scream hit an especially high piercing note right as the Regulator reached toward her neck with the pen-needle. A moment later, she was slumped between the two Regs.

The animal-like regression of anomalous subjects continues to be a concern. Treatment, however, is swift and effective. But only if every Subject remains vigilant to protect Humanity Sublime from this grow-ing menace. An anomaly observed is an anomaly reported. Order first, order always.

The vid and audio switched again, to a story about recent trade agreements with Sector 5, but the girl's screaming face seemed imprinted in my head no matter how much the vid flashed and changed.

She was so young. A shot of dread spiked through my veins. My brother Markan was fourteen. I thought he'd have a couple more years until I'd have to worry about the possibility of him glitching and getting caught.

But from what I'd just seen, it seemed like time was running out. I had to get my brother out of there, away from the Community and away from Chancellor Bright, before it was too late. The report had said family members of those confirmed as anomalous were being tested. Did that mean . . . I suddenly felt sick. Surely Bright would test the brother of the most notorious glitcher ever. I'd been a fool ever to think Markan was safe just because I was gone.

I un-Linked myself and swung the curtain from my bed back. "Taylor's still on site, right?" I asked Xona.

She looked up from the weapon she was polishing. "Yeah, why?"

"Thanks." I jumped down off the bed and pulled some slippers on my feet. I had already failed Max. There must still be time to rescue Markan, and the families of the other glitchers who'd been left behind.

All I could think about was Markan as I walked towards Taylor's office. I remembered the way I used to tiptoe into his room at night and watch him sleep. That was months ago. He might look very different now. I wondered if his soft cheeks had leaned out and how tall he'd gotten. As I got closer to Taylor's office, I saw the door was partially open already, and I could hear voices.

"Got the skeleton darn near done, but that don't mean nothin' if we don't have the contents to put in the godlam'd thing."

"Don't you think I know that, Henk?" Taylor's voice was sharp. "Obviously I know that."

"I got myself cracked puttin' this together for ya. You promised we could take them down for good. That's the only reason I risked my position to do this."

"Your position? That's right, here on the outer dregs of the Rez we don't get to eat caviar and drink gin."

"You know I don't care about any of that." Henk's voice got louder. "I wanna bring the whole thing crumblin' down on the shunters' heads, same as you."

I tiptoed closer to hear better. Henk sounded far different from the joking prankster he'd been when I'd last seen him.

"Then find me another way to get what we need."

"How am I supposed to do that if I'm watch-listed and on the run? This was your side of the bargain. You said if I designed the thing and brought you a prototype, you'd take care of the rest."

"Chancellor Bright always seems to be two steps ahead of us." Taylor grimaced like she'd eaten something rotten. "All we can do now is figure out another way to get what we need. You work things on your end and I'll work mine."

"I ain't got an end anymore, or haven't you heard a single

word I've said? I need access, machinery, resources. It's all gone."

"We both know you have clientele outside the Community you could talk to. You moved product between global Sectors all the time."

"You're trying to get me killed, is that it? Need your project all hush, hush, so let's get Henk to cut deals with the ganger bosses and get his throat slit?"

"I would die for the cause tomorrow," Taylor shot back. "A sacrifice that all of us should be willing to make, no questions asked."

"Dyin' for something that actually makes a difference is one thing. Takin' a suicide run is somethin' else entirely."

"I'm not saying you have to steal it—"

"Well it's gotta come from somewhere, don't it? And last I checked, the Rez ain't got near enough resources to buy—"

"Stop," Taylor said, and I heard feet approach the doorway. "You can't even close a door correctly, no wonder you got cracked trying to leave the factory with the prototype."

The door shut fast before I could hear his response.

I pulled back, my heart beating fast. What were they talking about? I was stunned, but I couldn't turn back to my dorm room. I'd come here with a purpose, and I was going to see it through.

I waited a few minutes, so they wouldn't know I'd heard them, then knocked on the chrome door until it slid open. I looked at Henk. He was staring at the General, his face mottled with anger. She looked down at her console screen as if purposefully ignoring him.

"I'm sorry if I'm interrupting."

"I was just leaving." Henk grabbed his jacket and strode out the door.

I looked around. Every ounce of wall space was covered with paper maps and a wall-wide monitor that had digital notes scribbled all over it. The clutter gave the room the look of a lair. And all the actual paper surprised me. I leaned in without thinking to try to read her small scratch. I was used to everything being digital. Other than me and my drawing stock, I didn't know anyone who used paper anymore.

"What?" the General asked, still not looking up.

Nervousness struck, but I held my ground. "I want to talk to you about something."

She finally looked up, but her eyes were narrowed. "What?"

"I saw over the Link News feed that glitchers are showing up younger and younger."

The General nodded, her face impassive. Of course she already knew.

"That means the Chancellor is getting access to even more glitchers every day," I went on, "building up her ranks when we haven't been able to rescue any new ones other than the few from the raid."

She didn't respond. I hesitated.

She stared at me, her face still expressionless. "And? Is there something else?"

"They say glitching runs in families sometimes," I rushed on. "So I want to put together a mission to rescue my brother and other people's siblings. We've got to get to them before the Chancellor does."

She stared at me blankly for a long moment, then took a deep breath. "Oh my, you're serious. Listen carefully, Zoel.

Chancellor Bright has your family's housing unit under constant surveillance because she thinks you would be stupid enough to try to attempt such a thing. It's probably the same for the family of every other glitcher we've rescued. There might be a lot of rumors and talk about you becoming a leader, but this army doesn't belong to you. These aren't your lives to risk. And if you think it's worthwhile to get good soldiers killed just so you can play happy family, you've got a hell of a lot to learn about being a leader."

"But his life could be in danger," I sputtered. "I have to try. And he might be a glitcher."

"*Might* is the operative word. And all of us have family." She turned her attention back to the file in her console screen.

"Which is why I'm not just talking about my brother, but the others' families too. There can't be that many of us with siblings, and if we organized coordinated strikes all at the same time—"

"No," Taylor said simply, looking back at her console screen.

"You don't understand." I sat down at the chair across from her. "I betrayed my older brother a long time ago, and I couldn't save my friend Max. I can't do the same to Markan. I have to try to get him out. I could disable any Regs who are assigned to follow him, then we could—"

The General looked back up at me, her face suddenly hard as marble. "I've already wasted too many of our resources in the hope that you might turn out to be useful. We built this entire facility with you in mind, to protect you. We saved you."

"But—" I started to protest, but she cut me off.

"No, Zoel, you have yet to pay back any of the great debts you owe. And that's fine. I have one task that I need you for, and then I'm happy never to work with any of you glitchers again. You're all unnatural anyway. A by-product of the enemy we are trying to destroy. I'll take care of mine, you can take care of yours."

I gasped, taken aback. "What does that mean?"

"It means I'll take care of freeing the drones. Your job is to get rid of Chancellor Bright."

"You can free them?" I leaned forward. My worries about my brother were momentarily sidelined. Getting rid of the V-chip was everything I'd always hoped for. "How? I'll do anything to help."

"Would you?" Taylor raised an eyebrow. "Would you really? You speak of sacrifice as if it were simple. As if choosing who can be saved and who can't is a burden easily carried. Yet you come in here begging me to risk losing countless good fighters, people who have their own families and lives worth protecting."

"But it's our families—"

"We all have families." Her voice caught for a moment before her eyes hardened again. "The question is not whether you are willing to give your own life, it's whether you're willing to give up the people you love most. Even if it was for the greater good, could you do it? Could you?" She waited a moment with her hawk eyes on me. "I thought not. But you can kill the Chancellor. You're powerful, you're immune to her compulsion, and she will kill you unless you take her down first. That is all you are here to do. You are dismissed."

I left Taylor's office both fuming and terrified. We couldn't get Markan back. They were watching him, all because of me. If he was a glitcher, the Chancellor would know first, and if he wasn't, she'd still make sure I never got to him before he turned eighteen and the final adult V-chip was implanted. He'd turn into a drone forever, just like our parents.

No. I wouldn't let the Chancellor take the only family I had left. Anger surged up inside me like a billowing red sheet. The idea of Markan glitching and being able to feel emotion— only to be made a slave to the Chancellor's compulsion— chilled me to the bone. If it was in my power to end the Chancellor's life, I could save my brother and so many others. This was my destiny, and, sooner or later, I had to face it.

Chapter 19

TRY AS I MIGHT, I could never seem to catch Adrien alone. I wanted to talk to him about everything the General had said, or just spend a couple of hours holding each other. But I never could. He'd show up late to meals and would disappear right after classes. He always seemed tired and drawn. He'd brushed me off when I asked if he was okay and said he was working on a special techer security program for the General. He looked like he never slept. What happened on the raid seemed to have ruined the peace he'd spoken of when we watched the sunset.

Meanwhile Tyryn was pushing us harder than ever in training. We ran a long loop up and down the stairwells between the two floors, over and over again.

"Faster," Tyryn yelled as Ginni and I ran by on our tenth lap.

"I take back ever thinking he was cute," Ginni said through huffing breaths.

Xona flew by, lapping us. Again. It seemed like she was in a race to keep up with the ex-Regs, whose pounding feet had run past us three times already.

I looked behind me, trying to see where Adrien was in the pack. He was so far back he must still be on the stairwell. I frowned. Adrien had been running slower than normal the past few days. His late nights must be taking their toll. Saminsa jogged down the hall behind us, carefully keeping her distance from Ginni and me.

"Rally up," Tyryn called on our next lap. I came to a stop inside the training center and leaned over with my hands on my knees. Ginni collapsed on the ground. Adrien and City were the last to finish their laps. Right when they came in, Tyryn called out, "Everybody on your feet!"

City let out a long complaining groan.

Xona smirked, bouncing around from foot to foot as if the workout hadn't even begun yet. City glared, her blond hair wet with sweat and matted on her forehead. Before she could fire off a snappy comment, Tyryn interrupted with his booming voice. "You all need to start acting more like a team. Until we get another chance at the Chancellor, you'll be called on for more and more dangerous missions, and your life will depend on the people standing around you now. You all did as well as could be expected on your first mission together, but when we go up against the Chancellor herself, we have to be flawless."

City nodded toward Xona. "Then I don't know why she's here. She's not even on our task force."

Xona's jaw tensed like she was barely keeping herself in check, but she didn't say anything. She looked at her brother.

"She is now," Tyryn said.

City's mouth dropped open. "What?"

"She's been testing through the Rez fighter training program and was just officially assigned yesterday. Taylor thinks she'll be good to have on your team."

City scoffed. "Why?"

"The General believes it's imperative to have non-glitchers

on every task force, and Xona is the perfect choice since she already lives and trains with you. I don't want to hear another word about it," he finished, staring at City. She put her hands on her hips and rolled her eyes.

"Stand at attention."

With another audible sigh, City dropped her arms and straightened her back.

"Now," Tyryn said, "as I said, you have to start working more as a team. You each have varied and unique gifts, but you have to start working as one. Which is why today instead of moving directly into weapons training, we are going to do some trust exercises."

We all stared at him.

"First, everyone needs to grab one of these poles." He pointed to a pile of poles on the ground. They were thin metal rods, each with a rubber hand grip on the bottom. They didn't look like anything we usually trained with.

"Each of you will hold this and let Filicity cast her electricity at you. You have to trust she'll hit the pole. Don't let go or drop it. And Filicity," he looked at her, "keep the amperage to a low stun just in case."

City nodded, her attitude suddenly changed now that she was the center of attention. She grinned and rubbed her hands together, sparks flying between her fingertips. Rand was the first to go and pick up a pole. I reluctantly followed. As much as I might not like City, I had seen her aim, and she was always spot-on.

Ginni tried to hand Saminsa a pole, but the pixie-haired girl took one look at the pole and City, then crossed her arms and turned to go sit by the wall. Tyryn let it go without comment.

I guessed there was a grace period for trust when you'd been the enemy on the last mission.

We lined up and let City attack us. It was unnerving to see the blue-white spiral coming straight toward me when it was my turn, but other than a faint vibration in the handle of the pole, I didn't feel a thing.

"Good," Tyryn said after we'd all gone. "Now we'll turn to Cole and Zoe. Cole," he looked at the ex-Reg, "I want you to hoist each team member gently by their waists and toss them up into the air a few feet. Zoe, you catch them with your telekinesis and return them safely to the ground."

Xona's eyes widened until I thought they'd pop out of her head, but she kept her mouth a tight-lipped line.

"Do I have any volunteers to go first?"

"Hell yeah, I'll try it." Rand stepped forward. He put his hand on Cole's shoulder. "Be gentle, my good man," he said with mock seriousness before turning to grin at the rest of us.

"Let us know when you're ready, Zoe," Tyryn said.

I closed my eyes and let the buzzing in my ears grow. I imagined my connection to everything around me. The people standing in front of me were just extensions of the floor which was merely an extension of myself. I still meditated every day, and accessing these connections came more and more naturally now. After only a moment's resistance, a projection cube of the entire room rose in my mind. I marveled for a moment at being able to call on my power so easily, then latched onto Rand's figure. "Ready."

Cole lifted him up by the waist. Rand was a big guy, surely over two hundred pounds, but Cole lifted him as if he were no heavier than a paperweight. He tossed him up. I'd had my power lassoed around him the whole time, but when he peaked in the air and began to fall again, I grabbed hold and lowered him slowly to the ground.

"That was awesome!" Rand said, pumping a fist in the air. "You could've let me fall faster though. Where's your sense of fun?"

One by one the rest of them went through. Adrien felt bulkier in the air than I expected, but I was glad because it meant he was still putting on weight. Finally no one was left but Xona. She gritted her teeth and walked over to Cole. She looked up at the ex-Reg who towered a good foot over her and took several quick breaths. I could see her arm trembling slightly as he reached toward her, but she managed to stand still. Cole hesitated before gently placing his metal-reinforced hand on her waist. She jerked away. "I can't."

"Xona," Tyryn started. Cole dropped his hand.

"I can't." She spun on her heel and ran out of the room.

For a second no one said anything, then Ginni grabbed my hand and we headed out the door. We caught up to Xona halfway down the hall. She'd slumped to her knees, her hands covering her face.

Ginni dropped down and smoothed her hair out of her face, rubbing Xona's back with her other hand. I crouched down too. "Talk to us," Ginni said. "Tell us what's wrong."

When Xona finally looked up, her face was tear-stained. I was stunned. The only emotions I'd ever seen from her were annoyance or anger.

"My mom and I were sleeping when they came." Xona's voice was a low guttural whisper. "Out of nowhere, there's this huge boom and the wall was blown in on us. A beam landed on Mom and me. I was able to crawl out from underneath it, but she was trapped. That's when the Regulators burst into the room.

"They were animals. Dad fired off a couple of rounds, but they all bounced off the Regs' chests. Then one Reg grabbed my dad by the neck. The snap of his spine was so loud." She winced. "I'll never forget that sound." Another tear escaped from one eye and ran down her cheek before she swiped it angrily away.

"Oh, hon." I reached out to put an arm on her shoulder, but she just shrugged me off and kept talking, staring at the wall like she was watching the memory play out.

"I should have made Tyryn stop and get the beam off of Mom. I should have made him save her instead of me. But I didn't." Another errant tear escaped. "Tyryn grabbed me up in his arms and took off. I watched over his shoulder as a Regulator crushed her chest like she was nothing." She looked up at Ginni and me. "I know everyone thinks I'm a jerk for not being able to stand the ex-Regs and saying they aren't human. But what human being could do that? And how could I ever see them as anything other than the monsters they are?"

Xona turned her face away and wept. This time she let Ginni and I get close to hug her, our arms around her like a shield.

Over her shoulder, I could see Cole standing in the doorway with a pained look on his face as he watched Xona's back shake with sobs. I didn't know how much he had overheard, but it was obviously enough. He looked over at me, raising his eyebrows and gesturing a question. I shook my head. No, I didn't think he should come talk to her.

Cole sighed, his shoulders limp as he turned to walk the opposite direction down the hallway. His reinforced legs made a rhythmic hydraulic hiss as he disappeared from view.

Chapter 20

I STARED AT ADRIEN over my steaming bowl of protein goo. Yesterday I'd finally tracked him down and asked him what was wrong.

"Nothing," he'd said with averted eyes. When I reached out and touched his arm, he flinched away from me. At first I thought he was still angry and hurt that I had accused him of foreseeing the sabotaged mission and not stopping it. And could I blame him? He already felt so guilty about his visions causing horrible things, and I'd just reinforced it with my accusations.

Still, it had been over a month since we'd been back. I couldn't help wondering if it was about more than him just being hurt at what I'd said. All kinds of doubts nagged at the edges of my mind. What if he simply didn't want to be with me anymore? Our romance had been a whirlwind from the start, but what if now that I was actually here, living in close proximity to him, he realized I wasn't the girl he'd built me up in his mind to be? He'd been walking around with these visions of this amazing leader in his head, but in person I didn't match up.

Today Adrien was sitting at the other end of the Caf with a guy I didn't know. He clearly wasn't a Rez fighter. I squinted.

"Who is that?" I nudged Ginni and pointed over to him.

"Oh," Ginni smiled. "That's . . ." She paused, eyebrows coming together. "It's . . . give me a second. I swear I know his name." She frowned. "But I can't seem to remember it now that I try to think of it."

Adrien suddenly looked up and caught me staring. I quickly glanced away. In case he was trying to avoid me, I didn't want to embarrass myself. I was glad when Saminsa walked past, and I shifted my gaze to pretend I'd been watching her as she dropped the rest of her food in the trash and left the Caf.

Adrien quickly stood up and headed towards us, the other boy with him following suit.

"Hey everyone," he said, his voice light and easy. "This is Simin."

"Hi," Ginni said, standing up. She grabbed his hand and pumped it. "It's so lovely to meet you, Simin!"

The boy pulled his hand away, pointing to the book open on Ginni's tablet by her plate. "You're reading that again? Doesn't it always make you cry?"

"How did you know that?" Ginni gasped. "Is your power telepathy?"

Simin sighed. "We've met like ten times already." He looked over at Adrien. "I told you this was a dumb idea."

"Nah," Adrien said, putting a hand on Simin's back and pushing him lightly into a chair at our table. "The more days in a row they see you, the better chance they'll have at remembering you."

"Remembering him?" I asked.

"Simin is the glitcher who keeps the Foundation's location safe. Anyone who meets him immediately forgets that they saw him. Taylor has anyone who visits talk to Simin before they leave, and they forget where they've been."

"So why can't I remember him?" Ginni asked. "I haven't left the Foundation."

"It doesn't just work on people leaving," the boy said, staring down at the ground uncomfortably. "Everyone forgets me."

"Whoa," Rand said. He stared at the boy, frowning. "You don't like, live in the dorms with us do ya?"

"I stay in the security hub," Simin mumbled. His eyes darted back to Ginni before quickly looking away.

I remembered going to the security hub once with Adrien, but when I tried to think about anyone else there, the details became indistinct.

"The hub's below the Foundation," Adrien continued. "Simin's a techer too. He handles all the communications for the Foundation."

"So how do you remember him?" I asked. Adrien looked at me, our eyes holding each other's gaze for a moment before he answered.

"I wrote it down and put a note on the side of my bed to look at each morning. Figured he could use some company."

My heart swelled. Despite everything weighing on his shoulders, Adrien still thought so much about other people.

"Can I sit here?" Adrien pointed at the empty chair beside me. He leaned over. "I'm sorry for how busy I've been lately," he whispered in my ear. "I've been researching with Simin on a task for the General. But I miss you."

His breath was warm on my neck and I felt the chills race up my arms. It was the closest we'd come to touching in so long. I felt a rush of relief. I'd been making a big deal out of nothing. He did still want to be with me, he'd just been busy.

"I missed you too," I said, and grabbed his hand. The second my skin connected with his I felt a wave of warmth and security wash down my body. I tugged him down and he sat. A shy smile warmed his face. I interwove my fingers with his, my hand a perfect fit.

But almost the instant he'd settled into his chair, his body went rigid. He stared at the wall beyond me, his eyes vacant. No matter how many times I witnessed one of Adrien's visions, they were still unsettling.

"What?" I asked as soon as he shook his head, his eyes refocusing and his face taking on a look of horror.

"Get down!" he yelled.

A billowing flame of fire blew outward from the kitchen.

Everyone except the ex-Regs immediately dove from the explosion, arms over faces. I raised my arms too, but my chair was jammed in too tightly to move. I looked behind me frantically. Adrien had dropped under the table and I thought I heard his voice screaming my name amid all the shouting. A blindingly orange fire had spread over half the cafeteria wall, filling the room with a haze of smoke.

It was a surreal moment—the ex-Reg Eli just sat against the wall completely still, even though the upper half of his body was in flames. Part of the skin on his face had been burned away, leaving only the metal of his reinforced jaw behind.

The buzzing in my head eclipsed the chaos. The sprinklers weren't coming on, I didn't know why. Tyryn had grabbed a fire extinguisher, but he was no match for the wall of flame. Other Rez fighters ran for the hallways to look for more.

Some people from tables near the door escaped through the doorway, but then the blaze moved toward the entrance. We were trapped.

I finally managed to push my chair back and stand up. The others had climbed out the other side of the table and were stumbling toward the wall farthest away from the blaze. It was hard to see much of anything beyond the basic outline of their bodies through the smoke. I turned back to the fire.

I had to do something. But when I sent my telek outward, I couldn't get a hold of the fire. It wasn't a solid object I could just surround like I normally did. It kept morphing and changing shapes and right when I thought I'd managed to catch some of it, it danced out of my grasp.

I grabbed all the glasses of water from the surrounding tables with my power and hurled them at the fire, but when they hit, it only seemed to make it spread.

The buzzing screamed in my mind, but there was nothing I could do. The ex-Reg continued to burn and the flame licked over to the table beside me. I yanked off the tablecloth with my telek and tried to smother some of the fire with it. But it barely made a dent in the blaze and quickly caught aflame itself.

I tripped backward, only barely managing to stay on my feet. The smoke and heat were disorienting. I coughed and covered my face with my tunic sleeve, my mind racing for something else to try.

Then an image popped into my head—of Saminsa, and how she'd covered herself with an orb of light. The picture took hold and I stopped trying to get a hold on the fire and instead imagined a bubble without oxygen surrounding me.

As I imagined it, I could suddenly feel the tingling of energy as the air around me shifted.

Finally, a surface to hold on to! Even though they were infinitesimal, I could feel the oxygen molecules clustered like a cloud. I took a deep breath and then pushed the cloud away from me right as the flame leapt closer. The flame stopped like it had hit an invisible wall.

I continued leeching the oxygen from the air around the fire, pushing the bubble outward. The flame on the tablecloth fizzled and died out. Next I immediately concentrated on the ex-Reg, stamping out the fire on his skin and clothing. I pushed past him toward the fiery wall.

I wasn't even sure exactly how I was doing it. I wasn't focusing anymore on the individual molecules, but it was like I'd gotten the feel of them and now I could just do it. My power was like a dampening wave. I felt light-headed from not taking a breath, but kept going anyway. Only a little bit longer. The people behind me were far enough away, they should still be able to breathe. I started at the edges and moved inward. The flame banked inch by inch, until I'd whittled it down to the counter. I finally stamped out the flame surrounding the blackened cooking unit that must have been the source.

I realized a moment too late that I'd forgotten to let oxygen back into the space surrounding me, and I blacked out.

"Eli just sat there. Why didn't he move?" I recognized Cole's low voice. I shifted on my cot in the Med Center. It was a little awkward with the oxygen tubes plugged in my nose, but I could see Cole standing beside the bed where the other ex-Reg lay. Eli was wrapped head to foot in burn ointment and the skin regrowth serum. It looked like Jilia had healed some of the minor burns, but she couldn't create skin where there was none.

Jilia's voice was kind. "His pain and reaction centers just haven't started working as naturally as yours have."

"But he's human," Cole said. "He can feel. He just doesn't know who he is without his Reg hardware." His hands curled into fists.

Jilia noticed I was awake and came over to do a quick scan before releasing me back to my dorm. My footsteps were heavy as I headed down the hallway. I didn't want to think about it anymore. I didn't want to think about any of it—the ex-Regs, the fire, or how I'd used my power. Of course, when I got back to my dorm room, Ginni had other ideas.

"Zoe, you were amazing today! Xona, did you see the way the fire just stopped? And all because of Zoe's power. No one will doubt what you can do now."

Xona didn't say anything, she just kept slowly scraping her knife across a whetstone. *Scrape. Scraaaaaaape.*

"Xona, wasn't it great?" Ginni pressed.

Xona looked up at me. "Magnificent." She pulled her feet up into the box and swung the curtain shut.

I looked at Ginni questioningly, but she shrugged.

"What started the fire anyway?" I asked.

"A circuit on the thermal unit blew," Ginni said. "A bottle of cooking oil was right beside it and sprayed everywhere at the same time the spark lit it all up." She shook her head. "Here we are worrying about these death-defying missions

and then something like this happens right in our own home."
She paused, shaking her head. "Life is weird."

I nodded. I'd never heard a better summation.

The scraping stopped. "It's not just weird." Xona hopped down from her bunk. "It's suspicious, that's what it is."

I blinked in confusion, both by the sudden change in her manner and by what she'd said.

"Suspicious?" I asked. "What do you mean?"

"The thermal unit circuit just happened to blow while we were all at lunch, and the bottle of oil just happened to have been sitting beside it?"

Ginni gasped. "Sabotage!"

"Normally I'd guess it was a Reg. But they're more the brute force types."

"Let's not jump to conclusions," I said quickly.

"You know, Saminsa did leave the room right before it all happened," Ginni said.

Xona leaned in, nodding. "It makes sense. Saminsa was already working for the Chancellor. She says she hates the Chancellor for being willing to blow her and her friends up, but what if that was just a lie to get in with us?"

I thought of how I'd felt when I'd come here, like a stranger without a home. But it was even worse for Saminsa, going from one cold dangerous place to what she thought was another. That didn't necessarily make her a threat. Then again, after everything she'd been through, maybe she wanted to strike back the only way she could.

The door slid open and we all jumped.

"Hi Saminsa," I said, my voice high and too-bright.

Saminsa's eyes narrowed as she took in the scene of the

three of us pretending we hadn't been huddled together whispering conspiratorially. Ginni's eyes widened in fear and she turned around abruptly. Xona arched an eyebrow at Ginni and me, looking pointedly at her ankle weapon before climbing back into her box.

Saminsa set her jaw and sat down on her mat by the door without saying a word.

I stared at her a moment longer than I should have. Could Xona be right? Did Saminsa secretly hate us and want to hurt us? I didn't want to believe it, but then I remembered the flesh melting off Eli's face. I knew we'd all be keeping a closer eye on Saminsa. Then I shook my head. No, I wouldn't accuse someone without any clear evidence again. Xona was probably just seeing enemies where there were none again, like she always did with the ex-Regs.

Chapter 21

THE PROFESSOR BROUGHT OUT new art supplies in Humanities. There were little pots of shocking colored paints and brushes. I picked one up and looked at it dubiously. I ran the bristles across my hand. It tickled.

It seemed like a very impractical instrument for making pictures—how could you be precise with tons of little flopping bristles? The sharp-tipped markers I'd always used before seemed like a far better idea.

I sat in front of one of the large blank pieces of canvas the Professor had set up at stations throughout the room. He gave brief instructions and set out a bowl of vegetables, but he said we could paint whatever we wanted. City was laughing and joking with Rand, who was quickly making a mess on his canvas. Cole immediately began working quietly in the corner, glancing around the room occasionally. Adrien had skipped class. Again.

I swallowed and dabbed the tip of my brush into the red, but stopped before it touched the canvas. The paint was globbed on the bristles. I'd picked up too much. I didn't know how to do this. I tried wiping some of the red off on the edge of the pot, but it still looked like too much on the brush. If I put it to the canvas now, it'd just be a mess. I screwed the tops back on the pots, feeling an embarrassed heat flush my neck. I was supposed to be the artist.

But then, I was supposed to be so many things.

I dropped the paint brush into the cleaning solution and moved my chair away from the canvas. I pulled out a piece of paper from a stack in the corner and a marker. There, that was better. I started sketching the room and the people in it. City and Rand kept moving around, and I wished I could tell them to stand still. I tried to get their proportions as correctly as I could. I almost wished I was connected to the Link so I could see the technical schematics laid across my vision. I could be so much more exact that way.

Professor Henry called me to stay after class. The heat in my neck returned.

"May I?" he asked, gesturing to the paper I'd been drawing on. I handed it over and watched him eye it critically.

"It's very . . ." he paused, "accurate."

"Is that good?" I asked in a small voice.

The Professor laughed. "Zoe, art isn't about good or bad." He handed the paper back to me. "It's about letting yourself feel things, and then trying to communicate those feelings. Here, let me show you something." He led me over to the canvas in the corner where Cole had been working. The canvas had been pointed at the wall, so it wasn't until we walked around that I could see it.

Tears immediately pricked my eyes. "It's beautiful."

There wasn't any clear image or figures in the picture. Instead, it was a wash of color, vibrant red spreading into shocking blue, with dabs of white and yellow throughout.

It looked like delight. Or maybe that's just what looking at it made me feel.

"But he's an ex-Reg," I turned to the Professor.

"It's harder for them than it was for the rest of you glitchers," the Professor said, "but Cole's living proof that no matter how much metal you put in a person, you can't take away their humanity. Cole just has to fight harder for it."

I immediately thought of how I always felt a rush of relief right before I clicked into the Link each night. It felt like a free pass. For a while I didn't have to try to sort out the emotions, I could just let them dull to gray. But here Cole was, fighting to keep them.

"But why?" I whispered. "Why does he try so hard?"

"Oh, Zoe," the Professor said with a smile, "look at the canvas. Can't you see why?"

I couldn't stop thinking about the canvas as I walked out of the class and down the empty hallway. I wanted to be like Cole and paint in color. I wanted to feel things, I was just tired of feeling bad things. I'd had enough of bad things. But I'd also felt the emotions Cole had captured in the painting before—beauty, color, delight. I'd felt them with Adrien.

My wrist com buzzed with a message:

I'm waiting for you at your dorm.

It was as if Adrien had read my thoughts. I felt a flush of warmth and smiled. I hurried down the hallway to my dorm.

He was waiting outside the door for me, his face dark and intense.

"I'm sorry," he said as soon as I got close. He pulled me into a tight embrace. His words were a whisper against my neck. "I've been an idiot. I let this project I was working on distract me from what's really important. So tonight," he pulled back and brought my hands to his lips. He kissed my fingertips. "We are going on a date."

"What's that?" I asked, my heart fluttering erratically at his touch.

"It's what they used to call them in the Old World," he grinned. "Just two people going out to dinner. And not at the Caf."

I scrunched up my face, confused. "Why not? We've repaired most of the fire damage. Everyone's been eating there all week."

"Because," he laughed, then leaned in to kiss my nose. "The whole point is that it's just the two of us together. Alone." His voice dropped on the last word in a way that sent a quick shiver up my spine.

He'd been so distant the past few weeks, but here he was, grinning genuinely like there wasn't a thing to worry about.

I shook away the confusion and smiled back at him. A night of forgetting about everything and simply being together sounded perfect.

"A date," I said. "Will I eat my gruel out of a fancy cup?"

"Don't ruin the surprise," he smiled. "I already know you're going to love it."

I started. "Wait, you've had a vision of our date? No fair!"

He winked at me. "Let's just say I have a good feeling

about it. I'll come back by your dorm room at seven so I can escort you to dinner."

"This is so romantic," Ginni squealed, and for once, Xona didn't even bother to roll her eyes.

Ginni had pulled me in front of the mirror for the last half hour and was curling and pinning my hair up in intricate ways.

"I wish I had a boy who would ask me on dates. We'd talk about the books I love and he wouldn't mind that I talk so much. In fact, that's what he'd like about me most. We'd talk for hours and . . ." She paused. I looked at her in the mirror and her face held a puzzled frown.

"What?"

"Oh," she giggled, shaking her head. "I just had the weirdest sense that I had met someone. But that's impossible."

"All those romantic books are giving you hallucinations. I knew reading that much couldn't be healthy," Xona said.

Ginni swatted at Xona with a spare piece of cloth from the sewing table. A knock sounded at the door.

I jumped up to open it. Adrien was wearing clothes I'd never seen before. His shirt was dark and fitted, and it slimmed into pants that hung a little off his hips. He'd even done something to tame his curls. My stomach did a little flip-flop.

He stared at me, his mouth dropping open a little. "You're so beautiful."

I was suddenly very glad I'd let Ginni talk me into wearing the skirt she'd made.

"I brought something for you." He held up a small rectangular box. I opened it and gasped. A small silver chain was nestled inside with a blue stone embedded in a circular pendant. I touched the delicate stone with the tip of my finger. The tiny facets sparkled in the light whenever I moved the box. I'd never seen anything like it.

"It's a necklace," Adrien said, his voice a little higher-pitched than normal. "Henk helped me get it. Here, allow me." He pulled the necklace from the box, then moved behind me and draped the chain over my neck, the little pendant hanging like a teardrop. His fingers trembled as he lifted my hair and closed the clasp. He leaned in from behind, his voice a whisper. "Don't take it off, even when you sleep. I want a little part of me to be with you all the time."

"It's so pretty!" Ginni squealed.

I put my hand to my neck and traced the chain down to the pendent. I'd never owned something so special in all my life. I turned to look at Adrien. He'd pulled back slightly, but he held out an arm.

"Shall we?" he said.

I glanced back and saw Ginni's swooning face. I laughed and grabbed Adrien's proffered arm.

"We shall," I said.

We walked down the hallway, and I felt a bit silly in the skirt. It whooshed around my legs in a way I wasn't used to, and my calves were bare. It was a strange sensation.

Adrien raised one eyebrow and grinned as we passed the Caf. He finally stopped when we came to the training room.

"Are we going to be lifting weights or perfecting my aim?"

He smirked. "Neither." He opened the door and I stepped in. The lights were dimmed like they were during meditation, but in the farthest corner I could see a small table set up.

Someone had draped a deep magenta fabric over the plain white walls beside the table, and as I came closer, I saw some of my newer drawings had been hung up. My brother's face, my parents, even Max.

"I thought you might like to be surrounded by all the people you love tonight."

I felt myself tearing up. I turned and hugged him. "It's perfect," I said.

He pulled back with a laugh. "But you haven't even seen everything tonight has to offer." The table itself had been covered in cloth too—a bright blue triangle piece was set over a bigger white cloth that draped over the edges of the table. A single rose spun in the light from a projection cube set in the center of the table.

Adrien popped the top of a tall bottle and poured sparkling liquid into our glasses.

"What is that?" I leaned in closer.

"The Community rations finally arrived, and I had Henk toss in some champagne as well."

"But won't I be allergic to it?"

"Nope. We've tested everything you're going to eat tonight. It was all produced in the underground Community hothouses, with zero Surface allergens."

"Wait," I paused as what he said sank in. "You mean I'll finally get to eat real food?"

He nodded, his grin so wide I thought it would split his face. "Surprise."

I let out a giddy squeal and clapped my hands like Ginni did when she was excited.

"My lady," he said, and held out a chair for me.

"Tonight you get to feast on braised beef and carrots, in a red wine sauce." He clicked his com, and a few moments later, Jilia walked in carrying two loaded plates. She set them down in front of us.

"Thank you," I said, but she didn't respond, she just smiled and then walked out again.

I took a deep drink of the champagne and almost coughed because of the bubbles that seemed to fizz in my nose.

"Start out slow," he said, patting my back as my coughs died down. "Take sips, not gulps."

"It stung," I said, my eyes watering.

Adrien laughed. "It does take a little while to get used to. But hurry, take a bite of the beef before it cools down too much."

I did as he said, and immediately closed my eyes to focus on the flavor. The beef seemed to melt on my tongue, it was so tender and juicy. I'd never had anything like it in my entire life. When Adrien said Community rations, I thought he meant the hard bread and protein patties I'd eaten every morning of my life, not this. A low groan escaped my throat.

I looked back up at him. He hadn't even taken a bite yet. He was just watching me. I blushed slightly and ducked my head.

We ate quietly for several minutes, both of us enjoying the sumptuous flavors.

"Remember how you used to explain emotion words to me?" I asked after I'd finished the last of the meat.

He nodded.

"I've been experiencing emotion for long enough now that

I think I understand most of them, but every now and then another one will surprise me."

He smiled. "Like what?"

"Like this right now." I put my hand to my chest. "I feel warm and happy, but that doesn't quite seem to describe it. It's something more than that. What do you call it?"

Adrien's face turned thoughtful, his eyebrows drawn together. He took a drink of champagne before answering. "I think," he said tentatively, "I think it's contentment. Where you have everything you ever wanted, all together in one place. It's quieter than excitement, but," he swallowed, "maybe it's better."

"Contentment," I said, trying the word out on my tongue.

"I haven't had a lot of it in my life," he said. "It's new to me, too."

"When was the last time you felt this content?"

His face darkened and he shook his head. "It doesn't matter. My past isn't me." His tone sounded strangely resolute. "All that matters is who I am now. Who I am when I'm with you."

I stood up and walked over to him, not hesitating before I leaned over and swooped in to kiss him. I could feel his surprise, but he quickly opened his soft lips to mine, his hands gently cupping my face.

I dropped into his lap, feeling pleasure bloom inside me. He slid his hands down my jaw and pulled me tighter. Something inside me began to soar, and my power buzzed to life. Instead of releasing it uncontrollably, it hummed inside my chest, sparking down my spine like electricity. Every inch of me felt alive and wild.

Reluctantly, I released his lips, and looked around. Even though we were alone, anyone could walk in. I pulled his hand to stand up and follow me. "Come on," I whispered.

Since we were already in the training room, we didn't have far to go to the equipment closet. We didn't touch as we walked across the room, but I felt the anticipation building. I pushed the button to open the door and tugged him over to the corner, grabbing a training mat from a shelf as I went. I tossed the mat on the ground in the corner. As soon as the door closed behind us, I pulled my top off over my head, then turned to him.

I didn't say anything more, just grabbed the bottom edge of his shirt, lingering for a moment to touch the skin at his waist. Then I stood up on my tiptoes to pull it over his head.

Adrien stared at me, his warm blue-green eyes full of heat, though the corner of his lips turned down with a touch of uncertainty.

"Zoe, wait—" he started saying, but I shook my head. He lifted his arms up to help me take his shirt off in spite of his protests. I paused, breathless and excited. His chest was lean and tanned, and taut with tension. He looked wiry but strong. I traced my finger down along his collar bone, down the small dipping line in the middle of his chest, then down his stomach to his navel. A shudder rippled though his body at my touch.

He wrapped one arm around my waist, burying his other hand in my hair. He cupped the back of my head and looked in my eyes. "You drive me crazy. All I want to do is make everything around us stop so I can just be with you. But I don't know if it's right . . ."

I knew the look on his face. It was one I'd seen more and

more lately. It was like he was fighting something deep inside himself. I held my breath, hoping that just this once he could forget about destiny and the future and everything else. His eyes were so bright. He closed them briefly, and then he grabbed the waistband of my skirt and pulled me close, crushing me to him, his mouth hot and passionate.

The sudden release was overwhelming. It lit me up and I opened my mouth to his searching tongue. He was gentle one moment, then rough and needy, then pulling away so that his lips barely nipped mine in a way that made me crazy. I'd chase his lips back with mine, and suddenly he'd stop and kiss me so deeply again it seemed to sear straight down to my stomach.

I gasped at the intensity of it. We'd kissed before, but it had been nothing like this.

He pushed me up against the wall, his hand sliding down my hip. A soft moan escaped my lips.

"Shh, we have to be quiet," he laughed into my ear, before kissing down my neck. He slid one bra strap to the side and kept kissing down my shoulder. I trembled.

Slowly, he led me to the mat on the ground, pulling me down beside him. I was all heat and sensation, deepened by the hum of my power tingling just beneath my skin. He nudged me over as one knee swung over mine, and then he hovered above me, before dipping down and sucking on my neck until I felt like I was going to erupt and light us both on fire.

He paused for a moment, and even though the alcove was shadowed, I could still see the glint of his eyes reflecting some bits of light from the main room.

I put my hand on the back of his neck and pulled him

nearer, so eager to close the final space between us. "I love you, Adrien. Adrien, Adrien." I said it languorously, delighted by the feeling that stirred within me at just the sound of his name.

He stiffened in my arms. I smiled and tried to pull him closer, but he didn't budge.

"Adrien?" My voice was small in the dark room. I couldn't see his face to tell whether he'd seen another vision, or if the weight of the world had suddenly secured itself back on his shoulders.

He swore under his breath, jumping back to his feet. "I'm sorry. I can't do this."

I sat up, all the wonderful feelings dissipating as if cold water had been thrown on me. I covered up my chest awkwardly. "But what—"

"I'm sorry," he said, still not looking at me. "I've gotta go."

"Wait!" I scrambled up.

But he'd already left. Just like that. The door slid shut behind him and I sat, pained and bewildered, clutching my top to my chest.

Chapter 22

THE NEXT MORNING Adrien wasn't at training. Rand mentioned he'd gone to spend the morning at the security hub. That was just fine with me. I didn't know if I could face him. I felt embarrassed and confused, but, more than anything, I felt angry. I was getting tired of being shut out. A relationship was supposed to work both ways.

When I walked into the Gifted training class, he was already there, sitting on a mat with his eyes closed. My anger roared to life. I sat down on the mat farthest away from him and glared, hoping he could feel the fury pulsing off me in invisible waves.

He looked miserable. There were dark circles under his closed eyes. His strong broad chest rose and fell softly with each breath, and his hands rested open on his knees. The aching hurt rose up all over again. In spite of myself, I felt my heart stretch in my chest for him. But he'd rejected me without even a word of explanation. I couldn't let go of the hurt yet.

I settled into a spot on the floor and tried to still the squirming thoughts in my head. I could only manage a few moments of focus at a time.

The door opened suddenly. General Taylor stormed in

with the ex-Regs and a half-squadron of Rez fighters behind her. I stared at her in confusion.

"What's going on?" City asked. We all stood up.

"Get her!" Taylor yelled, her face a mask of focused intent. She was looking right in my direction.

"What—" I started to ask, but then she strode right past me. I swung around and my heart dropped when I saw where they were headed.

Saminsa.

Wytt reached out his metal-infused hand toward Saminsa's shoulder.

"No!" she shouted, a blue orb immediately bursting to life around her. Wytt pulled his hand away. He stumbled backwards, looking back and forth between his hand and the orb in confusion. I followed his gaze and my stomach lurched when I saw four of his fingers lying inside the orb. They'd been sliced right off. Blood dripped from Wytt's hanging hand.

"Stay back!" Saminsa yelled. Between the shock of everything that was happening, I realized in a moment of absurdity that this was the first time I'd ever heard the girl's voice.

General Taylor advanced forward. "You're surrounded! There's nowhere to go. Did you really think we wouldn't catch you sneaking into the security hub and trying to send a transmission to the Chancellor about our location? Adrien and the other techer boy detected it and stopped it before it could be sent." The General glanced at me, then back at Saminsa. "Very clever, though, piggybacking off the signal created when Zoel Links herself at night."

I felt a wave of guilt and anger. Not being able to control

my powers at night was an embarrassing weakness, but I'd never expected anyone to be able to exploit it.

"I knew this day would come," Saminsa said, her voice calm now, eyes glowing from the blue light of the orb surrounding her. "I knew for all your talk of helping every glitcher that it was never really true. You were never trying to help me."

"That's not true!" I said.

Rand nodded at City and widened his stance beside her, preparing to fight.

I glared at both of them. Saminsa was right. We never really tried to make her part of the team or helped her see the good we were doing. But maybe it wouldn't have made a difference if she'd been set on working for the Chancellor the entire time. If she actually managed to get a message out, all the people closest to me would be in danger. I was torn between sympathy and anger.

Saminsa didn't look at me, but only held her hand out in warning. The orb's circumference inched farther outward. She kept her eyes trained on Taylor.

"You will let me pass from this place in peace."

"So you can go report straight back to the Chancellor?" Taylor said coolly. "I don't think so."

"If you don't let me pass, I'll take down everyone in the building as I go. Starting with your pet mutant," she nodded in my direction without taking her eyes off Taylor.

Saminsa held up her other hand and the orb doubled in size. Everyone scooted back, and City barely made it out of the way in time. The pillow she'd been sitting on was disintegrated as the outward curve of the orb passed it.

City let out a growl of anger and unleashed lightning from her fingertips toward the orb. It hit with a crackle of static, but it made no impact.

"Stop it, City, that didn't work before and it's not going to now!" I yelled at her, then turned back to Taylor. "Can't we just let her go? That boy's power makes it so she won't be able to tell them where we are, right?"

"Don't be a fool. If she leaves, she can send a message from the nearest city and the Chancellor would know the vicinity of the Foundation."

A thunderclap seemed to go off in the room with us. The shock wave of the orb's release rocked me backward. I hit the ground hard on my back and the air was knocked out of my lungs. I gasped to get another breath and tried dizzily to sit up. Most of the others were on the ground too. Some were bleeding from where they'd been tossed into the walls by the wave.

And Saminsa was gone.

General Taylor got up a moment later. I blinked in confusion as she raised her com and spoke into it. "Jilia, activate!"

"Activate what?" I tried to ask, but it came out as a whisper since I was still gasping for breath. Another shock wave rocked the floor, but it was far enough away from us now that, other than shaking some ceiling tiles loose, we barely felt it. Taylor held on to the wall and dragged herself to her feet.

"Jilia, report!" she said into the com.

There was no response. I managed to pull myself to my feet. "Jilia, REPORT!"

Another moment of silence. Then finally, Jilia's voice sounded over Taylor's com. "I activated the system and it's done. She's down. Access corridor north."

I got to my feet and turned to head out the door to the north corridor, but Taylor grabbed my arm to hold me back.

"No glitchers. Just Xona and Cole. Come with me."

"But Wytt," Cole protested, pointing to the injured ex-Reg cradling his bleeding hand. "I have to help him."

"Rand and City can get him to the Med Center." She looked at me, then pointed up at the cracked ceiling tiles above us. "Zoel, you need to go get into your biosuit in case of leaks in the air-filtration system. Come with me, Cole; that's an order."

Cole nodded and snapped to attention, following Taylor and Xona out the door. I stared after them for a quick second, disquieted by Taylor's tone and the way Cole immediately obeyed. And what had they done to Saminsa? Jilia had said Saminsa was "down." Did that mean dead? I shuddered at the thought, then went to my room to put on my biosuit.

Xona and Ginni came in not long after I had finished putting on the helmet and sealing the suit shut. "That was fast," I looked up at Xona. "What happened to Saminsa? Is she . . ." I couldn't quite bring myself to ask.

Xona sat backward on one of the chairs at the desk. "When we got to the north corridor, Saminsa was already on the ground unconscious. There was some kind of gas that had been released from the vents."

"Did Taylor get you masks?" I asked in confusion.

"Nah, most of it had been suctioned up by the time we got there. And Taylor said whatever was left in the air was harmless to non-glitchers. That it just might make us feel tired for a couple hours."

I felt my mouth go dry. Taylor had developed something that could take down a glitcher but was harmless to others?

I'd known General Taylor didn't trust glitchers . . . but this? She'd set up security measures against us in our own home.

"So Saminsa's still alive?" I finally managed to ask.

Xona nodded. "Cole picked her up and carried her to the Med Center. Doc said she'd keep her sedated for the time being."

"And then what? They can't just keep her knocked out forever."

Xona shrugged.

All the next day, I couldn't stop thinking about the possibility that Taylor had developed some kind of chemical weapon against glitchers. As disturbing as it was that she'd set it up here in the Foundation to use against us whenever she saw fit, I couldn't ignore the fact that it meant we might finally have a chance against the Chancellor. I didn't understand why we hadn't already set up a mission. I could get close enough to administer it, then the rest of my team could follow me in as backup without fear of her compulsion.

Instead of going to lunch with everybody else, I headed toward Taylor's office to talk to her about it. I was still in the suit while they repaired a cracked pipe in the air-filtration system and didn't feel like eating through a straw anyway.

When I knocked on Taylor's door, though, there was no answer. I stood outside her office for a minute feeling frustrated, then went to the Med Center. Jilia was the one who had activated the gas that had taken Saminsa down—surely she knew something about it.

But I slowed to a stop outside the open Med Center door when I heard voices inside.

"Henk, you know what she's doing is wrong, but you're building it for her anyway." It was Jilia talking. I leaned in closer, though I was careful to stay clear of the entryway.

"I don't know anythin' of the sort." Henk's voice responded. "Revolution's the only way to bring it all down, so we all can start over. We finally got the tech to make it happen. The Kill Switch Op is our chance." His tone was hopeful, urgent. "Maybe even give you and me a chance to get a fresh start."

I heard Jilia's feet tapping the floor, like she was walking away. "But at what cost?"

"Do you wanna sit here and see another generation enslaved? You think all those drones ain't mostly dead already? Gettin' that adult V-chip is the same as a death sentence. They just make the corpses walk around a few more years so they can work till they drop."

There was a pause and some shuffling, then Henk lowered his voice. I could just barely make out his words.

"It's our best chance to end the war and save countless lives. Taylor's finally tracked down the missing component. She's out gettin' it right now. I'll finish the device up for her, then you and me can get out of here. You could keep doin' your research, you don't have to see one bit o' blood. We'll hide out somewhere till it's all settled."

"I'm a doctor, Henk. If Taylor goes through with this, they'll need me more than ever."

"Tell me you'll at least think about it." Henk's voice was low and insistent.

I didn't hear Jilia's response. I backed away as Henk's footsteps came toward the doorway, wincing at the squeak my shoe made on the tile. When he reached the door, I reversed my direction, hoping it looked like I'd just arrived.

"Hi Henk," I said, trying to smile and do my best to pretend everything was fine.

"Hey," he said back as he brushed past me.

I stepped into the Med Center, but suddenly didn't know what to say after the conversation I'd overheard. Taylor was obviously planning something big, but if it was about taking down the Chancellor, why hadn't she briefed my team on it?

"Is there something you need, Zoe?" Jilia's hair was falling out of her bun and she looked disheveled.

"Is she okay?" I walked over to where Saminsa lay on one of the beds. Her face was unusually pale, her lips almost white.

"She's sedated."

"What did Taylor use on her? Xona said there was a gas of some kind?"

Jilia's messy hair flopped into her face, and she tucked some behind her ear. "We closed off the hallway leading to the elevator and gassed it. It's a mix of heavy antipsychotics and sedative."

"Antipsychotics?"

She stopped and rubbed her forehead, clearly uncomfortable. "We've been trying to develop a serum to neutralize glitcher abilities. It was one of Taylor's requirements in setting up the Foundation."

I'd known it must be something like this, but hearing it stated out loud made the air whoosh out of my lungs. "Neutralize abilities? You mean take away our Gifts?"

"No, no," Jilia said. "Not you guys! Only the enemy. Just for tactical . . ." Her voice trailed off.

"But you had it installed here. To use against us." I turned back to look at Saminsa. "Is her power totally gone?"

Jilia's shoulders sagged and she sat down on her lab chair. "It's not permanent. The antipsychotic numbs the norepinephrine transmitters and seems to disrupt whatever it is that makes Gifts possible. We don't even know how it works, just that the serum did work in sample patients."

"Sample patients? You experimented on glitchers?" I didn't even try to hide the accusation in my voice.

"You don't understand. We needed another way to try and combat the Chancellor's compulsion. Or at least to defend against her glitcher army without shedding blood. Just think, Zoe, without it, we might have had to kill Saminsa. Sometimes you have to go along with things you aren't comfortable with." She glanced at the door Henk had left through. "But if the end goal is important enough, the good outweighs the bad."

I stared at her, frowning reluctantly. It was what I wanted, wasn't it? A way to neutralize the Chancellor's compulsion powers? It was why I'd come looking for the General in the first place.

"If you've had this serum or gas or whatever, then why haven't we put together a mission against the Chancellor already?"

Jilia looked away. "Taylor's been busy pursuing another mission first."

"What mission?" I asked.

"I can't tell you."

Surely it had to be the one Henk was just discussing with her, but she obviously wasn't going to share. "Well, why didn't someone at least tell us about the serum you guys were developing? Even if you didn't want to tell everyone, you could have told our task force. We're all fighting on the same side here."

Jilia didn't say anything, she just looked at the ground.

My chest tightened. Jilia didn't have to say it. Taylor didn't think of us as on the same side. That was the crux of the whole issue. As much as she was willing to use glitchers to further her goals, she still considered us an enemy.

"She wants to find a way to make it permanent, doesn't she?" I looked up at Jilia. I didn't wait for her answer. "How can you help her with this? You're one of us!"

"I didn't want to at first," Jilia said earnestly. "I didn't want any part of it. But it was the only nonviolent solution on the table. And we would never use it on you, only the enemy." She shook her head. "You don't know how bad it's gotten out there. Everyone's scared and desperate. We're all afraid of what's coming."

Her words suddenly triggered a memory of watching Adrien, dripping wet at the sink. Staring with shadowed eyes into the mirror talking about how he'd told Taylor something he shouldn't have. Some vision that had changed her. Made her desperate.

Jilia's wrist com vibrated and she looked down at it. She turned back to me with a falsely cheerful smile. "They've finished repairs and all air systems checked out fine. It's safe for you to take off the suit. If you hurry, you can make it in time for lunch."

I didn't say anything but my mind was racing. It wasn't only about the General and her serum. Henk had spoken of blood and revolution. If Taylor was desperate, just how far was she willing to go?

I didn't know, but I was going to find out.

Chapter 23

I MESSAGED XONA AND GINNI to meet me later in the equipment room. They were the only two I trusted completely. Part of me longed to message Adrien, but I couldn't be sure where he stood in all this. If he'd seen something about the General in the future, he wouldn't tell us. And maybe it was petty, but I still couldn't forget what had happened the other night. I needed to be able to focus right now, and I couldn't do that with him around. Besides, the fewer in on this, the better chance we had of pulling it off.

"What's up?" Xona asked when she walked in. "Why not just talk in our room?"

"Because someone might overhear or come in. I didn't want to take any risks."

"What risks?" Xona asked. She put a hand to her waist, touching her weapon holster. Her eyes darted around anxiously. "Is it those ex-Reg bastards? Are they spying on us?"

"No, nothing like that." I took a deep breath. "I want to break into Taylor's office, and I need your help."

"What?" Ginni's eyes flew open wide. "We can't do that!"

But Xona looked as if I'd finally said something worth her time. "What are we looking for?"

"I overheard Jilia and Henk talking about an operation called Kill Switch. He's building her some kind of device." I looked at Ginni. "Have you heard anything about it?"

She shook her head.

I paced in the small space. "Look, Taylor's the leader of the Rez. But what if she's making the wrong decisions? I just learned today she and Jilia have been doing experiments on glitchers to take away their powers."

"What?" Ginni sounded shocked. "They wouldn't!"

Xona didn't seem as outraged. "It could be pretty handy against the Chancellor and her minions," she pointed out.

I nodded. "Exactly. That's how they justified it. And I don't know," I threw my hands in the air, "maybe it's the right thing to do. But they've done it all in secret. We're supposed to be on the same side, but she had the weaponized gas installed here at the Foundation to use against us.

"Taylor talked to me about sacrifice once, about being willing to give up the people you loved most for the greater good. Which might be a nice ideal, except I'm not sure she's going to give us a choice in the matter." I stopped pacing and looked at them. "We need to know what she's up to."

"What does Adrien say?" Ginni bit her lip nervously. "He'd know if she were planning something bad. He'd have a vision of it, right?"

"I think maybe he already has." I looked down. "But he won't tell me, and I'm not sure he'd help us with this. We need to get into that office. I'd do it by myself, but if I just rip off the door to get past the locks, it would set off alarms."

"Which is why you need me," Xona smiled and cracked her knuckles. "I may not be a computer whiz like Adrien or that other security kid, but I've been sneaking into places my whole life. I just have to steal the daily encryption key for the compound's locks."

"You won't be doing anything of the kind," said a deep voice from the doorway.

We all froze.

Tyryn walked into the light, striding quickly to where we were gathered in the corner. He held up a sonic listening device. He'd obviously heard our entire conversation.

Ginni stared at him open-mouthed.

"You gonna rat us out, Ty?" Xona narrowed her eyes.

Tyryn held up a hand. "Xona, I know better than to try to keep you out of trouble. I didn't come here to stop you. Something big is going on, but they won't tell us anything. And the way Taylor takes risks lately . . ." He shook his head. "I'm here to help."

"Can you get us the encryption key?" Xona asked.

Tyryn smiled and held up a small drive. "What, you mean this?"

Ginni pinpointed the General's location, confirming she was away at another Rez site. Tyryn agreed to go down to the military level and keep a lookout. If we triggered any alarms, the soldiers there would be the first to know. Ginni stayed behind too, but promised to watch with her power and com us if anyone was approaching.

We waited until everyone was asleep, then Xona and I crept over to Taylor's office. Xona waved the newly encrypted key card in front of the reader at the door. The metallic sound of the sliding door opening echoed down the empty hallway. I cringed, but Xona was calm. She made a sharp forward motion with her hand. I followed her inside.

I was nervous. We couldn't afford to make a mistake here. At least Xona was completely cool, a total professional at this. She closed the door behind us.

The lights clicked on, and I gasped.

"It's just the motion sensor," Xona whispered, then allowed a smile. "Don't be so tight, girl."

She went around Taylor's desk and began rifling through the papers tacked to the board all around the imaging panel.

"Bet if she knew we were in here she'd rethink her paper obsession," she said.

I nodded. "Ginni says it's because Taylor thinks paper is safest. There's no way it can be hacked digitally, and the Foundation is their most secure location. Secure to outsiders at least."

Xona pulled on one of the drawers in the desk.

"Locked." She raised an eyebrow at me. "When there's a lock, you know the good stuff's hidden inside."

I went over to the closet on the left side of the wall. It had an old manual slide door, and I opened it easily. "Well then I guess this is a very good thing."

Xona popped her head up from behind the desk and let out a low whistle. "A safe!" She hurried over to me. "The General sure likes her Old World stuff, huh?"

I crouched down to get a better look at the wide three-by-three-foot box that took up the entire floor of the small closet. I closed my eyes and raised my telek. It took a little longer than normal for the buzzing to sound in my ears because I was so anxious, but it finally came. I cast around the box.

"How do we open it?" I asked.

Xona pointed at a circle turnstile on the front and frowned. "It's an antique. No one bothers learning how to open these things anymore. We should have brought Rand. He could have melted through it."

"Yeah, along with whatever's inside," I said sarcastically. I finished my sweep of the surface with my telek. "If it's an antique, what is this wire on the back for?"

I could feel that it lead from inside the box straight into the wall.

Xona swore. She stood and felt quickly up and down the door frame of the closet. Her hand stopped about midway in the frame. "I should have known."

"What? Should have known what?"

"That opening the closet door would trip an alarm."

I pulled back as if stung.

Xona was still crouched down, whispering furiously. "Of course. She mixes in the Old World stuff to trip you up so you don't expect the tech."

The buzzing in my head eclipsed Xona's voice. Taylor was going to know someone had broken into her office. We couldn't change that. But we could still make sure it was worth it.

I projected my telek inside the box and felt the outline of a stack of thin sheets. More paper. And then I saw a vial of liquid perched above the papers and sensed vibration like a ticking noise.

Then the ticking stopped. It must have been counting down. I felt the first crack in the vial before I could react.

"No!" I clapped both hands to the sides of the safe to anchor myself inside. I surrounded the shattering vial with my telek just as the first drop of liquid beaded through.

At first I was afraid it would be like the fire and I wouldn't be able to hold on to it. But the liquid had enough surface area that I was able to catch it all with my invisible lasso, holding it in the shape of the splintered vial.

"Get back," I said through gritted teeth. Obviously we weren't getting out of here without Taylor knowing, so there was no reason to try to be smooth anymore. Xona moved out of the way. I let the buzzing build in my ears and then ripped the door off the safe. I was still careful not to let go of the liquid or let a drop spill. Now that the door was off, I could see what it was. Acid. If I'd been touching the liquid with anything other than my mind, I'd have been badly burned.

"Take the papers out," I instructed Xona, my heart thumping in my chest now.

She reached in carefully and retrieved them.

I raised the door gently off the floor where it had landed. Xona's eyes were wide as it floated past her and fitted it back onto the hinge as best I could. I forgot how much my glitcher power unnerved her sometimes.

Xona handed the papers to me. "Let's go."

I flipped through the top few pages. There were charts and schematics, none of which I immediately recognized. Xona headed for the door when I noticed my blinking arm panel. "Wait," I said. "Ginni's messaging—"

But Xona had already opened the door. Three ex-Regs stood in our path, tranq guns pointed toward us.

Chapter 24

XONA TENSED AND REACHED for the ten-inch blade holstered at her waist. I felt rather than saw the ex-Reg closest to her twitch his finger closer to the trigger. This was about to get bad quickly.

I looked at the ex-Reg in the middle. Cole, the boy who painted in color and wanted to feel human. "You don't have to do this."

He didn't say anything.

"You know I can rip these guns apart with my telek before you ever get a shot off." My voice was low and dangerous.

"We have orders to apprehend anyone who sets off this alarm," Cole said.

"Cole, you know us," I said. "We're part of the same team. You know we would never work for the Chancellor. Don't you want to see what we found?" I raised the pages in my hand. I may not have known what the plans were for, but I knew they were important.

I could see the conflict on his face. Taylor was at the top of his command structure now. If there was one thing that was ingrained in Regs since childhood, it was to obey orders. But I was the one who'd freed them. He trusted me, I could feel it. And there was something about the way Cole's eyes kept flicking over to Xona. Where did his loyalties lie now?

"We don't need to know," said Eli in a monotone. "We have our orders."

Unlike Cole, I knew there was no reasoning with Eli. His finger twitched on the trigger and I yanked the gun out of his hands with my telek before he could fire. He'd been gripping it so tightly, his whole body was jerked forward.

Xona attacked the third ex-Reg right in front of her the same moment. She kicked his gun upward so the tranq dart lodged into the ceiling. Her victory was short-lived, however, because the next second he had her by the throat up against the wall.

"Stop!" Cole and I said at the same time.

Xona struggled violently against the ex-Reg's grip. She was strong, but her eyes betrayed a terror I remembered well. She was thinking of her mother again. Her knife clattered to the ground and her blows landed harmlessly on the hard metal plating of his chest. He held her throat so tight she couldn't scream.

"Let her go." I worked hard to keep my voice calm. I stared at the ex-Reg's hand holding Xona's throat. There was a line where the fingers had been fused back together. "Wytt," I said, "Please let her go."

Xona turned her head sideways to free her windpipe. "Just rip his arm off already," she growled hoarsely.

I turned back to Cole and laid a hand gently on his forearm. "Please."

A long moment stretched. Cole swallowed hard and then his body relaxed. He dropped the gun to his side.

"Release her," he said.

"But there are orders—"

"Do it!" Cole's voice was commanding and Wytt finally obeyed. I grabbed Xona's arm the second she was released to keep her from grabbing the knife from the floor and attacking Wytt. I could see her fury boiling. She managed to restrain herself, if only barely.

Some of the papers I'd been holding had dropped to the ground and gotten shuffled. I picked them up hurriedly, but I froze when my eyes stopped on a diagram of a shape I recognized.

I gasped as I pulled the sheet closer. "You all need to see this. But we've got to get out of this hallway." I looked around us. "No telling what else Taylor has set up in case of a security breach."

Xona pinned Wytt to the wall with her piercing glare, but she spoke to me. "Fine, but if he tries anything, I'll blowtorch him in his sleep."

Judging by the look on everyone's face, it was clear no one doubted her.

Tyryn and Ginni met us in our dorm room. Ginni didn't wait for us to speak.

"I've been monitoring Taylor. She's on her way back to the Foundation." She brightened when she saw the ex-Regs come in behind us. "Oh, hi Wytt, hi Cole, hi Eli." None of them responded.

"What'd you find?" Tyryn asked.

I hurried past them and laid out the schematics on the table. Cole and Xona pressed in, almost bumping heads. Xona pulled back distastefully, and Cole stared at her for a moment before looking back down at the spread-out papers.

Ginni, who'd been peering over Xona's shoulder, straightened after a moment. The confusion was clear on her face. "Is that a—"

"Nuclear weapon." Cole's eyes widened.

"That's what I was afraid of," I said quietly. The diagram showed a large missile; I'd just been hoping it wasn't nuclear.

"But surely Taylor's not that stupid," Xona scoffed, looking up. "She wouldn't risk starting another D-day."

"Maybe she would if she were desperate," I said.

Tyryn pointed to the top diagram. "It's clearly a nuke, and it's a big one."

"Where would she even get nuclear material from?" Xona asked. "It's the most carefully regulated and guarded substance on the globe after D-day."

My eyes widened as I made the connection. "Like something the Underchancellor of Defense would have access to. What if this is what General Taylor was after in the raid?" My mind spun. Henk had told Jilia that Taylor had tracked down the missing component. And that he was building the rest of the device for her. Henk, who was the Rez's weapons specialist. All the pieces clicked into place. I put a hand over my stomach. I was going to be sick.

"What would be her target anyway?" Tyryn asked, his eyebrows furrowed. "It's not like Comm Corp is a snake you can kill just by cutting the head off. Uppers are spread out in cities all over the Sector."

"And in other Sectors across the globe," Ginni said.

"Maybe she doesn't care about killing the snake." I thought

about Adrien and his visions. "She wants to do something big, to make a difference. Maybe she simply wants to do the most damage she can."

"Here's the trajectory path," Cole said. He picked up one paper on the end and put it in the middle. The page was filled with numbers and readouts that were gibberish to me.

"You understand it?" I asked Cole.

He nodded.

"What's the target, then?" Xona asked.

"That's what's strange." He frowned. "These altitudes. It looks like they're planning to launch it up out of the atmosphere, but without it ever coming down."

"What's the point in that?" I asked.

Cole stared, his eyes widening in understanding. "It's an EMP."

"A what?" Ginni asked.

"Electromagnetic pulse," Cole said. "It's a burst of magnetic energy that disrupts electrical fields. You make one by detonating a nuclear weapon outside the earth's atmosphere." He pointed at the page with all the numbers. "And this one, set to detonate three hundred miles up, could burn out every electronic circuit over the entire continent. The radiation wouldn't affect humans physically, but all the energy grids would fail. All of Sector Six would go dark."

"But what's the point?" Ginni asked, cocking her head to the side.

"The EMP *is* the point," Xona cut in. "Don't you get it?" We all looked at her. "Zoe, you said they were calling the operation Kill Switch. Think about it. Fry all the electronic circuits, and you fry all the V-chips."

My mouth dropped open. Ginni's head swung back and forth as she looked around the room at our stunned faces.

"What is it? What am I missing?" she asked. "Isn't that a good thing? All the drones will finally be free of their hardware. They'll be able to think and live and feel like us. Isn't that what we want?"

"Not the adults," I said. "Everyone older than eighteen relies on the adult V-chip to regulate their limbic functions. It controls them completely. Without it, they'll all die."

Ginni gasped.

Cole shook his head in disgust. "It would be mass murder."

"So all the teenagers and kids are freed from the Link, and the adults are made catatonic or killed," Xona said. "But that doesn't make them free from the Community. What are they supposed to do?"

I remembered the rest of what I'd overheard. "Start a revolution against the Uppers who've been controlling them this whole time. Drones outnumber Uppers fifty to one. If there were some way to organize everyone quickly, they could fight back and defeat the Uppers. They could help us finally win the war."

Tyryn ran a hand over his head. "It's not a bad plan."

"It's not worth the cost," Cole spoke up angrily. I looked over at him. I'd never seen so much emotion displayed on his features.

Tyryn's lips tightened. "The Rez is getting stamped out. Children and whole families are being murdered. So many have already died." His eyes flicked over to Xona and then back down. "In a way, the adult drones are lost already to the V-chip. There's no way for them to ever be normal again."

Henk had said the same thing when he was talking to Jilia. If the adult V-chip was like a death sentence, was it still murder to shorten the adult drones' lives by a few years? I shuddered. I couldn't even consider the question.

"So that means their lives aren't worth anything?" Cole asked, his voice spiking half an octave.

Tyryn's eyes flashed. "I'm not saying that. I'm just saying if this plan works, we would save the next generation and all of the generations after. Every war has casualties, but this could end the war forever."

Xona hesitated, then reached out and put her hand on her brother's arm. "We can't do this. Remember what Mom always said? No matter how hard things get, there are lines we can't ever cross without becoming just like them."

There was a long beat of silence.

Finally Tyryn met her gaze and nodded. "But what else can we do?"

"What if we came up with another viable plan?" I asked. "Taylor's been taking a hardware approach. But what if we came at it from another angle? Maybe there's a way to hack the Link programming itself somehow."

"I'm sure they've already tried it," Tyryn said.

"Maybe," I said. "But with our powers, we can get to places the Rez couldn't before. Taylor hasn't even been taking us into account. She doesn't like us. Doesn't trust us."

I looked at Ginni. "How much time do we have before she gets back?"

Ginni closed her eyes a moment. "She's half an hour away, but she's moving fast."

"Okay," I said. "I'll go get Adrien. We could use his techer expertise on how the Link code works." As much as I was still uncomfortable around him, it was time to bring him in.

Ending the V-chip was everything both of us had hoped for. I knew he'd help.

"But what are we gonna do when Taylor gets here?" Ginni asked, her voice high.

"Try to convince her that we're on her side but that we can't let her use the EMP. Not when we know it will kill millions of innocent people," Cole said. I nodded.

"I'm not sure she'll be receptive," Tyryn said.

I had a feeling that was an understatement.

"Then we'll improvise," Xona said, her hand resting on the weapon holstered around her hip. Cole grinned at her.

I walked away, my heart racing. I didn't know what the General would do, or if there was any way we could get her to listen to us. But we had to try.

I softened the sound of my footsteps as I approached Adrien's dorm. I winced at the slight grating noise the door made as it opened. But no one seemed to have woken from it. The room was totally dark. I touched my arm panel and it lit up in response, giving enough light for me to creep toward the beds without stumbling on anything.

I held my breath and climbed up the short ladder to reach Adrien's box, alert to any sign of the other boys waking up. No one stirred as I pulled back the curtain on his bed.

I couldn't see much in the dim light. Adrien's blanket was pulled up to his chin and his arm was slung over his face. I reached for his shoulder and he shifted in his sleep, dropping his arm.

I gasped in shock.

Because it wasn't Adrien sleeping in the bed.

It was Max.

Chapter 25

I FELL BACKWARD in my surprise, tumbling off the lip of the box and falling hard on my tailbone. I barely looked up in time to see a dark shadow jumping deftly down from the bed.

"How are you here?" The breath was knocked out of me from my fall and the question came out as a whisper. Max was alive!

But then my eyes widened with the ramifications of what Max being here in Adrien's bed meant. How long had he been impersonating Adrien?

Max's bulky frame towered in front of me, his shock of blond hair catching the light from my forearm panel before it turned off again.

"What have you done?" I shrieked, my voice finally back. "Where's Adrien?"

I heard Rand swing his curtain open. "What's going on?" He sounded still half asleep and couldn't see us in the dark.

Max swept to the side and twirled behind me. One of his thick arms slipped around my neck, choking me so I couldn't call for help. Any question of Max's intentions were answered. After all the excuses I'd made for him, here he was attacking me after impersonating Adrien for who knew how long. The buzzing exploded in my head. I used my telek to send a shoe across the room, hitting the alarm button. A siren began wailing and the lights turned on bright overhead. Just in time for me to see Max reaching for a knife at his ankle and swinging it toward me.

I ripped the blade out of his hand with my telek and flung it to the ground.

Rand and Juan jumped down from their beds, ready to attack. I lifted a hand, trying to warn them to stay back. I knew everyone in the compound would be here any second, and we needed Max alive and conscious to find out what he'd done with Adrien. My buzzing power swarmed around him, but I was sure I would kill him in my panicked rage if I used it. He squeezed tighter, cutting off my air supply, and pulled me backward toward the exit. The pressure squeezed tears out of my eyes.

I turned my head sideways in his grip like Tyryn had taught us in training and then with my free arm reared back and elbowed Max hard in the stomach.

With a surprised gasp of pain, he lessened his grip, and I used the moment to drop to the ground and wriggle out of his grasp. Rand was on Max the next second, catching him and pinning both of his arms behind his back.

"Who are you? What are you doing here?" Rand growled as the door opened. Sophia ran into the room, with Tyryn and Professor Henry right behind. Tyryn started typing on his arm com and firing off commands.

"Where's Adrien?" Sophia asked, swirling one way and then the other as she searched the faces in the room.

252

All I could do was stare at Max. He blinked hard, like he was just waking up. Everyone was talking at once. Max looked down at the knife on the ground, then back at me.

"I didn't mean to attack you, Zo, I swear! Chancellor Bright must have implanted some kind of sleeper compulsion to kill you if my cover was blown. I would never hurt you, you have to believe me!"

It felt like I was watching the scene through a marbled pane of glass, separate from it. None of this made any sense.

Sophia screamed, knocking Max out of Rand's grasp and kicking him hard in the gut when he hit the ground. "Where is my son?"

Max didn't say anything and she kicked him hard again.

"Stop it, Sophia!" I crouched down beside him. Even though it repulsed me, I put my hand on Max's face. "If you ever had any love for me, just tell me where Adrien is."

Max looked up at me, his eyes unsure. "I don't know, Zoe, I swear. The Chancellor took him."

My legs threatened to give out from under me. "How long? How long ago did she take him? How long have you been here pretending to be him?"

Max looked down, avoiding my eyes. "Since your raid on our facility."

I stepped backward. No. It couldn't be true. He'd been imitating Adrien for a month and a half? I would have noticed. How could I not have noticed?

The buzzing became a screech in my head and I lost control for a moment. The table and chairs flew against the wall with a loud clatter, startling everyone. I backed up a few steps. None of this was real. It couldn't be.

A sudden explosion of pain across my cheek startled me back into my body. Adrien's mom had slapped me. I blinked and looked at her as she raised her arm to strike me again. Tyryn grabbed her, trapping her arms against her chest to hold her back.

"I knew you'd get him hurt!" she shrieked, fighting to get free from Tyryn. "I tried to keep him away from all this. But he wouldn't listen, because of you!"

Everyone's attention was turned toward us. Out of the corner of my eye, I saw Max disappear. Literally *disappear*.

One moment his body had been clearly there on the ground, and the next there was only air. I gasped and lurched forward to the space where he'd just been.

Tyryn turned to his com again. "Lockdown! Full facility lockdown," he said. It lit up everyone's forearm panels and came over the loudspeaker. "Intruder alert. I repeat, intruder alert. Everyone rendezvous at the training center and await further instructions."

Tyryn ran out the door, Rand and Juan on his heels. I raced after them.

"Max can make himself look like anyone, so don't get separated," I shouted. "And he can somehow make himself invisible now too. Make sure to com me if you bump into something that shouldn't be there." It felt ludicrous even as I said it. I wouldn't have believed it if I hadn't seen it with my own eyes. Jilia had said that most glitcher powers expanded as we grew into them. In a way it made sense. His power manipulated the minds of the people around him. Instead of making you see another person when you looked at him, now he could make you see nothing at all.

We turned a corner and saw City, Xona, and Ginni sprinting toward us.

"Stop right there!" Tyryn yelled to the approaching girls. "Don't move!"

Xona stopped immediately, grabbing the elbows of the girls on either side of her. "What is it?" Xona asked from about fifteen paces away.

"It's Max," I said hurriedly. "He's infiltrated the Foundation. He could be impersonating anyone."

"Have you been out of one another's presence for even a moment?" Tyryn asked, eyeing each of them intensely.

Ginni and Xona exchanged a look, then stepped back from City.

"What?" City asked in an affronted voice. "You think I'm him?"

"We just met you in the hall." Xona's voice was cold. "You were alone."

"We don't have time. Show us your power!" I yelled over the both of them.

City turned back to my group and huffed. She raised her middle finger, electricity exploding from the single fingertip in a spiral up to the ceiling.

"It's not her," I shouted, sprinting forward again, passing them and heading toward the central exits. My mind raced. The compound might be in lockdown, but if Max had been here for a month and a half already, he could have found a way to subvert the security system.

Then I frowned. I was sure I knew something about the security at the Foundation. The more I thought about it, though, the less I could remember. It was like the thought teased at the edges of my mind, but whenever I tried to look at it directly, it was gone. But obviously Max must have encountered some problem too, or else the Chancellor would have already come for us.

My mind flashed to every time Max had held my hand or kissed me since the raid, pretending to be Adrien. I felt sick to my stomach. I forced my legs to keep moving forward. As I turned into the foyer leading to the elevator, I saw General Taylor standing right inside the barrier security door. Her hair was still wet from the wash-down chambers.

"Don't move!" I shouted.

Taylor swirled around to me, surprise on her face. "What's going on?"

She took a step toward me, but I held up a hand. "Stay back."

Footsteps filled the space behind me as Tyryn, the Professor, and a group of Rez fighters came in.

"Stop," I said over my shoulder. "It could be Max."

"What's going on here?" the General asked. "I came back as soon as the remote alarm for my office was triggered and now the compound's on lockdown? I barely made it inside myself before the security door shut." She glared expectantly at all our uncertain faces. "Well?"

"Max would have to come this way to escape," I said, eyeing Taylor. "Which is conveniently right when she shows up. The security door could have trapped him inside before he could leave."

Taylor's face became rigid. "Max. You mean Maximin? The shape-shifter who works for the Chancellor? He is the security breach?"

The Professor stepped forward again. I put a hand on his sleeve to stop him, but he pulled away. "Ask her something only the real General would know," I said. "And Tyryn, restrain her while he does it."

"How quick you are to fulfill your destiny," Taylor said with a bitter smile at me. "I leave for a day and suddenly you're the one barking orders?"

My face reddened.

Tyryn pulled Taylor's arms behind her back while the Professor leaned in to ask his question. He spoke quietly in her ear, so we couldn't hear.

She pursed her lips. "Top of my left thigh," she said, not bothering to whisper. "Now let me go!" She pulled against Tyryn.

The Professor nodded.

As soon as Tyryn let her go, she straightened her tunic. "Now report about Maximin."

"He infiltrated six weeks ago," Tyryn said. "So far we haven't yet ascertained if he has been able to communicate with the Chancellor."

"We've got to get this door open." I pounded the door in frustration. He could be long gone already. "His powers changed. He can make himself invisible now. He could have gotten through the security door before it closed and run right past you without being seen."

The General turned to Tyryn. "The whole Foundation could be compromised. Get our best techers to the security hub. Maximin will have covered his tracks, but see if there's any trace of his outgoing communications. Anything. And get someone up here to open this door!"

Tyryn nodded, turning back to his com to relay the order. Taylor turned to me.

"Didn't you report seeing Maximin during the raid?" Taylor asked. "You said he was tied up when you left him behind!"

Her words stopped me short. "His powers are way more extensive than I ever knew. I don't know if he was keeping it from me or if they hadn't developed yet last year." My mind raced, working it out. "His power affects the minds of the people around him. If he can make himself disappear completely, then he can probably project his face onto other people's. That boy I saw could have been anyone."

I breathed out and closed my eyes. I kept seeing the building collapse after we escaped. Where had Adrien been when it fell? Did he survive? Max said the Chancellor wanted Adrien's power. She was the one who'd rigged the building to explode. That had to mean she would have protected him somehow. Max would have the answers.

I turned back to the door and tried to project my telek beyond it to see if I could feel the shape of Max's body, but my mind was too chaotic. I barely made it halfway up the elevator shaft before it cut out again. I took a deep breath. I had to get to the centered, calm place where I could access my power steadily.

A boy with round cheeks and unkempt dark hair ran in. He seemed somehow familiar, but I couldn't remember his name. He inserted a drive into the wall near the door projection panel. The heavy door slowly began moving in its tracks just as I got hold of my telek again.

"Stop!" I suddenly screamed and ran forward. The boy jumped, pulling out the drive so that the door closed again.

"What is it?" the boy asked nervously.

I closed my eyes, centering myself and managing to calmly call my telek. Something didn't feel right, but I couldn't pinpoint what.

"There are only ten of us in this room," I finally said, blinking hard and trying to sift through my confused overlapping senses, between what I saw and what I felt.

"And?" Tyryn asked, shifting so his hand was on his weapon.

"I feel eleven bodies."

Chapter 26

"WHERE?" TAYLOR ASKED. Everyone swung around to look at the people around them.

I closed my eyes, trying to feel out the shape I'd sensed a moment ago. But there was too much movement in the room. I couldn't track down which one was Max.

"Everyone stop moving!" I shouted in frustration.

They stilled, but then I was thrown by the entire lack of movement. Where did he go?

I opened my eyes and tried to match up the objects I sensed with the things I saw. I gasped. "There!" I pointed. "Hunched by the door!"

He bolted toward the hallway at the sound of my voice.

I ran after him. I sent my telek ahead and locked on to him as he sprinted down the hallway. It was easy now that there was no one else around. I expanded outward as we ran, keeping the projection of the whole corridor in my head. My fury focused my telek. I was single-minded. When Max ducked into the training center, I easily followed him.

I knew what he was doing—trying to get lost among the shapes of all the other people—but I wouldn't let him. Jilia and City looked up in surprise as I ran past, but my focus was

261

only on Max. He was still invisible to everyone else, but I'd locked my telek around him. I knew when he looked over his shoulder. I could feel the adrenaline pulsing off him. I could probably use my power to stop him mid-step, but I didn't dare do anything that might split my focus.

He made it out of the training center right as I got close. The door dropped shut behind him, and I slammed into it with my full body, unable to stop in time. The pain disrupted my telek for a second. I impatiently clicked the door open, the whole time feeling beyond it. I locked on to him again as he slipped through the next door into the equipment room. He was probably counting on me continuing to chase down the hallway, not realizing he'd stopped to hide. He'd either underestimated me or was too desperate to think straight. All he'd really done was trap himself.

I opened the equipment room door, then tore it off the tracks and lodged it mangled sideways into the door frame so it wouldn't open again. Max wasn't going anywhere.

"What have you done?" I screamed, barely conscious of the wild rage in my voice.

Only silence greeted me, but I could feel his form huddled in the far corner. I lifted my arms and shook the shelves around him with my telek.

He flattened down on the ground.

I lifted one arm, teleking a net around him and then hefting him upward by his neck. I heard a gasp of pain and walked closer, my arm still raised.

He flickered in and out of invisibility, probably from the shock of pain, and I could once again see his face. His hands were at his throat, trying to pry the invisible grip of my power off him. I threw him against the wall hard and pinned him there. I tightened my fingers, cinching his throat closed and lifting him higher off the ground.

"No more games. No more manipulation. Just the truth." My voice was ice. "What has she done with him?"

I dropped him to the ground so he could answer. He doubled over gasping for breath. "I don't know," he said, his voice raw. "I only know she always planned to keep him alive. She needed his visions. I was just supposed to switch places with him, drop him in the bomb-safe bunker, and then get on the transport with any survivors so I could infiltrate the Rez." His eyebrows furrowed. "Look, Zoe, you gotta believe me. I'll tell you everything now, I swear."

I scoffed. "Believe you? You're the Chancellor's spy. You helped her try to kill me during the raid!"

He bobbed his head and looked down. "I asked the Chancellor to use her compulsion to make me stop loving you. And she tried. For a while it worked. I hated you. But then," he looked back up at me, "when I saw you again at the raid and the Chancellor wasn't around to compel me, I just couldn't do it. I couldn't let you die. I cut the fuse that led to the explosives in the second half of the building. I'm trying to tell you I've changed." His voice was pleading. "Coming back here with you, getting away from the Chancellor's compulsion, I feel different. I see now that I was wrong—"

"Liar. You're only saying that now because you've been caught!" I yelled. "Did you manage to get any messages to the Chancellor?"

Max paused, breathing heavily like he was trying to get his emotions in check. "I tried. I planned to use my own Link signal to contact the Chancellor until I found out that part of the security system here jams all wireless signals. I started looking for other ways to rig the system, but there's a glitcher boy who's always in the security hub. Any headway I'd make in my plans to get a message out, I'd forget the next day because of him. I started writing everything down."

Max rubbed his throat and took a deep swallow. "But I was never a very good techer and Simin had insane redundancies for monitoring outgoing packet streams. I couldn't find a way to get past them, especially while he was there and always watching."

"What about the secret security project you were working on?" I asked, trying to reign in my anger and keep my voice as calm and reasonable as possible.

"There never was any project. I just made that up as an excuse for why I was busy all the time. I couldn't handle being around you at first. I was still so angry."

"And the kitchen fire," I said, clenching my hands into fists. "That was you, wasn't it? Not Saminsa."

He nodded. "A diversion. I tried to get a message out while everyone was distracted. But Simin had the system locked down while we were at lunch. He trusted me enough by that point to share the security codes, but like most things he told me, I forgot them before I had a chance to write them down. Then I learned that you were able to Link yourself at night when you sleep. I knew it had to mean they'd opened up a wireless channel just for your Link frequency. I came up with the idea of piggybacking off your signal. There was a transmitter hidden in the necklace I gave you that copied the frequency."

A rush of hatred choked me in spite of my determination

to stay calm. He'd used me. Used my weaknesses and my trust. And then let it all fall on Saminsa. I ripped the necklace off and flung it to the floor.

"And then you dared to pretend to be him. All this time. You let me kiss you. That date—" I shuddered even thinking about it and rubbed my lips harshly, as if I could scrub away all traces of him. I felt like mud had been wiped over every inch of my skin he'd touched. I squeezed my eyes closed. To think that I'd mourned him when I thought he'd died. Everyone else could see what I'd let myself be blind to—there had never been any redeeming qualities in the monster in front of me.

"But I couldn't bring myself to send the message, Zoe. I took the data from the necklace and was about to send the Chancellor a message. But then I couldn't. I couldn't do it, don't you get it? I still love you." He leaned toward me. I held up a hand, wrapping my power around him like a straight jacket to keep him away from me.

"Why did you blame it on Saminsa then?"

Max sighed, looking defeated. "Simin came in and saw the code ready on the screen, so I had to blame it on someone."

I gritted my teeth, trying to hold in all the pain. I tried to get to the peaceful place, tried to touch the shining calm like I was able to do in meditation practice. But all I could feel was rage.

"Is that all?"

He nodded. "I swear, Zoe, that's all."

I grabbed him roughly by the arm and dragged him up off the floor. "If you try to get away again, I'll kill you."

Max's eyes widened. He looked at me like he didn't know

me, and it was true—he didn't. I realized in that moment I was capable of much worse, and that if something happened to Adrien, I might even enjoy it.

He nodded slowly.

"Good." I forced him ahead of me with my grip like a steel band around his arm. The telek sang in my mind, a harsh screaming harmonic. I spoke into my arm com, trying to keep my voice as steady as possible. "I've got him. Meet me in the Caf." I pushed the mangled equipment room door out of the way and steered Max out into the hallway.

Hurried footsteps pounded down the hallway toward us. I looked up just as a shrill voice called. "Max! Max!"

Molla, stomach protruding far in front of her, was running straight toward us.

"Stop," I said, putting out an arm to keep her back with my power. Molla struggled like a wild animal against the soft invisible barrier my telek created. I heard more footsteps behind me and saw Cole and Juan running after her.

Tears gleamed in Molla's eyes. "They said you've been here all this time . . ."

"I'm sorry," Max said, his eyebrows knit in what looked like genuine remorse. But I knew him too well now. He slipped on masks like others did a fresh tunic. "I tried to talk to you, but you always turned me away."

"Because I thought you were Adrien!" she shouted. "You didn't come back for me, did you? You came for her." She spun on me, hatred in her eyes. "Why is it always her?"

She launched herself at me, but Cole and Juan caught her and held her tight. She struggled against them.

"Calm down, Molla, please," Max said, pleading. "Think of the baby."

Juan looked at Cole. "Can you take her out of here?"

Cole nodded and swept the weeping girl up into his arms.

"I'm sorry," Max called after her.

Juan looked at Max with loathing, pulling out a syringe from his pocket. "Jilia gave me this. He deserves much worse."

"I'll hold him still." I turned to look at Max and poured my telek over him so he couldn't move while Juan stepped closer and inserted the needle in his neck. "Take him to the Med Center and let Jilia know that Saminsa was innocent."

"Wait, Zoe, I'm so sorry," Max said. "You have to believe me, I'm so sorry—"

He slumped to the ground.

When I got into the Caf, I saw Adrien's mother pointing at a 3-D satellite map hovering in the cube over the central table. The rest of my team was sitting around the table and several Rez fighters stood nearby. I hurried in and grabbed a chair.

"Ginni says Adrien is in Portston, and the Chancellor is with him." Sophia pushed on the image and the map zoomed in. "Right here, in this building." She pulled back. "So we need to organize an extraction mission. Can we get the schematics of the building?"

"Wait," City said. "Shouldn't we think about this? Won't it be another trap?"

Sophia's eyes flashed. "He's my son!"

"And Bright is the Underchancellor of Defense." City's

voice rose. "She has squadrons of Regs at her command. It'd be suicide."

"The girl's right," said one of the Rez fighters, stepping forward. "We can't risk countless lives on a mission just to rescue one person." Things were quickly spiraling out of control, everyone arguing and panicking. The General slammed her hand on the table.

"Enough," she said. She turned to the Rez fighter. "Normally I would agree with you. But he's not just any boy. His visions make him an incredibly dangerous asset that is now in the Chancellor's hands. Leaving him with her could endanger us all. The Chancellor will know every step before we make it. She's already crippled us. If Adrien stays with her, she'll be able to finish us off."

"But you just said it. She knows every move we'll make. She'll see us coming if we try to rescue him," City said.

Taylor looked at her calmly. "Yes, she will most likely see it coming. But we still have to try."

"Even if we get past all the security measures she's sure to have, there's still her compulsion power to consider," Tyryn said quietly. "She could use her power to make us surrender, or even turn against each other."

"Tyryn's right," I said. "I've seen her make people throw themselves into concrete walls, stab themselves. As soon as you get within a hundred yards of her, she could make you all attack one another."

"What about the gas? That could take out her power," Xona said.

Taylor shook her head. "No one could get close enough to administer it without falling under her compulsion first."

A terrifying realization settled in my bones. I felt cold. Really, I'd known it all along. There could be no other way. "It has to be me, and me alone." My voice was loud in the suddenly still room.

Taylor nodded. I could see she'd long ago come to the same conclusions. "Yes. Every day he stays with the Chancellor is another day the Resistance's secrets are compromised. More and more Rez cells are getting cracked. We thought it was because her network of spies was increasing, but it's clear now it's because she has access to Adrien and his visions. The only way we have a fighting chance is if we remove him and kill the Chancellor. Then all knowledge of the future Adrien's already told her dies with her. She wouldn't have trusted anyone else with those secrets."

I nodded. "So I go in alone, kill her, and get Adrien." The words sounded absurd to me even as I said them. I had the urge to laugh hysterically. It was beyond impossible. I balled my hands into fists instead.

"And if the girl fails?" asked one of the Rez fighters. "What then?"

"That's why Zoel is not going alone," Taylor said.

"But I have to—" I started, but she interrupted me.

"You can't even operate a duo. How do you expect to get there?"

I thought about how much trouble Adrien had when he'd driven the thing during our escape from the alcove, and he'd grown up driving and flying. The panic I'd been trying to contain threatened to bubble out. "So what do we do?"

"I'll fly you in as close as I can get and still be out of the Chancellor's range of compulsion. We'll land here." She pointed to the rooftop of a building near where Ginni said Adrien and the Chancellor were. "There's a skywalk connecting the two buildings." She zoomed in and I saw a glass-enclosed walkway threaded between the top floors.

Sophia looked at the General. "But if the Chancellor does somehow manage to catch you in her compulsion web, you'll tell her all the Rez's secrets. I should be the one driving Zoel in. I'm no one, I don't matter."

"I will be taking her," Taylor said, her voice hard. "I'm the best pilot here, and I've pulled myself out of the inner circle of intelligence for quite some time now, since I come and go so often. Not that it will matter. I won't get close enough for the Chancellor to use her compulsion on me anyway."

Taylor directed her attention back to me. "You stay on coms with Ginni and she can direct you to where Adrien and the Chancellor are in the building. The rest of the team will follow at a distance behind us in an attack transport in case we encounter any difficulties trying to leave. Once the Chancellor is dead, they can move in without risking falling under her compulsion."

"But what if it doesn't work?" pressed the Rez fighter who'd spoken up earlier. "What if the girl is unable to kill the Chancellor? Then we'll have lost valuable resources and the Chancellor will still have the seer."

"That's the other reason I will be leading this mission," the General said. "Adrien's knowledge is too powerful a weapon. Many more will die if he's allowed to remain the Chancellor's pawn, so I take the burden on myself. Should Zoel fail, I will bomb the building with Adrien in it."

Her words were like a punch to my chest.

"No!" Sophia screamed. "You can't!"

"Restrain her," Taylor said, her voice steady. Two Rez fighters grabbed Sophia's arms to hold her back. She kicked and fought against them. "I'm sorry, Sophia, but there is no other choice. We will try to save him if we can. You will remain in lockdown until the mission is finished, one way or the other. Take her away." The Rez fighters dragged her from the room. My heart was in my throat as her screams echoed from the hallway.

Taylor turned her flinty gaze toward me, waiting to see if I too would object. But what could I say? If Adrien stayed with the Chancellor, I couldn't deny that others would certainly die because of the foreknowledge he would be forced to share. I tried to quiet the sudden wave of panic rushing to my head. I was Adrien's only hope. I must succeed.

"How do I get in?" I asked with only a slight tremor in my voice.

Taylor looked back at me. "Any way you can."

I nodded and swallowed hard.

She looked around at the rest of the group. "The second transport team will remain outside the city until the extraction is performed. We leave in two hours."

They nodded. Before anyone could ask any more questions, Taylor strode from the room.

I stepped into my dorm room to put on my biosuit. I put my legs in and pulled it up to my waist, consumed with worry about Adrien, when I stopped, startled. Saminsa was sitting on her pallet, back against the wall, watching me.

"Ginni said you are going to kill the Chancellor," Saminsa said, her voice quiet. She looked up, her dark eyes piercing. "Is that true?"

I paused, surprised. I'd barely heard her speak two words strung together since we rescued her during the raid.

"Look," I said. "I'm so sorry for everything that was done to you. We should have—"

"I'm coming with you."

"Oh." Of all the things that might have come out of her mouth at the moment, that was the last thing I would have expected.

"Jilia flushed the meds from my system. I could be an asset. I'm coming with you."

I paused, confused. "But why would you help us?"

"I don't care about helping you. I want my revenge." She didn't say anything for a moment, but then continued. "Do you remember how it went silent when you attacked?"

I nodded.

"His name was Din." She closed her eyes as if remembering. "In the part of the Sector where I lived, we stopped school at twelve and went to work in the factories. The machines were so loud. But then the Chancellor found me out and I met Din. For the first time in my life, I had quiet." She smiled a little, even though it looked like the memory brought her pain. "Being around him was so peaceful.

"Bright promised that if we helped her kill you we could be free." She shook her head. "It was my fault. I'm the one who spotted you and sent the com that triggered the explosives. I should have realized she considered us expendable. I thought his death was my fault for a long time. But then

I realized that I may have pushed the button, but she's the one who killed him." Her voice broke, but she gritted her teeth.

She looked up at me, her eyes hard. "I want the Chancellor dead. If you're the person who can make that happen, I want to go with you."

I hesitated. She could be lying. But then I looked at the fierceness in her face. I believed her. And Adrien had had a vision about her—that was why we'd brought her back with us from the raid in the first place. She may have some part yet to play in all this. I looked at the clock on the wall. "We leave in a little over an hour. Go find Tyryn, he'll tell you what to do."

Chapter 27

I PULLED ON THE TOP half of my suit, alone for the first time since the insanity of the past few hours had begun. I checked to make sure a fresh epi infuser was safely tucked in the pocket at my thigh, then tugged the thin blue sleeves over my arms. But before I could put my helmet on and fasten the suit closed, it all hit me. Adrien was gone. He had been captured all this time, and I hadn't even realized. The thought tore me apart inside. Now I had to face the most dangerous and powerful woman in the Sector, and if I didn't succeed, the love of my life would be killed.

I suddenly felt very small. Fear and self-doubt bubbled up. It was ludicrous. We didn't even have a plan. The Chancellor would know we were coming. I wasn't strong enough for this. How could I possibly—

Stop.

I squeezed my eyes shut and put my hands to my temples, as if I could physically force all the stray thoughts out of my head. I needed to empty my mind. I needed to focus. But the fear kept crowding back in.

I am that, I repeated desperately to myself, trying to find

my center. I am that. But they were just words without meaning.

Then Max's face popped into my head, and with it a swelling tide of rage. I am *that*. I visualized the billowing red rage and clung to it. Fear had no place here. The buzzing rose to a squealing pitch in my ears. I opened my eyes, awash with the power humming underneath my skin.

I pulled the helmet and face mask over my head, fastened everything in place, and headed toward the transport bay. It was time.

There was no moon, only the soft sifting of stars as we flew through the night sky. I looked up at Taylor's face in the rear-view mirror. "I understand why it couldn't be Adrien's mom, but why not let someone else take me?"

"It had to be me."

I paused a moment. "Adrien told you. He had a vision about this." It wasn't a question. Another thought struck. "Did he know he was going to get captured?"

Taylor was silent a moment before answering. "Yes, he knew he would be captured, but he didn't know when."

I almost jumped out of my seat. "Then how could you have let him go on the raid?"

"He didn't tell me." Her voice was calm and even. "He'd been keeping a vision journal full of everything he saw and his theories about how things might connect. It was an elaborate, spiderwebbed map. I found it when we returned from the raid. I forbade him from leaving the Foundation after that." In the mirror, I saw her frown. "Of course, it was already too late by then. I was talking to Maximin without knowing it."

I sat back, feeling baffled and angry at Adrien. I thought about when he'd taken me to watch the sunset before the raid. He'd talked about how precious time was, but I hadn't realized it was because he knew his was running out. "Why did he go? Why would he do that if he knew he'd be captured?"

She pursed her lips. "He didn't know when it would happen, and he insisted on going on the raid. He said it had to do with protecting the causality chain. Along with the vision journal, he had endless scribbled notes about research into temporal paradoxes and causality links."

"Causality? What does that even mean?"

She looked away. "He said he needed to make sure certain visions were fulfilled in order for others to come true."

I sat back in my seat. "If he needed to protect a vision and make it come true, it meant he believed they could still be altered," I said, stunned. After all Adrien's concern and doubt and despair about his visions, he'd still held on to hope. He'd still believed he could make a difference.

"Do you think they can be changed?" I asked.

"I sure as hell want to." Her grip on the control stick tightened. "But still, here I am, driving straight toward my fate anyway."

I let out a small gasp as another realization smacked me like a club to the face. All this time, I'd thought the vision Adrien had told the General—the one that had made her desperate—was about some mission or the future of the Rez. But it was suddenly clear that it was much more personal than that.

"Did he tell you—" I stopped, clutching the seat rest and bracing myself for the question I had to ask. "Does something happen to you on this mission?"

Her silence was answer enough.

"We have to go back. Find another way." My words tumbled over one another. "We can stop his vision from coming true. Maybe if someone else takes me it won't turn out the same—"

"I'm no coward," Taylor cut me off sharply. "Besides, I might not know how the causality chain works, but it's clear it's too important to disrupt." Her tone shifted, urgent. "I need you to do something for me. Should we fail to take down the Chancellor, there is an operation in motion that must continue. It's called Operation Kill Switch, and—"

"You mean the nuclear bomb you were going to use to create an EMP."

"You've seen the plans, then." She nodded, her voice only carrying a small note of surprise. "Good. That makes this simpler."

"But I'm not going to help you."

She let out a quick angry breath. "We have the means of ending this war forever, and you're saying no? Millions of lives could be saved. Civilization could be restored. This is the difference I am meant to make with my life.

"You're young. You still believe that if you just try hard enough, you can do good in the world without ever having to get your hands dirty. You have to promise me that when you're a leader you'll do what needs to be done." Her eyes met mine in the mirror with a burning intensity.

I swallowed. "I promise to do what I think is right."

Her mouth turned down at the edges, but she finally nodded. "I suppose in the end that's all any of us can ever do."

"We can still turn back, General." I leaned forward. "Adrien didn't try to change his fate, he just walked right into it. You can't do the same thing."

"You don't understand. I don't know if I believe in destiny, but I do believe that we must win this war if there is to be any hope for humanity. And I won't hide from a fight or let someone else die the death that was meant for me. Battles are fought every day with the knowledge that it might be our last. And as confident as the Chancellor might be, I guarantee she will be underestimating me. Because there is nothing more dangerous than a soldier who knows they have nothing left to lose."

Chapter 28

I WATCHED THE OUTLINE of the city come into view. Tall skinny buildings were stacked beside one another like a cluster of claws reaching into the sky. Taylor didn't say anything more.

"How are we going to get close without detection?" I asked.

"We're cloaked from their digital image scans. We just have to hope we're not spotted by the patrols."

She flew straight into the heart of the city and landed on the roof of a midsized building. I closed my eyes, letting my telek sense spread out. There was no movement below, and no army of Regs coming at us.

Yet.

I clicked my wrist coms. "Ginni, what is the Chancellor's position?"

"She hasn't moved at all. Adrien either. It looks like they're in adjoining rooms."

I met Taylor's frowning eyes in the mirror.

"Maybe you were right," I said to her. "Maybe she is underestimating us, . . . or we haven't sprung the trap yet."

I jumped over the side of the duo and hurried across the

rooftop. The wind rushed against my suit. I spared a glance outward at the cityscape and felt dizzy. It was so high up, higher off the ground than I'd ever been in my life outside of being in a transport. I tried to watch only the concrete ground in front of me. I came to the door in the corner and, without wasting any time, cast out my telek and made the door open sideways in its tracks.

I hurried down a staircase, and after a few more doors, I was out on the skywalk. The entire thing was made of glass, even the floor. The hundred-story drop spread out beneath my feet, but I barely glanced at it. I focused entirely on the building in front of me.

I was close enough now that I could feel past the walls of the building. Ginni said Adrien and the Chancellor were on the twenty-third floor. If I could disable the Chancellor before I even got into the building . . .

I tried to scan the floors, but quickly lost count. It appeared to be a housing unit of some kind. All the floors were laid out the same, and I could only push down about ten floors before my control started getting fuzzy around the edges. I could feel the prone shapes of people sleeping in each unit. None of them had the bulk of a Reg. I had no idea if they were soldiers or civilians or other glitchers, but there was no way I'd be able to locate the Chancellor among them. I could accidentally kill an innocent person. As much as I wanted Adrien back, I wasn't willing to go that far. I'd just have to get closer.

I pushed aside the door at the other end of the skywalk. No Regs. I wasn't sure if I should feel lucky. My uneasiness grew as I crept forward. All I could do was keep my telek on call and try to detect any traps before the snare clapped shut.

The door opened to a long white hallway. The lights were dim, probably still on nighttime settings. I jogged toward the elevator, all senses alert. Still no one was coming.

I frowned, but waved the card the dark-haired techer boy had given me in front of the elevator sensor. A few moments later, the door pinged open.

The cylindrical elevator pod felt extra small as I pushed the button for the twenty-third floor and waited as I dropped. I had the strangest sensation I was a mouse in a trap. I shook my head. Not hitting any resistance was just making me paranoid. Maybe by some miracle Adrien hadn't had a vision of me coming.

The elevator slowed and came to a halt. Before the door opened, I'd already closed my eyes, feeling out into the hallway beyond.

The hallway itself was clear, but I could sense something strange about the ceiling, like the edges didn't quite match. I pushed farther in and felt several gun barrels embedded behind the ceiling tiles. My heartbeat ratcheted up a notch, and I crumpled the guns in on themselves until they were mangled bundles of useless steel.

The elevator door pinged again and then opened. But what I saw didn't match what I'd sensed with my telek at all, and my mind reeled in confusion. Instead of a hallway, I stepped out into a large room that was blindingly white.

Children dressed in white tunics sat at desks, their small heads all turning in unison as I walked into the room. The room was unlike any I'd ever seen, but it was clearly a school. They were so young. Five or six years old.

"You have to get out," I said, my voice a frantic whisper. "It's not safe!"

The buzzing exploded in my ears. I closed my eyes and the room fell away. I felt the contours of what seemed like an empty hallway again. Where were the children? None of this made any sense. And then I noticed a lone figure standing just a few paces away from me. He raised a gun. I screeched and crumpled it like I had the weapons in the ceiling.

But when I blinked my eyes open again, I was back in the white room. I twirled around in confusion. My telek faded to a low buzz in my ears and then was gone completely. The children needed me. Suddenly nothing else mattered. I had to get them out of here.

One little girl came toward me, her blond hair in ringlets that framed her face.

Her tiny lip trembled. "Are you here to hurt us?"

"No," I crouched down so I was her height. "You don't have to be afraid of me. I'm here to help."

But all of a sudden, I couldn't remember why I was here at all. How was I going to help? Something was wrong, there was something I was supposed to be doing—

The girl pulled away from me.

"He's waiting for you," she said. She pointed to a boy sitting up front with his back to me. He was bigger than the other children, and the only one who hadn't turned around when I walked in.

I hurried to the front of the room. I didn't have much time. Then I frowned, not knowing why the thought had arisen. Other thoughts seemed to be wriggling at the back of my mind too, but when I tried to focus on them, they evaporated.

Of course I had all the time in the world. I carefully rounded the desk and saw the boy's face.

I knew him.

"Markan!" I leaned over and hugged him hard. My little brother. I looked around at all the other children. They watched me silently. The more I looked at them, the more something seemed wrong with their eyes.

What had felt like a peaceful sanctuary only moments before now felt sinister. There was something wrong with these children. With this whole situation.

"Come on, Markan," I said, a chill running up my spine. "We should go."

He didn't say anything, but he let me pull him to his feet. I grabbed his hand and was about to tug him forward when he cried out and sank to his knees. Blood bloomed on the front of his tunic.

"Markan!" I screamed. I looked around. I didn't see any Regs. How had he gotten hurt?

I reached to pull his tunic off over his head so I could see the wound and try to stop the bleeding, but he grabbed me with a surprisingly strong grip.

"Why didn't you save me?" Blood bubbled out of his mouth as his face paled. "Why didn't you save me?"

The children around us picked up the chant, a choir of accusing voices. "Why didn't you save me?"

I reached out to pull Markan into my arms, but as I touched him, he disintegrated into thin air.

"Markan!" I screamed, pawing the empty air in a panic. No! I'd had him, he'd been in my arms!

The children continued chanting, but all of them were bleeding now, from their noses, heads, chests. I screamed.

Another figure appeared in the spot where Markan had disappeared. Milton. Half his head was crushed in and blood poured down his face and neck. He reached out his arms to me. "Why didn't you save me?"

"No!" I screamed, backing away. "You're not real." I spun around, clutching my head. "None of you are real!"

I closed my eyes so I wouldn't see them. I had to use my telek, I had to—

"Why didn't you save me?" Another voice added to the chorus behind me. A voice I knew well.

"Adrien!" I turned around to him, and I remembered why I was here. The thought burned clear like a light piercing the fog. I was supposed to save Adrien. He didn't look like the others in the room. He wasn't as clean and he seemed more solid somehow.

He'd always been thin, but now he was positively skeletal. Dark, bruiselike shadows ringed his eyes. His hair was shaved and jagged, barely healed-over scars crisscrossed the left side of his head.

"Why didn't you save me?" He didn't reach out for me like Milton. He simply stood still looking like a broken toy. His eyes were vacant, constantly shifting this way and that as if he were seeing but not seeing.

"I will!" I said. "I will save you. Come with me. There's a transport coming."

He blinked and shook his head like he was clearing away a

fog. "Zoe?" he whispered, as if he was seeing me for the first time.

"Oh God, what have they done to you? We have to get out of here." I reached for his hand, but he pulled me into a hug. He was so skinny, I could feel each rib as he breathed in and out. I held back a sob. He'd known this would happen. No wonder he'd looked so haunted in the months leading up to the raid.

"Let me hold you," he whispered so softly I could barely hear him through my helmet. "They've done horrible things to me. The only thing that got me through was the thought of you."

I nodded, tears in my eyes. I glanced around me.

The children and the bright white classroom had faded. An errant thought in the back of my mind screamed that this wasn't normal. Rooms and people didn't just appear and disappear. But the next moment, I'd forgotten that it was strange at all.

Adrien and I were now in a room that looked like my old housing unit in the Community. It was dark with only the small sphere of the light cell near the head of my bed. Adrien pulled me down on the mattress beside him, just like he used to when he'd visit me in the middle of the night. The ceiling tile was shifted overhead, as if he hadn't bothered to close it behind him.

"You've had a bad dream," Adrien said. "I heard you cry out, so I came down. But you're awake now."

A bad dream. That didn't seem quite right, but when I held him, suddenly it made more and more sense. I'd had such a very long, very bad dream, and now everything was back as it was supposed to be. Adrien and me, together and hidden away from the world in the dark sanctuary of my room.

He laughed, the sound of it gentle in the quiet room. "Zoe, why are you wearing that suit?"

His laugh made me feel warm all the way down to my bones. I looked down at my gloved hands, then laughed with him. I giggled, confused. "I don't know."

"Let's get this off you," he said, a warm smile still on his face. He put a hand to the edge of my faceplate.

I nodded. All I wanted was his touch. Suddenly I needed it more than I'd ever needed anything in my life, more than food, more than air. I let him undo the clasps and pull my helmet off. He swooped in and kissed me as if he was breathing me in.

For a moment everything was perfect. Adrien was in my arms and his lips tasted sweet, like strawberries. I noticed a slight whirring noise start up around us, like one might notice the buzz of a fly in the background. I kissed him deeper.

But when I pulled back to take a breath, my chest felt tight and I couldn't get any air. At first I laughed, thinking about how kissing Adrien made me breathless. But the next second, I knew that wasn't it. My tongue felt wrong. It was a thick stone in my mouth.

I knew what this felt like. This had happened before. My thoughts were sluggish, but I finally remembered.

It was an allergy attack. I was having an allergy attack. I fumbled for the epi infuser I always carried with me. It should be safely tucked in a pocket at my thigh, but when I reached for it, there was nothing there.

"Help me," I gasped at Adrien. I clutched his arm.

He pulled away. I looked up in confusion. All the features fit—the eyebrows, long aquiline nose, thick lips—but it was like I was looking at a stranger's face. No emotion flickered. And he was holding the epi infuser in his hand as he backed away.

I put my hands to my throat and tried to get another breath. Only a tiny bit of air trickled through my swollen throat, not nearly enough for a proper breath. Adrien watched me writhing on the bed as if I were no more than a specimen in a lab.

"Help!"

Adrien continued to back away from me. In the next blink, he'd dropped to the ground from the loft bed and pushed the door to my room open. He was leaving me.

No. I had to stop him. I was supposed to save him. He was supposed to save me. My thoughts jumbled all together, but one thought burned clear. I couldn't let him go. I could stop him, I knew I could, if I could just remember how—

My telek! How had I forgotten about it? I cast it out immediately, reaching for Adrien. But when I did, none of it made sense. The cube projection in my mind didn't match what I saw. I couldn't feel the shape of my loft bed or the tiny contours of my room.

Instead, it felt like a hallway.

And Adrien and I weren't alone. There was someone else standing right beside me. I tried to scream, but only managed a whimpering sputter.

I opened my swollen eyes and tried to get another breath. My throat was swollen almost completely shut now. Panic rose even as I lashed out with my telek.

I threw the other person hard into the wall, headfirst.

The image of my bedroom evaporated instantly. Adrien and I were in a white hallway. I wasn't on my bed, I was laying on the ground. It was just like the hallway I'd been in right before I'd gotten on the elevator. A thick mist spewed into the room from vents at the top of the wall.

I tried to call out to Adrien, but no sound came out.

My eyes had swollen almost entirely shut, but through the slit I could see a red-haired young man laying unconscious at my feet. He must have been a glitcher, making me hallucinate all those things.

But Adrien hadn't been a hallucination. He kept backing away from me, my helmet still in his hand. He was real.

I tried to stand, but collapsed to the ground again. My mouth gaped open, trying desperately to fill my lungs with air, but the bit I did manage to gasp through my swollen throat was toxic. The vents must be pumping in allergens.

I reached for Adrien, crawling on my knees, but knew that even if I could manage to get the helmet on again, the allergens were already clogging my lungs. I hadn't taken a breath for at least two minutes now.

Adrien was at the end of the hallway now.

And then he was gone.

Watching him leave sapped the last ounce of fight I had in my body. I knew he must be under the Chancellor's compulsion. But I still felt the loss like a sledgehammer to my ribs.

My body shuddered, the muscles expanding and contracting involuntarily. My mouth opened wider, gaping like a dying fish. I tried desperately to get a center, to be able to cast my telek as I had in training so many times, as I could almost do in my sleep now.

But the objects and impressions were all skewed. My back arched and spasmed. Everything in me heaved, needing a breath.

Why didn't you save me?

I loved Adrien so much. But in the end I couldn't save him. Or myself.

Anger began to boil inside me even as I felt my body shutting down from lack of oxygen. It wasn't supposed to end this way. I didn't care about fate, or what Adrien had or had not seen. All of it was futile if it ended like this. The rage burned red and the buzzing that had been a hum in my ears became a howling scream.

No.

The projection in my mind shined with burning light. I felt the pulsing fury that obliterated every other thought.

I was pure rage.

I didn't even care where the rage was directed—at the Chancellor, at Max, at me, at death itself for trying to claim me before my time was up—I ignored everything but the fury.

And then suddenly I wasn't expanding outside my body. I was inside it. I pushed past my skin and tissue and muscles, zooming in closer and closer. I barely knew what I was doing, and I didn't let myself think about it. I just felt.

Like I'd done with the oxygen molecules in the kitchen fire, I surrounded all the mast cells in my body. I forced the release of histamines to stop, expelling the ones that had already been released through the pores in my skin.

I couldn't stop to think about the impossibility of what I was doing. It was millions of cells, billions probably. I'd lose it if I thought about it too much.

The swelling in my throat went down, and the passage opened up. I breathed. Breath after painful gasping breath. My heart was working again and it raced to pump the oxygen back into the rest of my limbs.

The swelling in my eyes calmed until I could see light first, and then objects started to take shape in front of me. My raging telek was still focused inward on my mast cells, and I could sense that if I let go for even a moment the swelling would start again. I tried to figure out what I'd done unconsciously with my telek and how to hold on to it willfully now.

Get up. Get up now, I ordered myself. I stayed still. Too much hurt. How could I move?

"GET UP!" I whispered in a rasping, barely audible voice. I closed my aching eyes for one last moment, then said it again. I tried to think of the strength of Taylor's voice when she gave commands. There was no other choice but to obey when she spoke. I had to do that now.

"Ginni," I rasped into my arm com. "Where's the Chancellor now?"

"Zoe!" Ginni's voice crackled in my ear. "I've been trying to com you for the last ten minutes. I saw Adrien come out of his room and join you, but then he left again and now he's with the Chancellor! What happened?"

The hallucinations the red-haired glitcher boy had cast on me had been so complete, I hadn't even heard her com.

"Where is he?" I asked again. I didn't have the energy to explain right now.

"On an elevator, heading up."

I rolled onto my knees, then slowly, achingly, grabbed on to the nearby wall and dragged myself to my feet. The movement cost my focus a bit—I could tell by the sudden itching on my left side. I breathed out and gathered it back. The itching calmed, but I felt split in two trying to hold on to all the mast cells internally while also moving my outer body. I took one step forward, then another, and then another. Every few moments I lost it and I'd feel a bit of swelling or itching. I caught it again just in time.

I staggered to the elevator behind me and swiped the card. It pinged open almost immediately. They must have gone up a different elevator.

"They're on the roof now," Ginni said over the com.

I pushed the button for roof access and then sagged against the wall while the elevator lifted. It stopped and pinged open. My breath was heaving and unsteady as I stepped out on to the roof. The morning sunlight hurt my eyes, but I could make out figures and two vehicles on the transport landing pad. I recognized Adrien's tall frame immediately. The Chancellor stood with her back to me, her hair oiled back slick like she always used to wear it. She whipped around and her eyes widened in shock.

I saw her reach for a weapon and gave up a moment's control over my mast cells. I thrust my telek outward and yanked the gun out of her hands. It clattered to the ground only a few feet away from me.

"It's not possible," she managed to choke out. "You're supposed to die. Adrien said he saw you go into an allergy attack and die!"

The effort of pulling the gun away was too much. I fell to my knees the next second and scrambled to get a hold of the instantly erupting cells.

I reached my hand in her direction. This was it. After all these months, she was finally in my grasp. If I'd been in my biosuit, I could have snapped her neck in an instant. But I wasn't, and the more I tried to split my telek focus between my mast cells and reaching outward toward her, the more it felt like I was caught between two magnets ripping me apart in opposite directions.

"Don't waste your energy on me, darling Zoe," the Chancellor called out. The fear that had flickered on her face had disappeared at the sight of my struggle. She smiled instead.

I looked up and saw that Adrien had walked away from her to the edge of the building. The very edge. And on the opposite side of the building, Taylor stood just as precariously perched.

My heart skipped a beat. Why was Taylor even still here? She'd promised she would take off again as soon as she'd dropped me off. We must have underestimated the Chancellor's reach.

I took a step forward.

"Stop," the Chancellor commanded. "They'll throw themselves off if I command it. In your condition, I don't think you'd be able to pull them back." Her eyes narrowed as she looked me over. "In fact, I'm not even sure you could save one of them if you tried. But there is another way. All you have to do is pick up that gun," she gestured at the weapon I'd ripped away from her, "and kill yourself."

I glanced at the gun, then back up at the Chancellor. Hatred poured off me in waves. If I could just manage to get control . . .

"Kill yourself and I will let them live."

"Stop," I said. "You don't have to do this!"

She cocked her head sideways at me. "No? You won't save anyone but yourself? What a disappointing savior you turned out to be." She waved her hand and both Adrien and Taylor leaned farther out off the roof. Each tottered on the edge, the wind swirling around them as they held on to unstable footholds.

"Wait!" I stooped over to reach for the gun. "I'll do it."

The Chancellor sighed. "I can tell you'll just try to shoot me. You always were so transparent." She stepped closer to her sleek black transport. "So impulsive and predictable."

I lunged for the weapon, but out of the corner of my eye saw Adrien and General Taylor throw themselves off the roof.

"No!" I screamed.

For a split second I saw the choice laid out before me. I could use the last tiny bit of telek left in my body to kill Chancellor Bright, but Taylor and Adrien would both fall to their deaths. Two lives lost in exchange for taking down the Chancellor forever. It was what Taylor would have wanted. She'd spoken so often of the need to be willing to sacrifice the lives of the people I loved for the good of all.

But I wasn't her. The second Adrien disappeared off the edge of the roof, I knew that there'd never really been any choice. He was my life.

I sprinted toward the spot where he'd jumped and dropped

on my stomach to look over the edge. Adrien plummeted down, growing smaller every millisecond as the Chancellor's transport took off behind me.

"Adrien!"

The Chancellor was wrong. I would give up my life for his. I let go of my mast cells completely and cast the telek down toward him like a lasso. He bobbed forty stories below, held only by the invisible line of my power.

I hauled him back up, trying to ignore my swelling tongue and keep only the projection of him in my mind.

Twenty stories.

Ten.

My throat had swollen all the way back up by the time he was only one floor away. Just a little farther. My body was on fire. It didn't matter.

But then the projection cube in my mind started blinking in and out. Adrien dropped a few feet as I lost control before I caught him again. I tugged him back upward and reached out, leaning farther off the building. Bright spots appeared at the edges of my vision.

My gloved fingers scrabbled to get a solid grip on his ankles, but right as I did, the projection cube blinked out completely.

He slipped an inch, and I poured every inch of strength I had left into holding on to him.

It wasn't enough.

We only managed a second of equilibrium, me holding tight to his leg before I was yanked forward by his weight off the building.

And then we were both free-falling.

Terror spiked. Every millisecond we flew through the air, I

knew I was supposed to be doing something. I was supposed to save Adrien.

The wind was like a freight train in my ears and every millisecond the ground rushed closer. I tried to reach out with my telek. But I'd used every drop of energy trying to grab Adrien at the top of the building. My throat closed up and my tongue swelled.

I had nothing left.

There was nothing I could do.

Strange disconnected images flashed in my mind. Adrien's bright blue-green eyes. The first time we'd met in the crowded Market Corridor. Our first kiss.

Any moment now, we'd hit. I closed my eyes and gripped Adrien's leg harder. At least we'd be together at the end.

But suddenly our momentum slowed down, like we'd landed on a sea of cotton. I opened my swollen eyes in confusion. Blinding blue light surrounding us, cradling us on all sides. I didn't know when I'd last taken a breath. Had I died?

"Get them inside!" someone shouted. "The armada's right behind us!"

The blue light dissipated around us. In my disorientation, I watched in bewilderment as Saminsa pulled Adrien to his feet. Buildings rose up on all sides, and the Rez's transport was parked in the center of an intersection.

Rand saw me and grinned. "Did you miss us?"

Cole jumped out of the transport while Xona held a rocket launcher over her shoulder and fired at a group of Regs running down the street toward us. Cole scooped me and Adrien up, one in each arm, just as the explosion lit up the street behind us.

"Saminsa, more Regs are coming, we need another orb!" Cole called as he deposited us inside the back of the transport.

Saminsa immediately raised her arms and blue light exploded from her fingertips. It looked like the same light that had created the otherworldly net to catch us, except this time it expanded outward. Before the orb could encompass the entire transport, a Regulator came from nowhere and leapt toward the still open door. Xona was reloading and couldn't fire. Cole threw himself in front of her as red light exploded from the charging Reg's laser weapon.

The instant before it hit, Saminsa's blue orb expanded and made a shield. The laser fire hit the barrier just an inch from Cole's face and dissipated harmlessly, absorbed by the blue light. Xona stared up at Cole in disbelief as Rand slammed the back of the transport shut.

"Go, Henk, get us out of here," Tyryn said, looking out the window. "Two more armada ships are flying in from the north."

My muscles started shuddering again. I was on the edge of consciousness, darkness threatening to swoop in. Tyryn's face was suddenly over mine. "We brought another epi infuser," he said, pushing my hair back from my face.

I felt a bite of fire in my chest. I jerked away from the hands holding me down as the blaze spread through my whole body. I wheezed and clutched my heart, and for the first time in who knows how many minutes, air whooshed through the small space that had opened in my throat and into my lungs.

Tyryn helped me lean back. I gasped and finally got a full breath. The transport jarred beneath us as we launched off the ground.

"There's three of 'em now!" Henk shouted.

I felt the momentum as our transport rose straight up into the air. Nausea and dizziness swarmed me, but I managed to keep my eyes open. As we lifted past the top of the buildings, I saw three fully loaded armada transports waiting in the air. They launched another volley of laser fire. The lasers rippled harmlessly into the blue orb still surrounding our vehicle.

"This one's disintegrating," Saminsa yelled from where she stood in the center aisle.

"Attack as soon as she releases it!" Henk said.

City and Rand lined up shoulder to shoulder and lowered the long window running along the side of the transport. Air rushed in as soon as it was open.

"Now!" Saminsa called, shifting her body forward. The blue orb expanded like a spherical wave outward. City sent a giant spiral of electricity in its wake. Right as the blue orb dissipated, City's electricity circled around one of the attack transports, slowly weaving into a web. Sparks and explosions crackled through the air.

Rand held out his arms too, and the air wavered like water as he sent out an intense wave of heat. The outer hull of the attack transport closest to us began to melt.

Saminsa launched a small burning blue orb toward the third transport, and it hit with an explosion that rocked the whole thing backward. It toppled into the transport Rand was working on, sending them both spiraling into the buildings below. The next moment, the transport City attacked dropped from the air like a dead weight too.

Bright explosions burst from below us where the transports

had hit, but Henk already had us speeding toward the horizon before I could even get a good look.

City closed the window, letting out a loud whoop. "Did you see that?"

Ginni laughed and hugged her. Rand grinned and clapped Saminsa on the back. "That was amazing!"

My mind was clearing a little now that the epi had taken effect. I pulled my tired body over to where Adrien was buckled in near the front of the transport.

I hugged him hard, fat tears seeping out of my swollen eyes as I thought about General Taylor and how close we'd all come to suffering the same fate. "We're safe." I clung to his skinny frame. "We made it."

He didn't hug me back.

"Adrien?" I pulled away.

That was when I finally looked into his eyes.

And knew something was horribly wrong.

His eyes had no vibrancy. Even the normal bright blue-green hue seemed leeched out of them.

"Adrien?" Even though he was looking straight at me, I wasn't sure he saw me at all.

"Adrien?" My voice raised to a hysterical pitch. "Adrien, you're scaring me."

He continued to stare ahead dumbly.

I grabbed his hand and put it to my beating heart. "It's Zoe, talk to me."

"Zoe," he echoed, his voice hollow and lifeless. "Why didn't you save me?"

Chapter 29

ADRIEN SAT ON JILIA'S MED TABLE as she finished her diagnostic. His mother sat beside him, squeezing his hand. Deep brown circles ringed his eyes, and I couldn't look away from the barely healed scars lining his head where his skull had been cut open.

"Adrien," Jilia said, her tone falsely bright as she lowered the imaging panel. "You've done very well. Please go back to your dorm room and rest now."

He stood up and did what she said. All he ever did now was follow orders. Nothing else. He'd stand for hours if no one told him to sit down.

Rand was waiting to escort Adrien back to his dorm room.

"What is it?" Sophia asked the doctor anxiously.

Jilia swallowed, then pulled out a projection tablet that loaded a 3-D image of Adrien's head.

"He's had multiple operations. From the bit that he is able to remember and relate, the Chancellor had him under compulsion for over a month. Until he had a vision of what he thought was Zoe's death." She looked at me. "He foresaw you going into the allergy attack with no one there to save you. He knew if he told the Chancellor, he'd be telling her how to kill you. His determination not to harm you somehow enabled him to finally break her control over his mind. He began successfully fighting back and refusing to tell her his visions anymore. That was when she started in on the surgical options."

I felt numb as she spoke. This had happened to him because of me.

"What, as some kind of torture?" Adrien's mother asked, stricken.

"She did torture him at first to try to get the answers out of him." Jilia looked down. "But in the end, she lobotomized him. She cut out portions of his brain, including almost the entire amygdala. He has his memories, but can no longer attach emotion to them. Or to anything he experiences. After the operations . . ." she swallowed again. "After the last operation it appears the Chancellor's compulsion did indeed work on him again. But he'd stopped having visions altogether." She looked at me. "The only reason the Chancellor even kept him alive was as collateral against you. She knew that he had to be alive for Ginni's power to locate him, so she could draw you into the trap."

"Is he ever going to be my Adrien again?" Sophia asked. I held my breath while I waited for Jilia's answer.

She looked at the floor again.

"Tell me!" Sophia said.

"The developments in organ-regrowth technology have been promising over the last fifty years, but no one has ever succeeded at regrowing entire portions of the brain. Any replication processes will be long and slow. We'll begin right away, but I can't make either of you any promises. I'm so sorry."

I stepped back, stunned.

"But you're a healer," Sophia shouted. "Can't you *do* something?"

The sorrow on Jilia's face clear. "I'm sorry, Sophia." She reached out to put a hand on Sophia's shoulder, but Sophia ripped her arm away from the contact. She spun and hurried from the room, I think so we wouldn't see her cry.

I couldn't handle it anymore. I had to get out of here too. Sophia was gone when I got to the hallway, and my steps echoed loudly in the empty space. This wasn't how it was supposed to go. Regardless of everything Jilia had said, I knew Adrien and I were destined to be together. There was supposed to be a happy ending. Adrien and I, standing in the sunlight at the end of the war. But then again, Adrien had never told me that's how it would end. In the vision he'd shared with me, I was in the sunlight, but I'd been all alone. And I'd been running toward danger, not celebrating victory.

I stopped when I came to the T in the hallway, looking up in surprise when I realized my feet had carried me to Adrien's dorm. I stood outside the door for a moment, preparing myself for what was on the other side, then pushed the button and stepped in.

Adrien sat at the study table, staring at the wall. My heart tightened in my chest at the sight of him. He looked so broken, but the strong cut of his nose and his rugged jaw were still so familiar. This was the boy I loved. Jilia had to be wrong. Even if the Chancellor had removed part of his brain, surely Adrien was still in there somewhere. We were more than our physical parts, more than our electrical synapses or brain tissue; that was what Adrien always said. That's what Cole had taught me. We had souls.

I sat down in the chair opposite him and reached for his hand. He let me take it. Maybe if we touched for long enough, it would spark him back to life. The memory of the diagrams Jilia had shown us popped up in my mind, but I expelled the images.

This was Adrien. My Adrien. Our love could surmount anything. He'd proven it already when he'd thrown off the yoke of the Chancellor's compulsion. It shouldn't have been possible, but his love for me was stronger even than her ability. He could find his way back to me again, I knew it.

"How are you feeling?" I asked.

He didn't look up at me. His hand was limp in mine. "The doctor says I am unwell."

"You're going to be fine." I tried to smile, but I was fighting back tears. "We just have to give it some time."

He didn't say anything or nod.

"Can I ask you a question?" I leaned in.

"Yes."

I swallowed, gripping his hand tighter. "Why did you go on that raid? Why did you leave the Foundation at all after you'd seen the visions of what would happen to you?"

"I had other visions, of you and me together at the Foundation. Several of them had not yet occurred, so I deduced that my capture would not be until later."

I felt hope flower in my belly. "So they'll still come true?"

He shook his head, but it looked like a mechanical movement, sharp jerks back and forth. "No. It was not me that I saw. It was Maximin wearing my face."

The bloom inside me wilted, replaced by an involuntary shudder. It was cruel and unfair. All those moments that

should have been Adrien's and mine had been shared instead
with Max. I felt another rush of choking hatred for Max.
He'd been locked up in a room on the lower level and was
kept under constant supervision. It was far better than he deserved. If Sophia or I had our way, he wouldn't be treated so
humanely.

"You thought you had more time," I said, my heart breaking.

"That is not the only reason," he said. "I could not interfere with the causality chain. If I did not rescue Saminsa on
the raid, she would not have been able to save you when you
fell from the roof."

"You idiot," I said, feeling guilt burn through my veins
like fire. He'd gone because of me. Risked his safety for me.
And worse, the only reason Saminsa had even needed to save
me was because Adrien had gotten captured. If he'd only
stayed home, none of it would have mattered. In trying to
make sure one vision happened, he'd *caused* the circumstances
leading up to it.

I swallowed down my grief. At least he was responding to
me. That was what I needed to focus on.

"Do you know who the red-haired glitcher was in that
hallway?"

"He creates hallucinations based on a subject's fears and
desires," Adrien explained in a completely blank monotone.
"While your mind was busy in the world he created around
you, the weapons from the ceiling were supposed to take you
down. But you detected them and the gun he had with him
as well. The Chancellor was afraid if she sent out more soldiers to kill you, you'd sense them with your telek in spite of

the hallucinations. So she sent me out to kill you instead by taking off your helmet. As I had foreseen."

"She said you saw me die." My voice was quiet.

"I saw flashes of you writhing on the ground, and then not moving at all. I assumed that indicated your death." His voice was still so empty and cold. He talked about my death with the same emotion as one might when discussing the components of a propulsion engine.

"Do you feel *anything*?" I asked, desperate for some spark of the old Adrien I'd known.

He raised his head, and his eyes met mine for a moment.

This was it. This was the moment our souls would recognize each other and I'd see the light come back into his eyes.

I clutched his hand tighter.

See me, I wished silently. Look into my eyes and remember.

"No," he said. "I do not feel anything." His gaze was just as empty as my brother's had always been under the control of the V-chip.

No. I couldn't lose him like this. I would make him remember. I scooted my chair closer to his, ignoring the screech of the chair legs scraping across the ground. His eyes did not follow me, but instead stared at the spot I had previously been.

I closed my eyes so I wouldn't see his hollow stare. I touched my lips to his.

He didn't respond. I kissed deeper, harder, pouring all of my desperation into it and willing him to remember.

His lips didn't move.

I pulled back and searched his eyes. He still wasn't looking at me.

And I knew.

We hadn't saved him, not really. We'd brought back his body, but that was all. The Chancellor hadn't given me a choice after all. She knew I was going to lose both Taylor and Adrien either way.

My body trembled as I stepped back. "You should get some rest," I said. "Everything will turn out okay." I tried to sound more confident than I felt.

And then I fled from the room. The tears I'd been holding back before now flooded my cheeks.

My arm com buzzed.

Compound-wide meeting in the training room, attendance is mandatory.

I swiped the tears from my eyes and took a deep breath. The last thing I wanted right now was to be around other people, but I knew everyone was afraid for the future of the Rez. The General had been killed and the Chancellor had escaped again. We needed solidarity more than ever right now. I changed directions and headed toward the training center.

By the time I got there, half the room was filled. All the Rez fighters from the lower level were there. Even the Professor stood in the corner. He looked just as bad as I felt, with his disheveled tunic and red-rimmed eyes. His grief was so thick it seemed to cloud the air around him.

Ginni hurried over and hugged me. "I heard about Jilia's prognosis for Adrien, I'm so sorry."

I didn't say anything, just blinked back more tears and let her take my arm to lead me to where she was sitting. I noted with brief surprise that Xona and Cole were already there, talking in hushed whispers. This wasn't the first time I'd caught them like this. The fact that he'd thrown himself in front of the laser fire for her had changed everything.

While Adrien was undergoing the battery of tests, I'd gone back to my dorm to change out of my suit. Xona was sitting on the edge of her bed, eyes wide. After asking me about Adrien, she opened up about it. "If Saminsa had gotten the orb up only a millisecond later, Cole would have died saving my life." She shook her head. "For so long, I could only see them as killing machines, but he protected life instead of taking it. I talked to him earlier and do you know what he said?"

"What?"

"He said that if *I* of all people could forgive him for what he was, then maybe he could too. Like in spite of everything he always said, he couldn't believe he was fully human until he'd proved it to me, who hated them the worst."

The Professor's voice broke into my thoughts. He'd made his way to the front of the room. "This is a difficult time for all of us," he said, his voice raw. He cleared his throat and tried again. "Rosalina tried to prepare me for this possibility. She always said that to accomplish anything truly great or make lasting change, sacrifices would be necessary. Honor, loyalty, courage. These qualities are her legacy, and ones that we will all need more than ever in the coming months."

He looked out at the crowd until his eyes stopped on me. "Zoe, will you please join me?"

I looked at him, bewildered, but I got up and walked to the front of the room. I paused beside him.

"Tyryn," the Professor nodded to the large man who'd been standing off to the side. Tyryn approached. The Professor

308

looked out again at the gathered crowd. "General Taylor's last act before leaving on the mission was to name Zoel Q-24 acting Colonel should she not return. Zoe will join the other four Colonels who head the Resistance."

"What?" I couldn't help the astonished question popping out.

The Professor looked at me. "She thought your generation of glitchers should be represented among the highest ranks of leadership, and you in particular. She's watched you closely these past few months and believes you are ready."

I stood still, completely stunned as Tyryn came forward and pinned a star on my tunic. A hundred thoughts raced through my head at once. I thought Taylor hated glitchers, but she'd made me a leader in the Rez. It was just as Adrien had foreseen, but not at all how it should have happened. None of this was.

The Professor turned back to the crowd. "We have suffered heavy losses recently and made sacrifices that at times seem too much to bear." His voice cracked slightly before he took another deep breath and continued. "More will be required in the months ahead. But hope remains as long as we have breath in our chests. We fight for our lives and for the ones we love. Rosalina always believed that, though we are few, we can still change the world."

The Professor stepped back and I dazedly walked to sit down again while Tyryn discussed heightened security measures and the need to ration supplies now that more and more people were seeking sanctuary at the Foundation.

I leaned my back and head against the cool hallway outside after everyone else headed to dinner. It stretched out empty on both sides of me. That was how I felt. Empty. I'd always taken for granted that Adrien would be by my side no matter what came. But now I faced it alone.

Terror pitched in my stomach like acid at the thought. I gritted my teeth and clenched my jaw. No. I wouldn't let fear rule me anymore. I would not be weak.

The future was coming, and I would be ready to face it this time. As a Colonel, I could make sure the EMP plan was never put into effect. We'd find another way to end the war once and for all. And by all the stars and shadows in the universe, I would make the Chancellor pay for the lives she'd destroyed.